THE DEVIL'S BEAT

Robert Edric

BLACK SWAN

TRANSWORLD PUBLISHERS
61–63 Uxbridge Road, London W5 5SA
A Random House Group Company
www.transworldbooks.co.uk

**THE DEVIL'S BEAT
A BLACK SWAN BOOK: 9780552777094**

First published in Great Britain
in 2012 by Doubleday
an imprint of Transworld Publishers
Black Swan edition published 2013

Addresses for Random House Group Ltd companies outside the UK
can be found at: www.randomhouse.co.uk
The Random House Group Ltd Reg. No. 954009

The Random House Group Limited supports The Forest Stewardship
Council® (FSC®), the leading international forest-certification organisation.
Our books carrying the FSC label are printed on FSC®-certified paper.
FSC is the only forest-certification scheme supported by the leading
environmental organisations, including Greenpeace. Our
paper procurement policy can be found at
www.randomhouse.co.uk/environment

Typeset in Granjon by
Kestrel Data, Exeter, Devon.
Printed and bound in Great Britain by Clays Ltd, St Ives plc

2 4 6 8 10 9 7 5 3

For James Macdonald Lockhart

The Devil prospers when a lie is told,
and silence is the Devil's gold.

Seventeenth-century proverb

Nottinghamshire, October 1910

Part One

Part One

1

FRANCIS MERRIT UNFOLDED THE MAP HE HELD AND STUDIED the path ahead of him. It was no true or properly marked route, simply a track created over the centuries by the passage of feet, hooves and wheels between the town and the expanse of woodland that surrounded it in most directions.

He turned in a circle and saw the higher chimneys above the canopy of trees beneath him. He had been conscious of the gentle rise of the land as he had walked, and he saw that where he now stood marked the high point along his journey before the path started its descent back into thicker growth.

It was a mild day, part of the uncertain passage between early and late autumn, and the leaves of many of the surrounding trees were already turning. Soon, he guessed, the woodland might be bare and flooded with sharper winter light, presenting a different aspect completely to anyone walking even that short distance into it.

The map had been drawn for him by Oliver Webb, the alderman and magistrate, whose immediate response upon hearing Merrit's request had been to say that no map would be needed, that the path was well enough known, and that it was marked and visible along its entire length.

But Merrit had insisted, pointing out to Webb that he was a stranger to the town and that the path was not well known to *him*. Clearly riled by this, Webb had then suggested accompanying him into the woods, and this too Merrit had rejected. And if the alderman and magistrate had been offended by Merrit's first rebuttal, he was even more offended by this second.

It had surprised Merrit to see how incapable the man appeared to be of both hiding his true feelings and of shaping and tempering his responses. Webb had then suggested that all four members of the investigative panel be contacted. He had first called it a 'committee' and Merrit had corrected him. And then he had referred to it as a 'police council' – clearly a more reassuring title to a local magistrate – and Merrit had insisted on correcting this too: four contradictions within only minutes of meeting the man.

Already assessing his losses, Webb had then repeated his suggestion that they contact the two remaining members of the 'panel' – he now invested the word with a cold edge – and that all four of them might make the journey into the woodland together. 'A starting point for our investigation,' he had called it. 'An excursion.' And yet again Merrit had denied him, adamant that he wished to visit the site alone.

Because he was a stranger; because he was a newcomer to the recent events in the town; and because all he so far knew of those events was what he had read in the newspapers and the various ancillary reports already given to him by his superiors. Because of all that; and because – though Merrit was careful to avoid any suggestion of this in front of the magistrate – he was there to establish the simple truth of the matter, and then to separate this from the multitude of burgeoning tales and rumours and other wild speculations that had already tangled themselves around that kernel of undeniable truth and verifiable fact.

The map he held was on Council-headed paper: this was the town, here was its central square, and here was the road leading out of that square. And here, at the foot of that gentle hill to the north of the town – more accurately north-west – was where that road ended and then turned by degrees into the track which ran ahead of Merrit now. This change – metalled and surfaced road to scattered cobbles and then to ruts and overgrown edges – was not lost on Francis Merrit. These were the details he noticed and remembered; these were the details he took a professional pride in interpreting and understanding. The road changed; the town was left behind; the hill rose; the woodland began and then swiftly thickened around him until it grew so close over the track that it became almost a tunnel. Everything ahead was a mystery to him, drawing him on.

So, the path rose to this low summit, paused to allow these two backward- and forward-looking perspectives, and then it fell into the trees below, where the world and all it contained might be changed completely.

The trunks rose high above him, and he craned his neck to look up at them. Ahead of him, the bulk of the foliage was beneath him. He had risen, and yet, surrounded and enclosed as he now was, he had simultaneously gained and lost a vantage point. He could see, say, twenty yards ahead of him and the same distance behind him along the track, but on either side of him he could see only a few feet into the trees and their undergrowth. It was something else to make a note of, and to put somewhere safe and retrievable amid the explosion of testimony-gathering upon which he and the others would soon be embarked.

'The girls read fairy tales,' he said aloud, the realization and the words coming simultaneously. They were familiar with the usual tales, and this woodland and the road leading into it and the paths passing through it and all its secret places were constituent parts of the tale they themselves were now telling.

The first thing Webb had said to him, their two hands still firmly locked, was that the five girls were not to be trusted, that they had a clear leader and that *she* was to be trusted least of all. Merrit had known – or perhaps guessed or surmised – most of this already from what he had read, much of the information looked over again during his diverted, four-hour train journey to the place the previous day. He had not responded to this clumsy prod by the magistrate, causing Webb to fall silent for a moment and then to ask equally bluntly if he, Merrit, had some reason to doubt him. Merrit had reassured him otherwise, but Webb had remained unconvinced and suspicious, only then withdrawing his hand and taking a step back from this unwelcome stranger.

All this had taken place in the town's small, empty court-room. It was Webb's domain, and Merrit had gone there to seek him out. It was where he had asked the magistrate for the map.

'There are proper maps, official maps, surveyed maps,' Webb had insisted. 'I can get them for you.' He was a man accustomed to commanding and supervising others, a man accustomed to being obeyed without question or delay. Merrit had asked quickly if Webb could not provide him with a simple sketch or directions even, to the place in the woods.

'It has a name,' Webb had insisted. 'It's hardly a wilderness that none of us knows. People here know those woods, all the surrounding countryside like—'

'The backs of their hands?' Merrit had said, almost as a joke.

'Precisely,' Webb had said. 'Precisely that. Like the backs of their hands.' And he had held up his own right hand, palm down, as though to prove this somehow vital point. He had behaved then as though he had gained no small victory over Merrit – this man who, though expected and awaited, had appeared before him with no proper warning or introduction, and who had then done nothing but create this succession of aggravations and conflicts.

Merrit continued walking, beginning his slow descent into the thickest part of the forest. Was it a forest? Woodland? Did woodland become a forest as it thickened? As it expanded? Did it grow denser overall or in this direction alone? The town was well served by roads, by the railway in most directions, and by a canal, so however far or thickly the forest spread, it did not restrict the place's communication or commerce with the wider world; it did not isolate or confine or restrict it.

In addition, there was a broad river running channelled and straightened a short distance from the square – he had crossed the stone bridge on his walk from the railway station to the hotel, and then again when he had gone out to the courtroom – and so perhaps the woodland only gave the *appearance* of surrounding the place. Or perhaps it was just that the reports he had so far read had concentrated so much upon it, and what the girls had allegedly seen within it, that it had acquired such a dominant part in all those tales of the place. Doubtless, too, those other writers understood something of those same fairy tales and of their vital and indispensable parts.

Webb had insisted that it was no more than a mile from the town to the place Merrit wished to see for himself. Perhaps not even that; perhaps closer to three-quarters of a mile; no distance at all. And perhaps even that lesser distance might be measured from the edge of the buildings rather than from the faltering end of the surfaced road. All these qualifying remarks; all these unnecessary and misleading clarifications; all these sudden uncertainties. It would have served no purpose for Merrit to have asked Webb if he himself was familiar with the track – the track and perhaps even the clearing in the trees from which all these hazy and excited ripples of rumour and speculation were now spreading unstoppably outwards.

Having walked downhill for several minutes, Merrit turned and considered the path behind him. It curved slightly and so the impression of the distance he had already come was lost to him. It curved and the trees came together to hide its course from him. It was still there, underfoot, but now its line up the gentle hillside was lost to view.

Looking back and forth, he saw too that the path was also lost ahead of him, the same continuing curve, encroaching trunks, interlocking branches and swallowed course.

He retraced his steps until he stood at the mid point of this curve. Like the crest of the hill, it was another boundary, another divide. In the half-light or darkness, standing precisely where Merrit now stood, mapless, directionless, and without a clear view of the narrowing path upon which he waited, a man might easily imagine himself at the centre of that dense, encircling and endless forest. And if a grown man might imagine this, then an impressionable and frightened young girl might certainly imagine it, and more, much more; and worse, much worse.

Resuming walking, Merrit started to whistle, and he noted how quickly the sound was absorbed by the trees and then lost. On his way up the hill he had heard birdsong – unidentified, he was no naturalist – but not here; here there was only silence. And again there was contradiction: no birdsong, and not even the slightest returning echo of his own whistling. But a dry stick he picked up and snapped sounded like a gunshot resounding all around him. Or if not a gunshot, then at least the careless footfall of a stalker, a follower, an unknown watcher intending harm.

He broke a second stick, and then a third, gauging both the noise he made and then the speed and completeness of the returning silence.

It was midday. The sun, hidden today by low, pewter-coloured cloud, might at other times have shone directly down on him where he stood. The woodland would be a different place again at dawn or dusk or on a less overcast day. Another small reckoning.

There was no curve to the path on the simple map Merrit held, leading him to suspect that Webb himself had never come this far into the trees on foot. Perhaps all Webb truly knew of the place was what the five girls had so far concocted among themselves and what the newspapers had been only too eager to repeat. And just as there was no marked curve to the path, so there was no suggestion of it narrowing as it approached his destination.

The clearing itself was represented by a small circle – Merrit could easily fit the tip of his forefinger into it – something fixed and definite amid so much otherwise featureless terrain.

Merrit knew from long experience that there was always a starting point, always a beginning, a pause to be made, a breath to be taken, and then a line to be crossed – stepping out of a railway carriage, say, or hearing a gavel struck on a desk; opening an envelope containing a summons, or hearing a clock strike the hour. Or turning a barely noticeable corner along a poorly marked woodland path – always a starting point and a beginning.

It was why he was there now, obeying these unwritten rules, observing these unspoken proprieties, alone, holding another man's map and only too aware of the true distance he had already come along his short journey: because there was always that starting point, always that beginning, that line to be discovered, then fixed, and then crossed.

And just as he considered all of this, preparing to take that next carefully measured step, so he unexpectedly arrived at the clearing itself. In truth, it was little more than a broadening of the path, a slight thinning of the trees on either side of him, an even slighter brightening of the sky above. An ordinary clearing in ordinary woodland in which such extraordinary events were alleged to have taken place. A clearing in a wood and a circle into which he could fit his fingertip. A line which neither rose nor fell, neither twisted nor turned, neither broadened nor narrowed, but which nevertheless, and with an undeniable and unavoidable inevitability, had led him here to this exact and unremarkable place.

Merrit looked around, gauged the centre of that small space, walked into it, and then stopped and looked around again.

2

H E RETURNED TO THE HOTEL AN HOUR LATER. THE BUILD-
ing had been recently completed, constructed of vivid
red brick, with stone sills and two thin brown marble columns
at its entrance.

Upon his arrival there, it had immediately struck Merrit
that the building looked out of place amid the older, smaller
properties on either side of it. It had been built to capitalize
on the recent increase in the number of trains arriving in
the town, but shortly before its completion, several of the
place's larger factories – mostly tanneries and engineering
works – had closed down, creating unemployment and
a sense of uncertainty and unease over the town's future.
Consequently, the anticipated increase in visitors and the
resident population had not materialized, and the hotel,
so obviously new and ready to embrace the hoped-for im-
provement in the town's future prospects, now had an
unavoidable air of abandonment about it. In addition, or so
it occurred to Merrit as he returned to it across the square,
the building seemed somehow to mock the place and all its
thwarted expectations.

He had stayed in fifty others like it, and knew what to
expect. Elsewhere, in larger, more prosperous places, the

hotels were better appointed and more anonymous, and he was able to remain detached and anonymous within them. But here, he knew, this was unlikely to happen. The square was the centre of the town, and the hotel was all too clearly intended to dominate that square.

Merrit entered the small lobby and nodded at the clerk behind the desk, expecting that the boy would retrieve his key and hand it to him. But instead the clerk nodded to the far side of the room, where a couple sat on a low sofa and watched his arrival.

'They're waiting for you,' the boy said, his voice low. 'An hour, at least.'

Merrit turned to look at the couple.

The man immediately rose from the sofa; his coat was un-fastened to reveal a black suit and a dog-collar around his thin neck. He took off the bowler he wore and then half-raised his hand to Merrit, at the same time looking down at the woman beside him, who remained where she sat.

Minister Firth, the third member of the appointed panel. And, presumably, his wife.

Merrit tried to remember their Christian names, but couldn't. He turned briefly back to the clerk and indicated where the key to his room remained on its hook. The boy still hesitated in retrieving this.

'They wanted to talk to you,' he said. He smiled at the minister, and Merrit guessed the connection between them, the source of the boy's uncomfortable obedience.

Merrit continued to hold out his hand until the boy finally took down the key and gave it to him.

'Is there somewhere we can talk?' Merrit asked him. 'Privately.'

The boy looked around him as though he hadn't understood the question. 'Privately?'

'The minister and myself.' Merrit was already starting to consider why the man had come to him like this. Their first official appointment was arranged for the following morning. The encounter with Webb had been unavoidable – protocol – but this impromptu meeting with the minister might be at best inadvisable and at worst somehow compromising, especially in the presence of his wife. The town was already filled with too many shadows and secrets and the stale air of whispered asides and personal interests, so why this now?

Merrit closed his hand around the key and turned back to the man and the woman.

'First he turns his back on us, and then he finally deigns to acknowledge our presence,' the woman said loudly, looking directly at Merrit and causing him to feel even more cautious concerning the encounter.

'My apologies,' he said. 'I didn't—'

'I am Aubrey Edward Firth,' the minister said, crossing the few paces to where Merrit stood.

'Merrit,' Merrit said.

The two men shook hands.

'We were told you would be here.'

By Webb? 'Oh?'

'It was no inconvenience to wait.'

Still on the sofa, the minister's wife made a noise intended to suggest to Merrit that she did not share her husband's opinion.

'Your wife?' Merrit said.

'Angelica,' the man said.

Merrit went to her and held out his hand. 'I was in the woods,' he said.

She looked at the mud on his shoes and trousers. 'Why?' she said.

'Is it so strange? I wanted to be where the girls—'

'You mean the liars,' she said abruptly. She took back her hand and then she too rose from the sofa. She was taller than her husband, and more heavily built. She wore a hat with a plain brim, and a coat buttoned from her throat to her shins, its only adornment a mother-of-pearl buckle on its narrow belt. She held a pair of soft kid gloves, which she caressed and drew back and forth through her palm as she spoke.

'I'm afraid neither I nor your husband is at liberty to discuss anything that might have any bearing on what he and I—'

'There's been talk of nothing else for the past month,' she said abruptly. She motioned for her husband to return to stand beside her.

Firth started to say something, but was interrupted by the arrival of another of the hotel's few guests, and his wife put a finger to her lips to silence him.

'I asked the clerk if there was somewhere more private,' Merrit said. 'But, as I was about to say, I believe all our opinion and conjecture might best be saved for when the inquiry is finally and properly under way.' He looked to Firth for his support, but saw that the man was powerless in the presence of his wife.

'I have, of course, discussed my own part in all of this with my wife,' Firth said eventually, his voice falling as he spoke, and leaving Merrit uncertain whether he was speaking in defence of himself or the woman.

'Of course,' Merrit said.

24

'And you are here to do what, to achieve what, exactly?' Angelica Firth said disdainfully.

'To lead and support the inquiry,' Merrit said. He wanted to tell her to leave and to take her weak and inadequate husband with her. He wanted to tell her that she played no part in their proceedings. She might be a witness, she might express her own opinion on what had or hadn't happened, she might even repeat publicly her assertion that the girls were all liars, but she still had no true or determining role in the proceedings, and certainly not at their outset. But even as Merrit considered all this, he saw only too clearly what power the woman exercised over her husband, and he knew it was something he would have to bear in mind as the proceedings progressed, and as the man played his own designated role within them.

Firth was a Man of God, there to represent the moral authority of the Church; he would need to be listened to. Everything might be challenged, everything denied, everything exposed, and Minister Firth, Merrit well understood, might have more to lose than any of them. Conversely, a great deal might yet hang in the balance, and the Church – whatever that meant in this place, whatever denominations or sects might be represented – would still carry a great deal of weight as that balance swung one way or the other. It was something else Merrit had hoped not to have to consider until the proceedings were under way.

'"To lead and support the inquiry"?' the woman repeated, drawing him back to her. 'Why – because you and your masters consider that we here are not capable of doing such a thing ourselves?'

'Not at all,' Merrit said. *Of course.* 'My masters? I prefer to think of them as my superiors, who exercise their own power and authority in a manner—'

'But *they* still exercise it,' she said. 'And *you* do their bidding. *They* still sent you, and *you* still came.'

There was nothing to be gained by contesting any of this, and so Merrit remained silent.

The woman now stood with her arms folded across her chest. She looked from Merrit to her husband to the boy at the desk and then back to her husband.

'It would be inadvisable for me to ask you to my room,' Merrit said eventually. 'And perhaps unwise.'

'Of course, of course,' Firth said. 'We merely wished to introduce ourselves and to extend a welcome to you. In addition, I sincerely hope that—'

'"Inadvisable"?' Angelica Firth said to Merrit. 'Why? Because it suits you to say so? Because from now on you alone are to determine the procedure and outcome of everything here? Because whatever is revealed here, your mind is already set on its course?'

Merrit felt himself relax at hearing the predictable accusations. He might later use this hostility to his own ends; perhaps all he needed to understand now was its source. Another hour with the woman and her husband and their whole lives would be revealed to him. But it would be a life-time of an hour, and nothing would induce him to spend it.

'You seem very certain of this,' Merrit said to the woman, half-turning to the minister as he spoke. 'I had hoped for a certain degree of . . .' – he pretended to think – 'open-mindedness' – the phrase sounded clumsy – 'and an ability to at least reconsider what might already have been revealed or suggested.'

'Exactly – a generosity of spirit,' Firth said, receiving another sharp glance from his wife.

'Precisely,' Merrit said. 'We shall, no doubt, encounter prejudice, bias and suspicion everywhere we look in the coming days, and I feel it incumbent upon we tribunal members . . .' He trailed off, his warning to the minister perfectly clear.

'Of course, of course,' Firth said again. 'And I'm sure Angelica understands that particular necessity completely.'

'See?' the woman said maliciously to Merrit. 'He's sure I understand what you're telling us.'

There was clearly no hiding place for the man.

'It's only natural that there will be people who resent my presence here, my role,' Merrit said, the words intended to both dampen and divert the woman's rising hostility.

'Your intrusion, you mean,' she said.

'Very well – my intrusion. But consider this – if there *are* difficult decisions to be made, then might it not be best if someone other than the figures of authority already well established and well respected here made them?'

'"Respected"?' the woman said, and was unable to prevent a sudden, cold laugh. If the remark was aimed solely at her husband, then it was her cruellest remark yet, and for the first time during their encounter, Merrit felt a stab of genuine sympathy for the man.

Firth himself merely continued looking at Merrit to suggest that he, Merrit, should forgive the woman her lack of restraint and understanding.

But rather than accede to this unspoken plea, Merrit chose to take advantage of what the woman had just said – and which, he sensed, even she now regretted – and he asked her why she had laughed.

'Surely,' he said, only too aware of his own cruelty, 'your husband is such a figure? Respected. Prominent. Why otherwise would he have been chosen to participate in the tribunal?'

But if he had expected her to seize this opportunity and somehow retract or apologize for her remark, he was mistaken.

'Because he was the only one stupid enough not to understand the true nature of the invitation to sit on your so-called panel when he was approached,' she said. 'All those other oh-so-concerned Men of God scattered like harvest rabbits the instant the investigation was announced. Go and ask them if you don't believe me. You've been here a day now – ' she looked pointedly at her watch, 'a little longer, in fact – and so you must surely be aware of how many churches, chapels, missions and Gospel Halls we have in this God-fearing place. Find them and ask them.' By now she was almost panting, her eyes shining.

For a moment, none of them spoke.

And then her husband said quietly, 'I accepted because I believed I might do some genuine good.'

A further short, awkward silence followed.

The words retrieved what little remained of Merrit's sympathy for the man. But even so, he still wanted to tell Firth that his wife was right in all that she was suggesting – whatever her own motives for doing so – and that he should have listened to her and stayed well away from everything that was about to happen there; that whatever 'good' he hoped to achieve would be questioned, mocked, unravelled, torn to pieces and then scattered on a never-ceasing, cold and uncaring wind. It had happened before, it would happen again; it could not be stopped. He himself had frequently grown numb and then indifferent in the face of that same cold wind.

'I also believed . . .' Firth began, but was then uncertain how to continue.

Merrit waited. 'What? You believed the girls might need an advocate?' he said.

Beside Firth, his wife shook her head. She seemed to Merrit to be a darkness into which her husband constantly stared.

'Then what?' Merrit asked her, tired of the woman's strategy.

'He believed he might do *himself* some good, this unselfish Man of God. Himself.'

Merrit didn't understand her.

'He is being considered for a living elsewhere, somewhere much larger.'

'Where?' Merrit said.

'We have been asked not to say. His own lords and masters. But somewhere much larger and more advanced than this place. Considerably more advanced. Somewhere with real society, and with educated, grateful, *willing* congregations.'

'Are they not educated, grateful or willing here, then?'

Neither the woman nor her husband answered him.

'I see,' Merrit said eventually. 'And you thought your appointment as a member of the tribunal might somehow improve your chances of securing this new post. When will it be decided?'

'A fortnight,' Angelica Firth said. 'Perhaps longer.' She seemed suddenly less certain of herself, less convinced of her husband's prospects.

The inquiry had been allocated twenty working days, four weeks of the local court's precious time.

'Are you still hopeful?' Merrit asked Firth directly, hoping to somehow encourage him by the remark.

'Oh, always hopeful,' Firth said. 'Always hopeful, always that.'

It seemed almost an epitaph for the man.

Several other guests arrived in the lobby, all of them strangers to the minister and his wife, and polite greetings were exchanged.

'What did you find?' Angelica Firth asked Merrit when they were again alone.

'Find?'

'Out in the blessed woods.'

'Just what is always there, I imagine – nothing more, nothing less. Trees, clearings, paths.'

'So, nothing to convince you that there might be one single iota of truth in what the girls are saying?'

'The liars?' Merrit said.

She ignored this and waited for his answer.

'All I know so far is what I've read in the newspaper reports,' Merrit said. It wasn't the whole truth, but near enough.

'I can imagine,' she said.

'Then you must surely understand the need for this investigation, the need to let in some clean air and strong light on these—'

She made another of her dismissive noises at the remark.

'Will you attend?' Merrit asked her.

'To hear them repeat their lies?'

'If need be, yes. But to hear them repeat their lies in that place and in front of myself, your husband and others,

30

instead of to their credulous, gullible friends and neighbours, or to the newspapermen waiting to turn everything they say to their own profit.'

'I knew you would say something like that,' she said.

'It's a completely different thing, telling their tales to—'

'To men like you? And him?'

'To men like us,' Merrit said. Even that seemed too great a concession to the woman.

'He spent nine years in China,' Angelica Firth then said unexpectedly. 'The Chinese Missionary Society. He almost died. Fever of the brain.'

Was there now something approaching affection in her voice, something as unlikely or as impossible as that?

People are always contradictory, Merrit's father – a true judge – had once told him. One moment you understand them completely, and the next they are beyond your understanding and your reach.

'I was well cared for,' Firth said. 'I met Angelica upon my return.'

'And they sent him here – *here* – as a reward for all the work he had done, for all his devotion and suffering.'

'We were once—' Firth began.

'Very happy here,' she said. 'I know.'

And to Merrit the words seemed like a knife sliced suddenly between them, though it was impossible to know which of them wielded it and which of them suffered from it.

A further pause followed.

'In answer to your question, I may attend,' Angelica Firth said. 'But, please, be aware that many who attend alongside me will consider your inquiry to be nothing more than a diversion and an entertainment, like a visiting fair or circus.'

'Why? Because, as you insist, the girls are all liars and nothing of any true worth or significance is going to be achieved by whatever might be revealed here?'

She smiled at the simultaneously evasive and self-serving phrase. 'And people think *I* have an inflated opinion of myself,' she said.

Merrit conceded the point in silence.

Without warning, the woman turned and left them, pausing only to pull on her gloves and then to speak briefly to the boy at the desk.

Merrit imagined she might beckon her husband to her, but instead she left the hotel without saying anything further to either of them.

3

THE ELDEST GIRL – A GIRL CALLED MARY COWAN, THOUGH some reports insisted on calling her Maryanne (already this subtle shading, these fractured outlines) – remained a stranger to Merrit. He believed he had read everything that had been written about her, and yet she remained this unknown presence – another unformed shape in the shifting light and shadows of the case.

He guessed that she had been cast by the newspapers as the ringleader of the girls as a convenience. At fifteen, almost sixteen, she was the eldest, and as such would be deemed the girl most capable of properly explaining the events in which they were all involved. Equally, Merrit understood, she was the one who might most legitimately and forcibly be held to account for whatever events and tales – some reports already said 'crimes' – the girls had so far concocted among themselves. Even more significantly, to Merrit's mind, she was the girl most likely to influence the course and the outcome of his inquiry.

His first encounter with Mary Cowan came much sooner than he had anticipated.

Several hours after the departure of Aubrey and Angelica Firth, and after Merrit had changed into fresh clothes, he left the hotel for a further brief investigation of the surrounding streets.

It was late afternoon by now, and the October light was starting to fade. In the lobby, the young clerk was filling and lighting the lamps on the desk and tables.

'They told us the electricity would be installed before the place was opened,' he said as Merrit passed behind him. 'It was in all the advertising.' He made it sound as though the failure had been his own.

A fire burned in the hearth beside the reception, another in the small room beyond. Merrit looked around him and the boy followed his gaze.

'You were expecting something else,' he said. 'Something more . . .'

'Not really,' Merrit said honestly. 'I go where I'm sent. One place quickly becomes another.'

The boy didn't understand him; perhaps this was the only place he knew.

'Will it rain, do you think?' Merrit said to break this stalled conversation.

The boy shrugged. 'Hard to say,' he said.

It had been Merrit's original intention upon his arrival to go to the place in the woods accompanied by the other members of the appointed panel, but having made the journey alone, and having seen nothing out of the ordinary there, he was now convinced that such a joint undertaking would only have worked against them. He had played no part in these other appointments, but he knew well enough from past experience what to expect from them. And he knew, too, how he, Merrit, would always be viewed differently and apart from them in the eyes of their local audience.

He went to the hotel entrance, fastened his coat and stepped outside. The setting sun cast one side of the square in its copper light, the other in almost impenetrable shadow. Uncertain which direction to take, he started walking towards the station. A train could be heard letting off steam in the distance.

Arriving at the corner of the square, he paused and looked back, and for the first time, amid the passers-by and sparse traffic there, he saw that a small group of people – adults and children – stood at the edge of the shadowed buildings and watched him. It was immediately clear to Merrit that he was the focus of their attention, and that he was not merely being idly watched as any passing stranger might be.

He remained where he stood for a moment. Four adults and two children. Three men, a woman and two girls. He guessed that these latter were perhaps two of the five girls he was there to question.

Reluctant to confront any of these watchers so soon, he turned away from them to look into a shop window. He pretended to look at the goods on display – it was the store of an agricultural merchant and the window was lined with half-filled boxes of various grains and seeds – and as he did this he saw in the glass that the small group – delegation? – was now approaching him. Someone called to him, one of the men, and he waited a moment before turning. The man had not used his name.

Merrit made a quick assessment: the man who had called to him was clearly the motivating force of the small group; the remainder seemed considerably more reluctant to be approaching him, held there only by this leading man. The man now stood with one hand on the shoulder of the eldest girl, whom he pushed ahead of him, and who seemed to Merrit to be more reluctant than most to be presented to him like this. The man's other hand was round the shoulders of the woman beside him, and she too seemed reluctant to come any closer. Husband and wife, then, mother and father. Daughter.

The second girl was younger, perhaps ten or eleven, and she stood with another of the men. This second man seemed even less certain of his role in these proceedings and held himself back. The child at his side seemed agitated, and she kept her head bowed and repeatedly moved her hands in and out of each other, watching them intently, mesmerized by her own simple actions. She wore a long pinafore, and what Merrit had at first taken to be its pattern he now realized was a mass of convergent stains which covered the garment from the child's chin down to its hem.

There had been suggestions in some of the newspaper reports that one of the girls had exhibited 'simple' or 'imbecilic' behaviour, and so perhaps this was her, and perhaps the man beside her was her father, and perhaps his reluctance to come forward was connected to his daughter's ailment, whatever that might be. All these assessments were the work of a moment, but they were made, and Merrit felt reassured by them.

The man who had called to him called again, this time with an undisguised note of hostility in his voice.

Merrit waited. First Webb, then the Firths, and now this. *Let hostilities commence.* He regretted having abandoned the warmth and privacy of the hotel. He would have been left alone there, unseen, unapproachable, unassailable even – an alien being in the one place which itself seemed alien to the town. These people had waited outside for him and were now gathered between him and the building. He smiled at the realization.

'You're Merrit,' the leading man said provocatively.

'I am.' Merrit took a pace towards them and saw how the rest of them looked suddenly anxious at this. He took a further step, fixing them where they stood. Only the man at the front continued to look directly at him. It was all an act, another carefully staged encounter, and both men knew this.

The girl held by the man looked quickly at Merrit and then she bowed her head and kept her eyes on her feet.

Merrit looked beyond the two of them to the others; they too swiftly avoided his eyes.

'I'm the one who's talking to you,' the man said to Merrit. 'Not them.' He removed his hand from his wife and clasped it to his daughter's other shoulder. He then flicked her cheek and chin with the back of his fingers, causing her to raise her head and look directly at Merrit.

'Mary Cowan,' Merrit said. 'I'm pleased to meet you. I imagined I would have to wait until tomorrow, if not later, for the pleasure.' If she had been older, not a child, he would have held out his hand to her.

But the girl made no response to this hopefully disarming greeting, and her father countered it by pulling her back to him so that she was pressed even more closely to his chest and stomach.

The younger girl, Merrit noticed, continued to disregard completely everything that was happening, her attention still fixed on her restless hands. Merrit tried to remember her name – either Agnes Foley or Margaret Seaton – but he couldn't be certain. He took a chance.

37

'And that must be Agnes,' he said, causing an equally dramatic response from the man who held her. Why should his knowing their names come as such a great and unsettling surprise to them? He tried to remember the exact nature of the girl's affliction, anything he might have read concerning her own history, but this still eluded him.

'You were in the woods,' Cowan said, drawing Merrit back to him.

'Is that an accusation?' Merrit said.

'A what?'

'An accusation. Am I being accused of something? Should I not have gone there? Should I have spoken to you first? Are you the landowner?' They were not true questions, merely a succession of jabs to assert his own as yet untested authority, and, if this failed, simply to keep the man away from him.

'Landowner?' Cowan said.

'I just wondered . . .' Merrit left the remark unfinished, its work done.

'I'm no landowner,' Cowan said. He whispered something behind his hand to the two other men and they both laughed nervously at his words.

Merrit saw even more precisely where Cowan stood with the group, and he took a further step towards him. He looked around them and saw that others in the square had paused to watch the confrontation. Not many, a dozen perhaps, mostly men and women trying their best to appear otherwise engaged, but a few putting on no pretence and watching intently what was happening. It was Merrit's guess that they kept their distance on account of Cowan rather than because of his own presence.

'We have an audience,' he said to the man. 'Perhaps for the

children's sake all this might be postponed until tomorrow. I'm sure—'

'When *you*'ll be in charge of everything, when everything gets written down and shown to others, and when the world can have a proper gawp at us.'

'"Gawp"?' Merrit said. He knew exactly what the man was telling him.

'Look. He means a closer look.' This time it was the man's wife who had spoken, surprising both Merrit and her husband.

Merrit seized this small opportunity.

'Are you Mary's mother?' he asked her.

'I am. Also Mary.'

Cowan turned to look at her and the woman immediately lost her confidence.

Merrit looked again at the girl at the rear of the group. Her fingers were now tightly locked and she showed this knot to those around her and waited for their compliments. The distraction further angered Cowan, and he called to Agnes Foley's father to hold the girl more firmly.

'Agnes,' Merrit called to the girl.

Cowan smiled at hearing this. 'She won't hear you,' he said. 'What, you think she might even *answer* you?'

'Is she deaf?' Merrit said. He regretted the easy advantage he had tried to take and then so quickly lost.

Cowan's smile broadened, revealing a line of dark teeth. 'Something like that.'

'Then what?' Merrit said. He understood how the girl's presence undermined him, and he guessed that Cowan had brought her and her father with him for this precise purpose. It was also clear to him by then that the girl would almost certainly now be excluded from his own formal questioning.

He looked back to Mary Cowan and saw that she was still watching him closely. This time she did not avert her eyes from him, and he sensed a change in her – a growing defiance, perhaps, of the role she herself was there to play.

'Have you been waiting long?' he said directly to her.

'Waiting?' Cowan said before his daughter could speak. 'What makes you think we'd wait for you?'

Merrit almost laughed at the remark.

'An hour,' Mary Cowan said, causing her father to fall silent.

'You should have asked for me at the hotel,' Merrit said.

'That place?' her father said, confirming Merrit's suspicions about the building.

Merrit kept his eyes on the girl, and she in turn continued looking at him.

'You don't know what you're doing here,' Cowan said, angry that he no longer controlled what was being said, and demanding that attention shift back to him.

'It's a straightforward procedure, I can assure you,' Merrit said.

'So straightforward you can't even look at me when I'm talking to you?'

'I was referring to the inquiry,' Merrit said. 'The inquiry itself is straightforward in its aims and methods.'

'If you think for one minute—'

'And, please, don't mistake it for a court of law. No one is here – I am not here – to judge or to punish your daughter, merely to establish the facts of the matter.' He paused. 'And then perhaps for certain recommendations to be made.' He was tired of the man's posturing in front of his audience, and so he continued to jab back at him with this unsettling and vaguely threatening language.

'And *then* you'll judge us,' Cowan said.

'You weren't there,' Merrit said simply. 'In the woods.' And the instant he said it, he saw a smile form and then just as swiftly vanish from the girl's lips. She finally looked away from him, rubbing a hand across her face. She looked briefly at Agnes Foley, watching as her father prised apart the tight knot of his daughter's fingers.

'Did the others not wish to accompany you?' Merrit asked Cowan, catching him off-guard.

'What others?'

Merrit waited.

'He means the other girls,' Agnes Foley's father said. 'Their own families.' Even he seemed to have finally lost patience with Cowan's posturing.

'I know what he—' Cowan stopped himself.

'Anything you wish to know, to learn, you are at perfect liberty to ask,' Merrit called to Foley. 'Not now, perhaps, but at the inquiry. And I shall do my utmost to see that your own daughter is caused no undue distress.'

'Her?' the man said, uncertain what Merrit was suggesting to him. But in a tone which was all the confirmation Merrit needed.

By then the crowd of onlookers had doubled in number, and more of these were doing nothing now to hide their curiosity. But, tellingly, no one else had yet come forward to participate in the encounter. This growing crowd, Merrit realized, would do more to undermine Cowan than anything *he* might say to the man.

'What will you ask her?' Mary Cowan's mother said to Merrit, distracting him from his thoughts, and again causing her husband to suppress his anger at her words.

'I can't say,' Merrit said.

'You don't know?'

'I can't say. The thing must take its course. Nothing will be done in secret; everything will be open, made public. There will be ample opportunity for your own comments and observations to be recorded, should you—'

'Recorded?' the woman said.

'In the official record of proceedings. Of the inquiry. The usual court recorder will be in attendance throughout.'

'Recorded?' the woman repeated.

'So that no mistakes are made, so that everything is clear and above contention or misunderstanding.' He had intended to reassure the woman, but his words had clearly had the opposite effect.

'What did I tell you?' Cowan said loudly, stroking his wife's arm.

'Everyone concerned will be invited' – Merrit almost said 'called' – 'to give their own testimony.'

'Like I said – and *then* we'll all be judged,' Cowan repeated triumphantly.

And then *you will all be judged.*

Merrit took a step back. He felt the kerb at his heel. Another inch and he might have lost his balance and fallen.

'Watch yourself,' Cowan said, his voice lower but still with its malicious edge. 'Can't have an important man like yourself falling over in the street and making a spectacle of himself. What would people think?' He expected laughter at this, but none came. After this, he put his hands lower over his daughter's chest and announced that it was time for them all to return to their homes.

Merrit saw how quickly the others turned and started walking away. And it was only then, as he watched them leave, that Merrit noticed Oliver Webb standing at the far side of the square. The magistrate stood with his wife and two younger, grown women; his own daughters, perhaps. It was clear to Merrit that the man was unhappy at having been seen like this. He raised his hand to Webb, but received no response. In turn, he too felt uncomfortable at having been seen by the man.

'That's high-and-mighty Webb,' Cowan said. 'I hope you're not expecting great things from *him*.' He hawked a ball of phlegm into his mouth and then let this drip to his feet.

'I know who he is,' Merrit said.

'Of course you do,' Cowan said. He wiped his sleeve across his mouth. 'You know everything.' He turned his daughter and pushed her ahead of him towards the others.

Merrit watched them go. They approached close to where Webb still stood with his family, but if either man spoke to the other they were too distant for Merrit to hear. Waiting until Cowan and his daughter had turned into a side street, Webb also left the square, quickly followed by the three women.

Abandoning his plans of walking to the station, Merrit waited until the last of the small crowd had dispersed around him and then he returned to the sanctuary of his room.

4

H E TOOK FROM HIS CASE THE FOLDER OF NOTES, INSTRUC-
tions and documents he had been given by the Director
of Public Law, who had himself received it only ten days
earlier from the Assistant Chief Constable of the county.

Mostly, the folder contained newspaper cuttings and
the few local police reports on the matter so far. It was an
inadequate and unsteady foundation upon which to begin,
and Merrit understood this. For him, now, it was a matter of
establishing what few verifiable facts were known, and then
of compiling for possible further investigation a succession of
names, events, places and times.

There was a handwritten note from the Assistant Chief
Constable asking whether or not the events already listed
might lead to any prosecutions under criminal or, as seemed
more likely, civil law. It seemed an unnecessary remark to
make, however telling in its inclusion, and Merrit quickly decided that this was not a genuine concern or conviction on
the man's part, merely a further passing-on of the baton of
responsibility and recommendation-making – from him to
the Chief Constable to Merrit's Director to Merrit himself.
Reading the note, Merrit smiled at the thought that perhaps
Oliver Webb or Aubrey Firth might now consider themselves

close enough – and unfortunate enough – to have that same baton handed on to either of them upon his departure from the place.

It took him less than an hour to read again everything that had been collected – or, more accurately, everything that had so far been considered worthy by his superiors of retrieval and inclusion. Already there were these clues, these faint paths forward, these gently prodded sticks and whispering, beckoning voices. But in the absence yet of anything recorded by himself – the few police reports did little more than perform their own perfunctory duty – most of what he read came from the newspaper accounts. And because of this, there was duplication, embellishment and repetition: the same few headlines, the same few reported events drawn out into ever-growing and ever-changing tales. Little appeared to have been omitted, though as yet it was impossible to know this for certain.

No strong and reliable foundation stones then, merely a hundred loose straws blowing in the wind, with nothing but the five girls' shared story to bind them into a strong or cohesive whole. Shadows and whispers, and he, Merrit, was clutching at both.

The remains of a meal sat on the table beside the scattered papers. The clerk had brought Merrit a glass of soda and a large tumbler of whisky with the food. The wine he had ordered had failed to appear – something mumbled about the wine merchant and delivery dates – and so the boy had brought this other drink instead, clearly considering it a reasonable substitute to accompany the meal.

The clerk had then turned up the lamps in Merrit's room – one beside the bed, two on the walls, and one on the table by the window where Merrit sat – and had shovelled coal on to the small fire, briefly filling the room with smoke before adding to its already airless warmth. He had paused at the table, looking at the papers over Merrit's shoulder. 'Is that here?' he'd said. 'All those things?' Merrit had confirmed that it was indeed 'here' and 'all those things', intrigued by what the clerk might go on to reveal to him. But the boy had then drawn back, reluctant even to look at the papers, let alone speculate on them. Merrit had not pushed him, merely cleared a space for him to set the plate and glasses down.

An hour had passed since the clerk's departure, and in the scattered pages before him, the whole of a month had unfolded.

Outside, it was now fully night. Gas lights had been lit around the square, their balls of yellow light never quite coalescing and leaving their intervening strips of darkness. The centre of the square was similarly darkened. A few people still passed beneath the lights, but no one now congregated in the space. He imagined his own silhouette through the pane of glass and the patterned lace of the curtains. It was another of the things the place had once been renowned for – its lace-making – but not any longer.

In the final memorandum from his own Director, the man had written 'something or nothing?' as though a broad spectrum of choice truly existed – creating the illusion of a vast and empty land in which Merrit alone was now at liberty to wander as the place revealed itself to him.

It was a simple case of hysteria, the Director had told him when the two men had met the day before Merrit's departure, slapping his palm on the same pile of papers. Hysteria. Something or nothing, something *and* nothing. Hysterical girls, malicious intent; perhaps conniving, perhaps manipulative girls, anyway creatures beyond all rational understanding. It was hysteria, pure and simple, and the question now was one of public unrest, public confidence and public disorder. Order, it was a question of order. Order, above all else. Things must not – *would* not – be allowed to get out of hand. Order, yes, and reason, and both of them supported and held firmly in place by the rule of law. The rule of law and the voice of reason.

Hysteria. The spark of the word had spread in a sudden blaze and ignited countless other fires. Its repetition – and now that the newspapers had seized on the word it was seldom *not* included in their lurid headlines – might mean nothing or it might mean everything. But, the Director had said, pausing and drawing breath, what we are dealing with above all else here – what *you* and *I* are dealing with above all else here (and by 'you and I' Merrit knew, of course, that he meant Merrit alone) is public opinion. It was an altar to the man, and Merrit knew this, too. What had happened so far – all these rumours and lies and scarcely credible tales – was something out of hand, something uncontrollable, uncontained and unshaped. The man had said all this as though building a solid and dependable wall around that sudden blaze. He would retire in less than a year, whereupon he would be honoured for his services to the State. The same palm slammed down upon the same papers. A situation awaiting only a measure of external and rational control, imposed with conviction, and afterwards maintained by both reason and necessity. The man's very words. It sounded like a sermon, loud and clear and unforgettable in both its message and its intent. That same slippery and dangerous baton moving from hand to hand to hand.

Merrit had afterwards discovered – a word of caution whispered in his ear – that the Chief Constable of the county – the man already maintaining his own carefully measured distance from *his* assistant – and the Director had been at school and then university together. Harrow, then Cambridge. And then the two of them had worked in the same government departments as their careers had progressed. A measure of external control, a safe pair of hands, containment.

Facts, the Director had insisted. The facts of the matter, these were what now counted. Substance, evidence, confirmation. Not tales, not stories, not the attention-seeking fictions of these ridiculous girls. Not . . . not . . . not . . . The man had stuttered to this halt and his eyes had met Merrit's, the file still held under his heavy palm, waiting only to be reassured that Merrit understood him completely. Perfectly, Merrit had said. He understood the man perfectly. And the man had said, Good, good, good, no stuttering now, and had finally raised his hand from the papers and reports and all the inflammatory and contradictory tales they contained.

Merrit drank more of the whisky, regretting not having told the clerk to bring him the bottle and leave it in his room.

There had been other events before the affair in the clearing in the woods.

Seven weeks ago, Margaret Seaton, aged fourteen, had woken her parents and three older brothers in the middle of the night with her shouts and screams, and when they had rushed to her she'd told them that a man had been in her room and that he had pulled the covers from her bed. A small window was open, and Margaret Seaton insisted that this had been closed and bolted by her before getting into bed.

Because she could not be calmed or reassured, her father had gone to the police station and reported the event.

The following day, a constable visited the household to establish the details of the case. It was then that Margaret Seaton said that not only had the man appeared in her bedroom and pulled the bed sheets from her, but that he had also attempted to climb into bed beside her, putting his hand on her legs and attempting to raise her nightdress. This was when she had started screaming, she said, alerting her parents and brothers, none of whom could add anything to the story except to confirm that no one and nothing else had been disturbed or tampered with, and that the bolts on the two downstairs doors were still firmly in place.

It had been a rainy night and there were no wet footprints or pools of water anywhere in the house. In his report, the constable recorded that he had asked Margaret Seaton if she might have been dreaming. In response, he said, she screamed at him and then attacked him with her fists until restrained by her father, an unemployed harness-maker. He noted that the man was clearly embarrassed by his daughter's unaccountable and, he insisted, uncharacteristic behaviour.

It was the first of a succession of events. 'Similar' events, most reports suggested and then concurred, thus providing the first of countless tenuous connections and afterthoughts.

Margaret Seaton was kept at home for several days after the alleged assault, and then she was allowed to return to the school she attended.

A week later, the family of a girl called Edith Lisset, two years younger than Margaret Seaton, was woken by the sudden, loud and unmistakeable crashing and clatter of crockery being smashed, again in the middle of the night

– three a.m., according to the police report. Edith Lisset's parents had gone downstairs together to find a whole dinner service, two dozen pieces, smashed and scattered across the flagged floor of their small kitchen. The crockery – Staffordshire, a wedding present, six settings, plates, bowls, cups and saucers, no detail of the precious service was omitted – had been previously displayed on the kitchen dresser, and now here was everything smashed into a thousand pieces on the stone floor and gathered in drifts against the skirting.

Edith Lisset's mother had wept at the loss throughout the following day's interview. Again, doors and windows had been locked and bolted from within and there was no evidence of any intruder. Edith, her father said, had been the last to wake and come downstairs on that eventful night. She had appeared in the dimly lit kitchen – one of only two downstairs rooms – barefoot and rubbing her eyes, her long hair covering her face. She, too, had cried at the sight of the shattered crockery, and at the sight of her inconsolable mother. According to her father, the girl had gone to comfort the crying woman, treading on the shards and cutting the soles of both her feet as she went. She appeared not to notice this, however, and only acceded to her father's attention an hour later, when her feet were finally washed and bound with cloths. There were signs of slight bleeding, the police report noted, at several places on the floor.

The scattered pieces of pottery were left where they lay until the constable finished compiling his report. Edith Lisset, he recorded, had heard nothing of what had happened, waking only when her father had called up to her. The same constable said that the girl seemed oblivious to all that was happening around her, still more asleep than awake. For instance, he said, she felt no pain from her bleeding feet, insisting over and over that she be allowed to comfort her weeping mother. He noted that the roles of the pair of them – mother and daughter – seemed to him to have been somehow reversed for the duration of his time in the house.

Edith Lisset was an only child. It was, apparently, well known in the town that her mother had suffered a succession of miscarriages in the years following her daughter's birth, and that she had afterwards lived her life in a state of indeterminate invalidity.

Both Margaret Seaton and Edith Lisset attended the same school. They lived only a few hundred yards apart; they were friends, saw a good deal of each other and could often be found in each other's homes. It was not a particularly surprising or significant connection in so small a place, but a connection all the same.

Edith Lisset had been attended before this event by Doctor Simeon Nash, the fourth member of Merrit's panel, and his notes, though marked 'confidential', were now included in the sparse documentary evidence.

Two years previously, Nash had attended the girl when she had fallen and badly cut her head while – so it was then assumed – sleepwalking. She had been found shortly after midnight on the road outside her home, unconscious, naked, with a cut on her head and with blood smeared over her face and chest. And then, too, Nash had noted that the child had seemed oblivious to her injury and the pain it must have been causing her. It was why, he later said, he had concurred with the consensus of opinion that the girl had been sleepwalking when she'd fallen.

During the two years between this incident and the night

of the smashed crockery, Nash had seen little of the girl professionally, but had either visited or been visited by her mother on an almost monthly basis, sometimes accompanied by her husband and her daughter, and sometimes by her daughter alone. It was Nash's belief, he wrote, that when the woman came with the girl alone, it was to keep her visits secret from her husband. So, more collusion and secrecy to add to the growing mix.

It was the beginning. The girls' teacher was visited and questioned. The intruder in Margaret Seaton's bedroom was sought; sparks already falling into the waiting tinder. A man was arrested in a town fifteen miles away, brought to the local police station and interviewed, jailed for a night, questioned again and then released when his alibi was confirmed.

Cuts on Edith Lisset's forearm and palm were caused, she said, when wiping the shards from the seat beside her mother. There was no evidence to suggest that the injuries – in truth little more than scratches – had been otherwise inflicted.

It was the beginning. The girls, two events, separate and yet connected, completely different in all their particulars and implications, and yet –

Merrit laid his hand on the uppermost sheet of paper, pressing down and spreading his fingers, as though by this simple expedient everything might be held firmly in check. *Things must not be allowed to get out of hand.* The glass beside him was now empty. A further gust of smoke blew from his fire, leaving its haze over the hearth and mantel. The same draught caused his lamp wicks to gutter, and the low flames to falter and then fade for a moment before burning steadily again and resuming their glow.

5

THE INQUIRY WAS FINALLY CONVENED THE FOLLOWING morning. The small courtroom was prepared and the local staff were assembled; rooms and corridors were swept, windows washed, fires stoked; paper and pencils and ledgers were laid out, opened, closed, rearranged, opened again; public notices were posted, ushers positioned and the gathering, restless queues shown where to form.

And then a note from Doctor Nash was handed to a constable, who handed it to his sergeant, who then sought out Magistrate Webb and gave it to him.

Apologies. Emergency summons. Delay. Nash.

Webb read and re-read the note with growing disbelief. He then showed it to Aubrey Firth, who in turn suggested delivering it to Merrit.

Merrit, meanwhile, watched this sudden flurry of activity from his seat on the low stage. Everywhere he looked, it seemed to him – every action, every expression, every utterance – there was this excited, unnecessary drama.

'What is it?' he called down to the two men. Webb would sit

to his left, the minister to his right. Nash, when he eventually arrived, would sit beyond Firth.

For a moment, neither man answered him, making him cautious. He looked at the piece of paper Firth still held, knowing nothing yet of its contents or of its telling course towards him.

'This,' Webb finally called up to him, taking the paper from Firth and waving it at Merrit.

Merrit read the note and gave it back to Webb. He had expected something more.

'We'll still proceed,' he said calmly.

'Impossible,' Webb said. 'Court of Inquiry regulations. Every member of the investigating panel to be present and to register at the outset of proceedings.'

'Surely we can start and hope that Doctor Nash is able to join us soon?'

Webb shook his head. He turned to Firth for support, and the man came reluctantly to stand beside him. Merrit saw again how it was in the place.

'Rules of Commencement,' Webb said, this time only half-turning to Firth for his support.

'It does seem to be the proper procedure,' Firth said uncertainly.

Merrit knew not to insist. He wondered how many similar investigations – if any – had ever been held in the place. He might have more profitably spent the previous evening refamiliarizing himself with all these procedural minutiae and better preparing himself for eventualities such as this.

'Then what do you suggest?' he said, looking from Webb to the silhouettes of the waiting crowd in the frosted glass of the doors.

'It isn't a question of what *I* suggest,' Webb said.

'Of course. Then the inquiry shall adjourn until—'

'We haven't yet convened,' Webb said. 'So, on a further point of procedure—'

'The convening of the inquiry shall be postponed until Doctor Nash is able to appear,' Merrit said firmly. 'But might we at least open the doors and explain the situation to everyone who wishes to wait?'

A clerk had earlier told Merrit that the room would hold two hundred people and that at least that number were already gathered outside.

'Impossible,' Webb said. He said something to Firth, which Merrit did not hear. Then the two men walked together to the door and Webb commanded the man there to let them out.

Merrit heard the magistrate addressing the waiting queue, heard their angry protestations. He then heard the flowing line of these disappointed responses as the magistrate and the minister walked further along the corridor and out of the building.

The clerk at the door locked it and came back to where Merrit now sat alone in the otherwise empty room.

'What shall we do?' the man asked him.

'Go and wait outside,' Merrit told him. 'Lock the door and tell those who want to wait to wait. Explain what's happened, the cause of the delay.'

'No need,' the man said. 'I'll just tell them to wait. I doubt many will leave.'

'It might be hours,' Merrit suggested.

'They'll still wait.' The man returned to the door and made his own announcement. A further outburst greeted this. Merrit heard the door being locked and saw the man's back pressed to the glass.

It was not the beginning he had wanted. Now when the inquiry started, the room would be filled with a heightened and unnecessary tension.

A further hour passed, during which Merrit read for the first time in a decade those same rules and regulations so beloved of Webb. It was an advantage he was determined to cede no further to the man. The clerk remained at the door and the queue of waiting people remained stretched along the corridor, mostly quieter now, talking and calling to each other, all of them determined to secure their places in the room. Merrit saw what an even greater disappointment these opening rituals were now likely to be to them all. Or perhaps it was better for their anger to be vented like this, today, rather than when the proceedings were properly under way and the first of the girls was put before them.

After that hour there was a rap at the door immediately behind Merrit, the one which led into the room's small ante-chamber, in which he, Webb and Firth had first gathered.

The door opened and a man, stooping to avoid its low frame, came into the room. He smoked a slender cigar and was clearly surprised to find the room empty. At first he didn't see Merrit, and Merrit coughed to alert him to his presence.

'Has the witch trial finished?' the man said to him. 'Have they all been found guilty and dragged off to be drowned or burned?' He took a watch from his pocket and looked at it.

'Our doctor, apparently, had urgent business elsewhere, and our magistrate insisted on following to the letter—' He stopped speaking, guessing then that this was Nash.

'I'm sure he did.' The man held out his hand. 'Simeon Nash.'

'I'm Merrit,' Merrit said, wishing he'd added his own Christian name.

Nash smiled. 'I doubt there's anyone within a ten-mile radius of the place who doesn't know who you are. And "Go-Forth"?'

'Sorry?'

'"Go-Forth Firth". I imagine the man hears the unspoken words every time his name is said. Did he trot out after Webb like the calculating and obedient little lapdog he is?'

'They left together,' Merrit said simply.

'Forgive me,' Nash said. 'I imagine that underneath it all, Firth is the best among us.'

'I suggested starting pending your imminent arrival,' Merrit said.

'"Imminent"?' Nash said, smiling again. 'I imagine that went down well with *Alderman* Webb.'

'You clearly know the man considerably better than I do.'

'Everything there is to know about him, you learned during your first half-minute with him.'

Merrit conceded this in silence.

'*Apparently*, my patient died,' Nash said. 'She fell, I was sent for, and then she died a few minutes before I arrived.'

'My apologies,' Merrit said. 'I didn't mean—'

'She was sixty-three. An irregular heart. It was a bad fall. I would have been here sooner, but I had to arrange for a message to be sent to Proctor.'

'Proctor?'

'Our undertaker. When that was done, I came as quickly as I could. Was nothing whatsoever achieved here? Nothing at all?' He looked around him for a dish in which to press out the stub of his cigar. Merrit handed him one from the table.

'And Lady Bountiful?' Nash said. 'Angelica Firth.'

'I met her yesterday. She seemed concerned that—'

'She's concerned about everything, mostly her husband's lost, wasted, ungrasped and unfairly snatched-away opportunities.'

'It was the impression she gave,' Merrit said.

'She gives the impression like a boxer gives the impression he's punching you in the face. And Webb himself?'

'What about him?'

'Surely he's made his own unhappiness clear to you.'

'I spoke to him for more than half a minute,' Merrit said, causing Nash to laugh. 'Is there anything specific – Webb's own concerns, I mean?'

'*You*'re here – it's enough. You're here and you're usurping his own all-powerful and never-questioned authority at the centre of his very own little kingdom.' He waved a hand at the room around them, noticing for the first time the silhouette of the man at the door. 'Are they all still waiting?' he said.

'For the witch trial?'

'I knew who you were before I said it,' Nash said, unconcerned.

Merrit considered this and all it was intended to imply. 'I should send word to Webb and Firth that we're ready to begin,' he said.

Nash turned away at the suggestion.

'Is there anything else you think I should know?' Merrit asked him. 'Before the circus is under way.'

'This,' Nash said. 'All this . . . You do understand, I suppose – hope – you do understand what's happening here – the girls, everything they're claiming has happened, everything they say they've seen, the woods.' Nash turned back to him and waited.

'You believe it's all a fabrication,' Merrit said.

'Of course it is. It's all lies, all tales. They're revelling in it and all the attention it's bringing them.'

Merrit wanted to counter the remark with what he'd seen of Agnes Foley, but said nothing. 'Do you know them all?' he said eventually.

'I do,' Nash said. 'And I concur that some are gaining considerably more than others from all this. As you will already know, I was called to examine Margaret Seaton on the night of her so-called assault.'

'Perhaps this might wait to be put on record,' Merrit suggested, concerned about what the man might have been about to reveal to him.

'I'll say it, anyway,' Nash said. 'Publicly, privately, whenever.'

'What did you find?'

'Nothing. I see in all the reports that I "examined" her and found her to have come to no harm. That so-called examination was, shall we say, extremely cursory. There was no blood, no bruising, and everyone present – parents, brothers, the girl herself – insisted that nothing had happened to her. She woke, the man was in her room, he possibly lay on the bed, he perhaps touched her nightclothes, she screamed, the man disappeared, her parents appeared. I gave her a mild sedative and made every reassuring noise I knew how to make.'

'The reports suggested something more thorough, something more . . . definite, conclusive.'

'I know they do.'

'And you believe the girl made the whole thing up. To what end?'

Nash shrugged. 'I can think of a dozen reasons, but all of them would be speculation. I imagine they' – he gestured to the door and the waiting crowd – 'could give you a dozen more.'

'More speculation,' Merrit said, making his own point clear. 'And is it the consensus of opinion – locally, I mean – that the girls are concocting *all* of this among themselves?' It was no more or less than he himself already believed.

And Nash understood this and remained silent, this firm, unspoken understanding fixed between them.

'Wait until you meet Cowan,' he said eventually.

'It's already happened,' Merrit said. 'Father *and* daughter.'

'Then you'll know the man is already keeping his eye on the main chance.'

'I know he's—'

'Money,' Nash said. He rubbed his thumb and fingers together. 'Remuneration, I believe they call it. The newspapers. The man hasn't worked full-time for years. Too fond of a drink. Stories, articles, background information on all the other girls. And I daresay all this – you, me, us, the inquiry – has done nothing to dampen the reading public's salacious enthusiasm for any of that.'

'I have no real authority to restrict or deny the reporting of whatever happens here,' Merrit said. He had read the new regulations concerning the reporting of public inquiries only minutes earlier.

'Perhaps not, but both Cowan and Webb will be considerably more aware of that particular aspect of your powerlessness than you yourself will ever be.'

'Do you imagine Webb might seek some way to——?'

'To impose some magisterial and unassailable power of his own over all of this? Perhaps. Or perhaps he'll be content to watch you fail to impose your own barely existent authority here and make a fool of yourself that way.'

'How many ways are there, do you imagine?' Merrit said, smiling.

Nash began counting on each of his slowly outstretched fingers. 'After which, of course – and following your own premature and ignominious departure – he'll be only too happy to tell his own little story to the pencil-lickers.'

'A story of how he would have done everything differently and to a completely different end? I think——'

'And *I* think that whatever *you* try to achieve here, whatever measure of reason and understanding *you* try to impose over everything, the girls – and Mary Cowan in particular – will run rings around us all.'

The remark, and Nash's sudden change of tone, surprised Merrit. 'Webb and Firth included?'

'Webb and Firth included,' Nash said. 'Whatever else the girls are, they're all still children – even Cowan and Seaton. They're all children. All this is too . . . too . . .'

'Heavy-handed?'

'That's the least of it. But whatever else it is, and whatever its outcome, surely you can see how it will all look to the watching world once everything is actually under way.'

Again, Merrit understood precisely what Nash was telling him. And again, it was something he had himself already long understood and considered – if not here, then at a dozen other places and events like it.

'What happened between you and Cowan the elder?' Nash said.

'Nothing of consequence. I imagine he just wanted to make himself known to me.'

'I imagine he did. "INQUISITOR BACKS DOWN IN FACE OF LOCAL MAN'S QUESTIONS". If the profitable story doesn't exist, then conjure it up out of thin air.'

'"Inquisitor"?' Merrit said.

'You've heard it before,' Nash said. 'Surely. And you do understand and accept by now, I hope, that his daughter is the instigator and leader in all of this.'

'It seems fairly clear.'

'The others follow her, look up to her, though God knows why. She leads them and she manipulates them.'

'Even the Foley girl?' Merrit said.

'You've seen Agnes Foley?' Nash fell silent for a moment, and then said, 'Until nine months ago, she lived in a home for imbeciles in Wellingborough. I was appointed to attend to her by the County Charity Commissioners when her father insisted on bringing her back home under the new Asylum legislation.'

'Why?' Merrit said.

'Why did he want her back home? You'd have to ask him that. Whatever the reason, they share a particularly miserable existence.'

'What are her prospects?' Merrit said.

'You've seen her. I'm a medical practitioner; I know very little about that side of things. But whatever else afflicts her, she suffers from fits and seizures on an alarmingly frequent basis.'

'I imagine she must be easily led,' Merrit said, immediately regretting how callous the remark sounded.

'I imagine you're right,' Nash said. 'But, like I said, Mary Cowan is the one you need to keep the closest and keenest eye on.'

'Have you attended her, too?'

'On occasion. Nothing out of the ordinary. All the usual childhood injuries and ailments. Perhaps a few more cuts and bruises than most, but nothing more. And as you might also imagine, having met him, her father didn't exactly consider my fees money well spent.'

'But nothing in direct connection with what we're here to consider now?'

Nash shook his head.

It had been Merrit's intention to call for a full physical examination of all the girls, but he saw now how detrimental this would be to the remainder of his work.

'The girl was reluctant to say much to me in the presence of her father,' he said.

'You watch her,' Nash said. 'She behaves like two completely different people depending on his presence. He keeps her a dependent, obedient child when she's with him, but without him she imagines herself to be considerably more.'

'And you believe that's part of her motivation for everything that's happening now?'

'It must have *something* to do with it. He exercises control over her, she exercises an even greater control over the others. Last year, the man broke his wife's nose and her wrist. The year before that, she came to me with three broken fingers.'

'All caused by him?'

'Of course not. All accidents. She broke her nose by falling on a boulder while crossing the river, her fingers

63

by trapping her hand in a door. Her husband wasn't within a mile of her on any occasion. She told me as much ten times over.'

'I see,' Merrit said.

'Then also see that you are about to find yourself in an identical situation with the girl. She will lie to you, you will know she is lying to you, and yet there will be nothing whatsoever you can do about it.'

'But, surely—'

'But surely, what?' Nash said, raising his voice. 'Surely the truth will be plain for all to see? Surely all that is at issue here is establishing that truth and making it plain and clear and simple so that everyone might accept it and be convinced and then reassured by it? Surely the truth will be made plain and then this makeshift court will become, in its way, one great and vital act of redemption or atonement and everything will be made honest and open and straightforward again?' Nash paused, breathless, regaining his composure. He signalled his apology to Merrit.

Then he lit another of his cigars and offered one to Merrit, finally coming to sit beside him at the heavy table.

'Send word,' he said. 'To Don Quixote and Pancho Villa. The sooner all this begins, the sooner it all ends. What is it they say about sunlight being the best antiseptic?'

'And in between that beginning and that end?' Merrit said.

'We'll fumble and grope our way towards some half-satisfactory, half-convenient conclusion,' Nash said. 'What else?'

'You talk as though terrible secrets and not simple children's tales were about to be revealed.'

'Perhaps they are,' Nash said. 'Or perhaps just a succession of those common, everyday, tawdry revelations that are sometimes mistaken for – and which, in their own way, are much *worse* than – secrets. There will be four of us sitting up here, a courtroom, an eager audience, and all we'll have in front of us will be a ten-year-old imbecile. I ask you again – how do you imagine *that*'s going to appear to the watching world? Are *you* going to be the first to condemn her for everything that's happening here, for all the lies they've told, or do you want *me* to do it for you?'

After this, neither man spoke for a moment.

Then Nash said, 'My dead patient. She and her husband lived on the road leading into woods towards Warley.'

'I walked it,' Merrit said.

'I know – the old man saw you. He told me he regularly saw the girls going along there together.'

'Into the woods?'

'Into the woods. According to him, they met by arrangement and then did everything together.'

'Meaning they would have had ample opportunity to make up their tales and to ensure they all understood what they were saying and doing?'

'He said that the three eldest walked together and that the idiot girl and the youngest – he called her a baby, he means Maud Venn – followed behind. He said he saw Mary Cowan try to turn these two youngest back, to stop them from following them into the trees. He said he saw Cowan once take a switch and strap Agnes Foley on her bare legs to stop her from following. I saw the marks. He said she simply stood there while she was being struck and that she only laughed at whatever pain she felt.'

'And the man was certain it was Mary Cowan hitting her?'

'It's a small town. When Foley first brought his daughter home—'

He was interrupted by a loud and sudden rapping at the glass panel of the door and they heard Webb calling to be let in. The clerk unlocked the door and Webb pushed past him into the courtroom, followed a few paces behind by Firth.

'Surprise, surprise,' Nash said under his breath.

The magistrate walked noisily to the centre of the room and stood pointedly looking up to where Merrit and Nash sat together with their cigars.

'Doctor Nash,' he said loudly. 'How good of you to find the time to join us in pursuance of your civic duty.'

'My pleasure,' Nash called back. 'As you can see, Mr Merrit and I were enjoying a rare moment of calm before the coming storm.' He blew smoke in the direction of Webb.

Merrit wanted to intervene, to say something conciliatory to the magistrate, but he could think of nothing. 'Are we ready to proceed?' he said eventually.

He was surprised to be answered not by Webb but by Firth, who came ahead of Webb to the low stage and said, 'Of course, of course,' and who then took his seat at the side of Merrit.

'Alderman Webb?' Nash called down to Webb.

But before Webb could respond to this, there was a further rapping at the door, and the clerk reappeared to ask what was happening.

Webb told him to get out.

'Five minutes,' Merrit called to the man.

The man waited where he stood. Behind him, the waiting others pressed themselves against the frosted glass, all palms and fingers and flattened, unseeing faces.

6

THE EVENTUAL OPENING OF THE INQUIRY PROVED TO BE THE disappointment Merrit had always known it would be.

Proceedings were commenced after the delay, the room was filled and the formal opening duly announced. Everyone waited in silence – or near-silence in a room so full of so many eager would-be participants – for what revelations were to come. After which, Merrit rose to his feet at the centre of the low stage and announced that, in effect, all that would be undertaken on that particular day was this official declaration of the opening, followed by a listing of its objectives and the likely course of events thereafter.

This, in turn, would be followed by further introductory remarks – first from himself as the representative of both the Chief Constable and the Board of Inquiry, and then, if desired, from the remaining members of the appointed panel.

The first of the evidential hearings – he explained what these were and how they too would proceed – would commence in two days' time.

The rest of the day, he announced, would be spent in registering the names and interests of all those who wished to participate once the inquiry was fully under way. It all seemed far too small a reward for everyone's patience and eagerness, and at the first opportunity, Merrit sat back down.

There was a moment of silence, followed by a rising clamour as people digested what they had just been told. Many rose to their feet and shouted out that there was no need for this delay, that they already knew what would – what *should* – now happen in the days ahead. Delay would only become division, diversion and concealment; people had taken time from their work to attend; it was an outrage that so much formality should attend so little achievement; why was he there if not finally to expose the girls and their behaviour? Why was he there if not to give the remainder of the law-abiding, hard-working, God-fearing, tax-paying people of the place their say?

More people rose from their seats and gesticulated at the panel. The two ushers moved up and down the narrow aisle at the centre of the room ineffectually calling for silence.

Beside him on the stage, Merrit knew that the others were as disappointed as the shouting crowd by these opening formalities in which they were constrained to participate. Only Nash, Merrit saw, shared his own lack of concern at the unrest and the uproar over which they all now officially presided.

To confirm this, Nash leaned past Firth and said to Merrit in a loud whisper, 'Well, you pushed in the stick and you rattled it.'

Firth shared an uncomfortable glance with Merrit at hearing this. 'Perhaps you might add a few further words of encouragement. Something to . . . perhaps to . . .' But Firth was uncertain what he wanted to say, clearly expecting help from Merrit.

Merrit turned away from him and remained silent. He had opened fifty other inquests and inquiries and the same thing had happened at many of them. People didn't understand the nature of the proceedings; they expected too much; they expected to be heard immediately, to be allowed to participate from the very beginning, every one of them convinced that their own evidence was the only evidence worth hearing. What they did not expect was to have to put their names down on a list of countless others and then to have to wait – for how long? For how many more lost workdays? – to be heard.

Merrit looked at Webb, who, it occurred to him, had also witnessed similar scenes before. There was a look of both contempt and disdain on the man's face, which he did nothing to conceal, and Merrit guessed by the way Webb tapped his fingers on the desk that he wanted nothing more than to rise from his own seat, hold up his arms and then to wait for the silence and calm that would surely follow. After which, Webb would then tell the silenced crowd that Merrit was only doing his duty, only performing his sta-tu-tory and legal obligations. It was not *his* – Merrit's – fault that the proceedings might now appear to be delayed or diverted or allowed to move so slowly. Webb would then announce that he shared the crowd's disappointment and offer his own – his *personal* – reassurances that things would be under way soon enough. He knew these people and they knew him. There was a bond between them and they would be reassured by his promises. Everyone would be heard; everyone would be allowed to have their say; no one would be ignored or dismissed. A full and accurate record would be kept, nothing omitted, nothing avoided. Promises. *His* promises.

Everything the man might say would be a finger prodded into Merrit's chest, a warning, a signal, an affirmation. They were all dancers arranged on a dance floor and the distant music could already be heard.

Merrit slid the documents he held into a file and fastened it shut. It would all now be a matter of papers and files and cases, of boxes of papers, sealed boxes, cross-referenced files and other files held in complete secrecy.

'Do you wish to speak?' he said finally to Webb, his own small measure of authority still intact.

But Webb surprised him by shaking his head. The magistrate looked out over the subsiding clamour. 'As Nash says, *you*'re the one who has poked his stick into the cage. I imagine the wisest thing for the rest of us to do now is to stand well clear until everything settles.' He said this behind his raised hand and with a barely suppressed smile on his lips.

'Of course,' Merrit said. He waited a moment longer, detecting a further falling off in this first wave of outrage, and then he rose back to his feet and held up his hands, his palms to the court, his fingers spread, and waited for a further degree of calm. A few people noticed him and waited for him to speak; those around them followed their lead.

Judging the point at which he might finally make himself heard, Merrit shouted that he would explain further the proceedings about to get under way. There were a few shouted responses to this – men, mostly – but the main body of the crowd finally fell silent, allowing him to lower his voice.

He told them he understood their frustration at this seeming delay, but that it was a *necessary* delay. The preceding weeks of endless, often harmful, misleading and groundless speculation and accusation must now come to an end. There must be a new beginning, and that new beginning must start here, in this room, with this properly sanctioned and properly orchestrated inquiry. There must be a clear divide, an accepted and definite point from which to put the events of the past few weeks into some kind of order, and from which to move forward.

'Everything might be again repeated and recorded,' he said. 'But everything *now* must be a discovery of the truth, the establishment of a sound foundation from which to start moving ahead.'

Beside him, he saw, only Nash grimaced at the glib and overwrought phrases. All this talk of foundations; all this talk of order and moving forward. Firth, however, nodded vigorously at every word, and though Merrit appreciated this support, he knew that in the eyes of many it would count for little, and might even undermine what he was trying to impress upon the unsettled crowd.

'The time of unrest and anger and accusation' – he regretted this repetition, but the word came so easily and seemed to make its own important point amid even the subdued murmuring of his audience – 'is over. The time for clarity, understanding and explanation has arrived.'

He paused in the silence which followed the remark.

'You've made this particular little speech before,' Nash said to him in a whisper, his eyes fixed on the audience.

This time, Merrit hesitated too long before continuing, and people again rose to their feet and resumed shouting their complaints and questions at him. He saw that he was fooling only himself if he believed that all this confusion and anger was being left behind them. Tangled knots were still being tied and pulled tight; accusations were still being wielded and swung like blades. Perhaps he had dangerously misjudged the strength of all this scarcely suppressed hostility towards the girls, and perhaps also towards himself. And perhaps, as Webb had already smugly implied, he had also misunderstood its true nature and causes.

He waited where he stood, knowing that to sit back down now would be to concede completely. Besides, he knew what satisfaction this small defeat would afford Webb.

He raised his arms again. This expedient might work once, twice even; it seldom worked a third time.

'We shall proceed by means of taking depositions and testimony,' he said. There was a difference, but it would serve no purpose to make that distinction now. The court was not a permanent, full-time or continuous thing. They would, in effect, proceed as he saw fit. And they would proceed in a manner which best suited the gathering of all the necessary evidence. The hearings would reconvene in two days' time, and advance notice of everything to follow would be posted outside the court and announced in the local newspaper. The inquiry would continue for perhaps only a few hours each morning or afternoon, but it would proceed on a regular basis and at regular times.

Merrit knew better than any of them how much now depended on recording and compiling this spoken testimony. There was little actual physical or documented evidence, and this would necessitate a very particular way of proceeding.

'What I mean by that,' he said, 'is that a great deal of what needs to be recorded and collated—'

'About all the mischief the girls have caused,' someone called out.

72

'Evil, not mischief,' someone else shouted, to the obvious appeal of the crowd.

'Everything that needs to be recorded concerning recent events here must, of necessity, be collected in confidence, either by myself or a member of this panel.' He paused and swung his hand both left and right of him.

There was further discord at this, a second, lesser wave spreading from the stage to the outer reaches of the room.

'So – this is how we will proceed,' he said loudly. 'Everyone will be heard, and overlapping testimonies will be corroborated. We must begin to prise opinion from fact, belief from supposition, and guesswork from whatever actual evidence may exist. Hearsay and fabrication must be suppressed in favour of clear, straightforward and verifiable testimony. I doubt that we shall rid ourselves completely of all this speculation and make-believe, but it is my intention, as the head of this inquiry, to do my utmost to arrive at those simple facts, however meagre or elusive or unspectacular or disappointing they may ultimately prove to be.' He paused, looking at every corner of the room. 'And if we do not begin this process now, here, today, in the manner I have just outlined, then who is to say that this place will not be mired in them for all eternity, that you shall never rid yourselves of their burden and their shadow, and that you shall never move forward without the weight of their association forever dragging you back?'

The words were met with silence, but he knew that he was again speaking too easily and losing his way; his oratory was certainly more concerned with impressing his audience than with explaining in any great or particular detail how the inquiry would actually proceed.

Beside him, Nash patted his hands in near-silent applause.

But whatever his own doubts, Merrit sensed that his words had done their work. Most in the room now sat either silently or talking quietly to their neighbours.

He sat back down, convinced that he had achieved something in those few minutes, but not entirely certain what. If nothing else, then at least the net of authority had finally been cast over the restless, formless mass of everything about to be gathered in.

He looked out. A murmuring, whispering crowd was seldom settled or suppressed for long.

'None of the girls,' Firth said to him unexpectedly.

'Pardon?'

'None of the girls are present.' Firth flicked his hand at the room.

'No,' Merrit said. He had anticipated that at least Mary Cowan's father might appear, if only to further vent his hostility or to create new opportunities for himself where the newspapers were concerned. It had not surprised him in the slightest to see that the girls themselves had not come to the courtroom. 'Nothing would have been achieved by having them here,' he said. 'Quite the opposite, in fact. Besides, I doubt—'

'My wife,' Firth said. 'She visited their homes yesterday evening.'

'Oh?' The remark surprised and then angered Merrit, but also made him cautious. Beyond Firth, he saw that Nash was also taking an interest in what the minister was saying.

'I told her that any intervention may be unwelcome – contrary to protocol or etiquette, perhaps – but she insisted.'

'To any particular end?' Merrit asked him.

'To keep them away from this,' Firth said simply.

To postpone the inevitable, Merrit thought, but said nothing.

'I told her you might consider it to be interference.'

Which, prior to the inquiry having officially been declared open, it could not be.

'Perhaps,' Merrit said.

'She said that the Cowan man threw her out of his home, pushed her physically from his door and told her to mind her own business. Profanities were used.'

'I can imagine,' Merrit said. 'Was she injured, hurt?'

'Angelica is a very determined woman,' Firth said.

'And elsewhere?' Merrit said. 'The other girls' homes?'

'They mostly told her that they had no intention of coming to the court until they were called to it.'

'Of course. Because the inquiry had not yet been convened when your wife made her visits, I might overlook the intervention.'

'Of course,' Firth said, causing Merrit to wonder whether or not he heard a note of mockery in the repetition. 'Besides,' Firth went on, his voice raised slightly, more confident now, 'there have been plenty of other visits to their homes over these past weeks, plenty of other angry confrontations.'

'I can imagine,' Merrit said, unwilling to indulge the man in whatever point he was about to make.

'Ah,' Firth said slowly. 'But that is *all* you can do – imagine.'

'Granted,' Merrit said. 'But that now is the intent and purpose of all this.' He turned away from the minister and looked again at the watching crowd.

'You have no idea,' Firth said, his voice low again.

'Of what?' Merrit regretted prolonging the exchange when he might just as easily have ignored the remark completely.

But Firth, too, perhaps understanding that he had already said too much, shook his head and looked away.

Merrit felt a tug at his sleeve and turned to face Webb, who was leaning towards him. 'You need to stand up and tell them what happens next,' he said. 'About giving their names to the clerks. They're like children – they need to be told.'

'Of course,' Merrit said, and he again rose to his feet and held up his hands for silence.

7

THE FOLLOWING MORNING, AS MERRIT WAS PREPARING to leave, there was a knock on his door followed by the appearance of the hotel clerk, who said immediately that 'something had happened' and that 'his presence was required'. He then added that Nash was waiting for Merrit downstairs, almost as though these two events were not connected.

'Why Nash?' Merrit asked him.

The boy looked perplexed. 'Because he came and told me to fetch you.'

'Is it a medical emergency? Something connected to the inquiry?'

The boy looked even more puzzled. Merrit told him to leave, and to ask Nash to wait for him.

A few minutes later, in the lobby, he saw Nash sitting in one of the armchairs there reading a newspaper and drinking tea. A pot and crockery sat on a tray beside him.

Merrit went to him. 'You appear not to share our young friend's sense of urgency,' he said.

Nash shrugged. 'He's a messenger. It's in the nature of these things.' He continued sipping his tea.

'Are we leaving?' Merrit asked him.

'Sit down,' Nash said. He indicated a second cup.

'Is there no emergency, then?'

'Daubings,' Nash said cryptically.

'Daubings?'

'Someone's been painting on a wall in the night.'

Merrit began to understand. 'Concerning the inquiry, the girls?'

'Concerning *you*, us.' Nash finally put down his unwieldy paper, attempting first to fold it and then pressing the crumpled sheets flat beside his chair.

Back at his desk, the clerk watched him do this and then came and retrieved the paper.

'Sorry,' Nash said to him, only to be pointedly ignored. To Merrit, he said, 'He thinks we should be dashing off to share in the shock, outrage, disgust and horror of it all.' He watched the boy go into the room behind the reception desk.

'And are any of those things applicable?' Merrit knew from Nash's tone that they were not.

Nash shook his head and Merrit sat beside him.

'What do these daubings portray, say?'

'Much as you might expect. Four men – us, presumably – a hangman's noose, a few scattered initials and whatever the dauber in question understood to be symbols of some dark or satanic sort.'

'Symbols? Satanic?'

'Markings. Warnings. Nothing,' Nash said. He poured Merrit a cup of tea. 'Here. We'll go, we'll look, you can make some official pronouncement or other, and then we'll come away again. Responsibility acknowledged, duty done, discharged.'

Merrit sipped the hot tea.

'Of perhaps more pressing concern are the two men out-side,' Nash said.

Merrit looked to the doorway, but saw nothing.

'Newspapermen. Newly arrived newspapermen. Here for the meat and blood of the inquiry. Others have been drifting in and out, on and off for the past month.'

'I've seen a few of the stories they write,' Merrit said. He imagined he'd seen most, if not all, of the lurid tales the papers had been reporting and then embellishing over the previous weeks. It seemed that everything the five girls had said or done in that time had been of great interest to the vast and voracious newspaper-reading public.

'I can imagine,' Nash said. 'They're back now because you're finally here. Seemingly, you "legitimize" things.' He pronounced the word slowly and with humour.

'They can sit in the court and accurately report what happens there,' Merrit said.

'You don't believe that's their intention any more than I or they do,' Nash said. 'For a start, they're endlessly at the girls' doors, demanding every lurid, sordid, titillating, mendacious detail of what they insist they saw in the woods, and every-thing else that's been happening to them since. Everything.'

'And if there *are* no lurid, sordid, titillating details to impart?'

'Precisely,' Nash said.

'You believe the girls and their families – some of them, at least – have been only too happy to do that embellishment for them?'

'And when the few sparse details are finally exhausted, then to go on adding to that profitable stock. Most of what you've already read will have come either directly or indirectly from Cowan.' There was nothing in Nash's voice or manner to suggest any real alarm or concern at what he was saying.

'Why you?' Merrit asked him.

'You mean why am I here now? Because I was unfortunate enough to be out prowling around at dawn when the writing was first discovered.'

'Prowling?'

'Walking my dogs. The writing is on the wall of a small, empty warehouse down by the river. I go there most mornings. I arrived at the path leading past the building and, lo and behold, even at that ungodly hour, a small crowd had somehow already been alerted to this fascinating new revelation and been induced to gather there and start their unfettered speculation. I imagine my own unexpected though clearly fortuitous appearance on the scene only served to stoke the rising flames of outrage and horror even further.'

Merrit said nothing in response to this.

The clerk returned to his desk with the folded newspaper. He put it on the counter and laid a baton over it. The fire in the small grate settled and dripped ash into the clean hearth.

'So you're still convinced the girls are making all this up?' Merrit said finally, his voice low.

'Nothing will convince me otherwise,' Nash said. 'And if you weren't so constrained regarding your own public protestations – wrong word – of impartiality, then you would admit the same and make your time here in the heathen-filled wilderness considerably easier for yourself. Has it not occurred to you that most of the people here are simply waiting for you to make that denunciation so they can all get on with their lives, and so that the watching world – or its representatives outside at least – will withdraw and let everything settle back to its slow and predictable routine?'

Merrit conceded both points in silence.

'What?' Nash prompted him. 'Do you seriously expect me to believe that you *aren't* convinced that this is all something the girls have concocted among themselves?'

Again, Merrit said nothing.

Across the room a clock struck the quarter-hour.

'I still need to be seen to maintain that impartiality,' Merrit said eventually. 'I had hoped you might understand that much at least.' To have said any more, even to this man he now considered his ally, would have been too much.

'Of course,' Nash said. He emptied his cup and rose from his chair. 'I told the boy to put this on your bill,' he said.

'You did?'

'No, I didn't. I paid him with a handful of shekels out of my own threadbare pocket.'

Merrit smiled at the remark and finished his own drink. 'I appreciate this,' he said. 'Your being here, accompanying me, I mean.'

'Don't mention it. Like I said, most people here just want all of this explained away and then quickly forgotten. The daubing is the work of troublemakers.' He pointed to the door and stood aside. 'A word,' he said as they prepared to leave. 'Don't over-react. Just look at the things and shrug them off. And then come back to the inquiry and let everything that needs to be said and heard be said and heard there.'

It was good advice. It did not need to be said, but Merrit appreciated hearing it all the same. The man was a valuable balance against the resentful Webb and the ineffectual Firth.

They stepped out into the square. On every side,

shopkeepers were setting out their wares and brushing the pavements. A few stalls had been erected at the centre of the space, and carts had been drawn up alongside these. Half a dozen workhorses stood untethered at the polished granite trough opposite the hotel.

'There,' Nash said, touching Merrit's arm and surreptitiously indicating the two men already approaching them.

The first of these men held a notebook and a rolled paper, the second a camera, which he carried on a broad strap around his shoulders, and to which he attended as he came. Both men were almost running while trying to give the appearance of walking calmly.

'Mr Merrit, Mr Merrit,' the first called to Merrit, attracting the attention of all those around him.

'It's how they operate,' Nash said. 'Just smile at him and keep walking. First he gets his audience, then he builds a stage, then he shines a light on you, and then he reads from his script. Everything you say will be a stumble or a fall. He knows exactly what he wants to hear from you, and he'll prod and probe until, one way or another, he hears it. Keep walking.'

Merrit and Nash arrived where the two men were now blocking their way.

'A few words about your work here,' the journalist said loudly to Merrit.

'You're blocking our path,' Merrit said to him.

'And is that the same as saying we're obstructing you in your inquiry? Are you on your way to see the mysterious paintings that have appeared out of nowhere in the night? Are they the work of some malign – dare one say it, *demonic* – hand?'

Merrit smiled at the word.

'Strike a chord?' the journalist said quickly. 'Is that what you believe you're here to uncover, to expose?'

'My task here is very simple,' Merrit said.

'To establish if there is any truth or substance to all these other demonic occurrences which have surrounded these strange, blighted girls?'

'They are perfectly ordinary children,' Merrit said.

'Careful,' Nash whispered to him.

'So, them being perfectly ordinary *children*, you'd be at an even greater loss to explain what it is that has *possessed* them in this manner to make them behave in such an *extra*ordinary fashion.'

'That wasn't what I said. I am here to hear all the testimony and to establish the facts of the matter. It is as simple and as unexciting as that.' Merrit wondered how many times he would have to repeat this.

The journalist paused to write in his notebook, and both Merrit and Nash walked past him. He called after them, running to catch up.

'Keep moving,' Nash said.

'How far is it?'

'A few minutes. The same as everywhere in this place – a few minutes, near by, well known.' It was another warning, of sorts, and Merrit understood this, too.

By then, a small crowd – no more than a dozen early shoppers – was following the four men.

'Do you think they know where we're going?' Merrit asked Nash.

'Of course they know. Besides, your every appearance is a show for them, something they deserve to participate in. You could go for a stroll round the square and someone would follow you.'

The journalist and photographer ran ahead of them and then turned. The photographer steadied his camera, pointing it directly at Merrit.

'Can the other man stand to one side?' he called to Nash. 'Just for a moment.'

'No, the other man can't,' Nash said to him and walked even closer to Merrit.

But as he finished speaking, the photographer's flash bulb exploded in his face, leaving the pair of them briefly blinded by the glare.

'Apologies, gents,' the journalist said. 'What shall I caption it? "Judge and Accomplice Confront Blinding Light of Reason"?' He laughed at his cleverness. 'Is that Nash with or without an "e"?'

Nash said nothing and continued walking, Merrit keeping pace beside him.

'So, back to all this demonic occurrence,' the journalist went on. 'Are the girls now denying that they saw the Devil – *a* devil, at least – in the woods? Is all this other stuff, all this cutting and bruising, all this broken pottery, painted signs and whatever – is all this not the result of some *lesser* demonic intervention, some kind of possession, even?'

Merrit now regretted everything the man said in front of these watching others. His own silence was no true denial in their eyes. And to attempt to contest anything the man said would be even worse; he needed no encouragement to play to this crowd.

'No response?' the journalist said directly to Merrit, his face only a few feet away. 'Shall I put that, "No Comment"?

Does that mean you *do* believe in these stories of possession or that you *don't*?' He waited with a grin on his face. But it was an easy victory, and eventually even he seemed disappointed that Merrit had not confronted him more forcibly.

'May I?' Nash asked Merrit, and before Merrit could respond, he pushed himself directly in front of the man until their faces were only a few inches apart. 'No "e" in Nash,' he said. 'And for the further titillation of your poor readers, you may confirm that I, Doctor Simeon Nash, most certainly *do* believe that the girls are possessed by demons and that the great Prince of Darkness himself – Satan, Lucifer, Beelzebub, call him what you will – certainly *did* appear to them in that clearing in the woods, and that they are all now working at his command in carrying out their evil misdeeds. What other explanation could there possibly be? The Antichrist has chosen to return to Earth, here, now, and these poor, uneducated girls are the frail and broken vessels he has chosen to inhabit. Where else would he go? What does this place not possess that Babylon or Sodom or even Gomorrah does not also have to tempt him with? Should you not be writing all this down?'

Merrit resisted smiling at the ridiculous speech.

Nash went on. 'What more perfect specimens of woman-hood might he not find to inhabit in pursuance of his evil and destructive intent?'

The journalist closed his notebook and slipped it into his pocket. 'I might need to check on Gomorrah,' he said.

'For scriptural accuracy?' Nash said.

'For the spelling,' the man said, and this time Merrit was unable to resist laughing.

Nash turned to him. 'What? You don't believe me, you

don't concur?' He indicated for the pair of them to resume walking.

'You missed your calling,' Merrit said as they finally left their small audience behind. 'You should have been on the stage.'

'I was,' Nash said. 'Once. At Oxford.'

'And now you're a doctor.'

'And now I'm a doctor.'

They quickened their pace, leaving the square and continuing downhill along a cobbled road towards the river.

Turning a corner, they paused. The journalist and photographer, though still intent on following them, were now at a distance.

Nash pointed to a track leading into the sparse woodland. 'It's through here.'

More trees, Merrit thought. He knew that this made a difference.

'Does anyone truly believe in this notion of demonic possession?' he asked Nash as they reached the first of the trees.

'It hardly matters. They might not truly believe in it themselves, but they're only too happy to be titillated and shocked by the tales of others' belief. Sensationalism, that's all most of the papers deal in these days. If we'd given that man another minute, I'm sure the notion of witchcraft would have raised its cackling head.'

'It's been mentioned in some of the reports already,' Merrit said, remembering.

'Some of which *he* probably wrote. It might be mentioned, but that's all. They mention a lot of things – apparitions, poltergeists, possession – but it doesn't mean they're doing anything other than keeping their options open and their readers entertained and clamouring for more. When everything blows over, he'll write articles mocking us for our indulgence and gullibility.'

Merrit understood all this, and he knew the same charges would be repeated soon enough to him in the court.

They continued to pass through the trees, pale, thin trunks with little undergrowth. The track ahead of them was laid with cinders.

After only a minute, the river appeared to their right. Its banks were stone-lined, and the bed itself was broad and shallow, filled with discarded stone blocks and pieces of rusted metal. The far bank was considerably steeper and covered with denser woodland.

They arrived at an open gate and Nash pointed to the building beyond. 'They've gone,' he said, meaning the people who had been gathered there earlier.

They walked to the front of the empty warehouse, a wall facing the river. It was a double-storey building, its dozen windows either boarded over or smashed. A row of joists and pulleys overhung where they stood.

'There,' Nash said, indicating the crudely painted symbols and initials. 'The writing on the wall.'

The two men went closer and Nash pointed out the paint splashed on the ground beneath.

'What is it, exactly?' Merrit asked him, stepping back.

'Four heads. Those are our initials above them – you qualify for only one. And that' – he pointed to the left of the heads – 'I take to be a gallows. And that' – he swung his arm to the right – 'I imagine is intended to be a skull. The paint appears to have run. Or whitewash, rather.' He went to the skull and drew his fingers through it, turning to show this to Merrit. 'You'll find a bucket of the stuff in every house in the place.'

'And these symbols?' Merrit said, indicating a row of smaller markings across the bottom of the heads.

Nash shrugged. 'Demonic symbols no one has yet been able or brave enough to identify? The fevered scrawling of Beelzebub himself? The flung paint pot of Hell's own twisted Michelangelo? I don't know. What do you want them to be? They're just marks. Presumably, whoever painted them intends them to be taken as warnings, portents of some sort. I don't know. They're nothing, complete fabrications. Their purpose is clear, but that's all.'

One of these symbols was merely a circle with a cross inside it; another a circle with what appeared to be eyes and horns added; a third was a triangle and an inverted triangle, a crude Star of David. Merrit considered this to be of little true significance. Nash was right: they were the fabrications of someone wishing to add a further note of threat and unease to an otherwise easily decipherable message. A fourth symbol looked like a child's drawing of a cat with a skeletal hand beneath it.

'There's your witchcraft,' Nash said. 'And here' – he drew Merrit to one side and cleared a space in the wet grass at their feet – 'is a footprint of the man who did it all. Is it a cloven hoof?' The print was white. 'The idiot stood in his own spilled whitewash.'

'You don't think the girls themselves did this?' Merrit said.

Nash held his hand against the uppermost initial. 'I'm six feet tall and it's at the top of my reach.'

'They could have stood on something.' Merrit looked

around him, but nothing suggested itself. 'So is it intended merely as a warning? To me?'

'To all of us. We three will be here long after you've gone, remember. Or it might simply be intended to add a touch of intrigue or drama to the proceedings, now that they're finally under way.'

They were interrupted by the arrival of the journalist and the photographer.

'Can I have a picture of the judge standing beside the symbols?' the photographer called to them.

Both Merrit and Nash moved away from the wall, Nash covering over the footprint as they went.

'Can't you oblige me just this once?' the photographer shouted, exasperated, clearly accustomed to instructing more willing participants.

'*Is* it Satan's handwriting, then?' the journalist said, standing close to the symbols. He, too, tested their wetness.

'Even you would have difficulty persuading anyone that they hadn't been done by an incompetent and unimaginative hand,' Nash said.

'You've got me there,' the man said. 'Still . . .'

'We came, we saw, we considered,' Nash said to him. 'Whitewash, still wet, clumsily applied. If it is the work of the great Beelzebub, come to claim his hellish kingdom on Earth, then we have little to fear from him. Perhaps Minister Firth might be the man to consult on that score.'

'Him?' the journalist said dismissively.

'Precisely,' Nash said.

'And if it's the work of the girls while they were *possessed* by the Devil?' the journalist said.

'Then he held them up so they might daub so high,' Nash

said. 'Imagine that – or perhaps you already have done – innocent young girls in their nightdresses in the middle of the night and the Devil himself with his horny hands around their waists or thighs, or pulling them up barelegged to squat on his shoulders while he directs them.' He stopped speaking, aware of already having suggested too much to the man.

'You're sick,' the journalist told him, but with considerably more amusement than surprise or disgust in his voice.

'Possibly,' Nash said. 'Very possibly.'

A further flash exploded in the dim light as the photographer took a picture of the painted symbols. He wasn't happy with the likely result of this and asked the journalist if it would be possible to add a new coat of white to the faces and initials.

'No need,' the journalist shouted to him, his gaze still fixed on Nash as Nash and Merrit walked away from the abandoned building and back into the surrounding trees.

8

A LIST OF EARLY WITNESSES TO BE CALLED WAS READ OUT, followed by a considerably longer list of all those others who had applied to submit their own written or spoken accounts of what had been happening in the town.

Both the journalist and the photographer were present at this second beginning. Merrit had instructed the clerks that there should be no photographs taken inside the room; he could not control what happened outside. The journalist, catching his eye, raised a pen to him, but Merrit looked past the man to all the other newspapermen gathered there. Previously, there had been only three or four in the place; now there were close to a dozen.

The rest of his audience consisted mostly of townspeople, but some, he guessed, had come from further afield to watch and to be entertained. He wondered if the Assistant Chief Constable had sent anyone to observe and then report back on the nature and progress of the proceedings, and he looked around the room in the hope of spotting someone who might fit the part. But he saw no one; besides, he would know soon enough if what happened in the court was being relayed to the man.

There was a narrow, semi-circular mezzanine floor to the

room – though he doubted if anyone in the place had ever called it that – and today it was empty. The space was little more than an internal balcony, but he saw that it would be a perfect place for the journalists to be gathered together, over-seeing the proceedings from this slight distance and detached from the main body of the crowd, where they would soon enough go in search of their countless other stories. For the next session, he decided, he would open up this balcony and tell the ushers to direct the newspapermen to it. It was beyond his authority to banish them entirely from the inquiry, but he doubted if many of them would know this and contest their separation.

At eleven, Merrit raised a hand for silence, both surprised and gratified when it came so swiftly. All these ragged and disappointing preliminaries were finally over. It was time to begin. And because everyone understood this as well as Merrit, a sudden air of expectation filled the room.

At Merrit's signal, one of the clerks walked from the door and stood directly in front of the crowd, where, after a moment of complete silence, he read out a succession of preliminary remarks concerning the conduct of the inquiry and the behaviour expected of its audience, stumbling occasionally over the convoluted language.

Merrit looked over the man's head as he spoke. Mary Cowan sat with her father on the front row. It was where all the chief witnesses would sit and await their turn. There was no one else on the row. The girl was the eldest, the most mature and the most assured – some might say the most 'worldly' – of the five, and Merrit remained convinced that she was the key to them all.

She was their leader and their instigator. She was in charge of the others: they followed her; they looked up to her; they obeyed her. A speedy confession or explanation from her and the proceedings here would be quickly concluded. A line might be drawn. She was perhaps a clever and manipulative girl, but she would not outwit the court. Her claims might be swaddled in childish pleading or false sincerity, but they would quickly be revealed for what they truly were in this room of watching, assessing others.

Merrit looked at the girl and saw that she was careful to avoid his gaze. She knew he was watching her, but her head was either down, studying her hands in her lap, or she looked slowly from side to side, at her father and the others close behind her.

It surprised Merrit to see only her father with her, the pair of them arriving when the room was almost full, the man making his entrance alongside his precious daughter. No mother, no brother or sister. It also surprised him to see that none of the other girls were present. They might not have yet been called to give their own testimonies – hopefully creating a scatter of contradiction and confusion around each repeated tale – but they still had the right to attend and to listen to what Mary Cowan might now have to say on their behalf.

It pleased Merrit to realize that perhaps their own parents also understood something of the power Mary Cowan exercised over the others, and that they were happy for her to be the sole focus of the inquiry in these early days. Perhaps, after all, their own daughters might not now be required to attend and tell their stories; perhaps Mary Cowan would explain everything, and their own innocent and all too easily led children might be allowed to step back into the shadows and resume their interrupted young lives unobserved and unremarked.

Merrit was distracted from these thoughts by the sudden realization that the man beneath him had finished talking, and that everyone in the room was now silently watching him and waiting for him to speak.

He rose to his feet and thanked the clerk. The man put the papers he held on the desk, neatly squared them, and then walked back to the door, clearly relieved that his own public part in the proceedings was over. He positioned himself beside an equally young constable – a further, obvious presence of the law. The boy would call for order when required; he would shake his finger and cast his glances at the trouble-makers. People would know he was there and they would know precisely *why* he was there – what he now represented in this room of two worlds.

Merrit cleared his throat and began by asking those who had been listed to give their testimony later in the proceedings to be patient.

He then told the broader audience that he would tolerate no interruption to the serious business they were there to undertake. Anyone who called out to contradict or threaten the witnesses or the girls themselves would be evicted from the room. He was careful in all of this to avoid using the words 'court' or 'trial'; the inquiry, strictly speaking, was neither of those things. But he knew others would remain either oblivious or careless of the distinction. And some, he guessed – Webb among them – would deliberately confuse or ignore that distinction and thus provide themselves with a power and an authority they did not possess.

At the mention of eviction, Merrit cast a glance at the

constable by the door, causing him to stiffen and to nod officiously.

He then told his audience that it was in all their interests to investigate thoroughly everything that had happened and then to attempt to understand the background and the possible causes of all these events. Afterwards, and as a direct result of this investigation, it would, he hoped, be possible to restore a measure of order and calm to the town. And once again, he regretted this imprecise and all-encompassing language. In another place, and with a more straightforward inquiry, he would have been more direct, less evasive, less suggestive.

But here, in this place, and in front of these people, he knew that these half-promises and reassuring suggestions would serve him better.

He had almost said 'peace' and 'sanity' rather than 'order' and 'calm', but he saw an instant beforehand what a gift these words would be to the waiting journalists. 'Madness', he knew, would be a much-repeated accusation or explanation in the days to come. There was plenty of opportunity for the notion to be established or dismissed in the words of others.

Finishing these remarks, he paused again.

'Some of you may already be aware of the symbols that have been painted on the warehouse wall.' A day had passed since their appearance; the whole town would know of them. A sudden draught of whispering filled the room and then just as quickly died. 'This inquiry, these members' – he gestured to left and right of where he stood – 'will not succumb to threats or intimidation of any kind, however directly or indirectly those threats are made. I fully – *we* fully – understand the nature of these symbols and their true intent. They are no part of what has already happened here; they are part of what is happening *now*. We understand them for what they are, and we understand why they have appeared.'

Had he sounded officious and knowing and threatening enough? Had he said the same thing three times over? He glanced at Nash, but saw that Nash's attention was directed fully at Mary Cowan, who sat immediately beneath him.

'Thank you,' Merrit said. The speech he had originally prepared was much longer, but already he felt the room's rising impatience. He had made an accusation. Had he accused them all? Had he accused them all of being complicit by their silence? He looked down at Cowan's father, and the man returned his gaze, smiling and shaking his head slightly. Merrit found himself looking for signs of whitewash on the man's hands or clothing or feet, but saw nothing.

Beside him, Webb coughed to attract his attention. Merrit nodded to him, and before he had sat down, Webb was on his feet and addressing the crowd.

'You all know me,' he began. He paused, perhaps expecting some gratifying acknowledgement of this. Perhaps he was even expecting applause or some other signal from the crowd to let him know that they understood and appreciated the difference between himself and this other man, this stranger so suddenly among them and sent to sit in judgement on them.

But there was no such response.

Some, Merrit saw – mainly the journalists and the out-siders – smirked and whispered behind their hands.

'Yes, well, you know me,' Webb went on, 'and you know, I hope, that I am a fair man and a just man, and with only the interests of this town uppermost in my mind.'

There was further murmuring at this, and Mary Cowan's father turned to whisper to the men sitting behind him.

'These are *our* children,' Webb continued, his voice raised. 'Born here and brought up here. *Our* responsibility. This is *our* home; our livelihoods are here, our families, our histories, even.'

Merrit began to regret having given him this opportunity to speak. Webb's standing in the place was nowhere near as high as he himself clearly imagined it to be. His speech might have looked good on paper – emotional appeal, common bonds, shared understanding – but it was playing poorly to this roomful of people who lived without his advantages, who might have stood before him in his court, and who were now growing increasingly impatient to hear what the first of the girls might finally have to say for herself.

Cowan, Merrit saw, was openly enjoying Webb's growing unease. The man took the stub of a cigarette from his pocket, lit it and then smoked it down to his fingers in a succession of sharp draws. He let the smoke drift over his daughter and along the empty bench.

Webb continued in this vein for a further five minutes, concluding with an appeal for nothing less than reason, honesty, decency, understanding and forgiveness.

Merrit looked back to Nash at hearing the empty words, and this time Nash flicked his eyes to the ceiling.

Webb finally sat down. There was some applause, but it was scattered and quickly died.

Merrit thanked him, but Webb barely acknowledged this, intent on looking out at all those ungrateful listeners who had not even clapped their hands together once.

And because Webb had spoken, it was incumbent

upon Merrit to offer the same opportunity to both Nash and Firth.

Firth was quick to rise. He held up a large black Bible, from which hung a slender scarlet ribbon.

'You all know what this is,' he said. 'I was told that there would be no *legal* requirement for binding oaths to be made at this inquiry. Then I was told that witnesses might do so if they *chose* to. I told myself then that I knew what choice those witnesses would make. I told myself that they would surely look into their hearts and see there what *moral*, what *Christian* demand was being asked of them.'

Beside him, Nash again looked up at the ceiling.

Merrit saw Angelica Firth at the rear of the crowd. She was watching her husband intently, and mouthing everything he was saying. The speech was hers, a perverse way of ensuring Firth stamped his own early mark on these proceedings, and that he was not, as was perhaps more usual, pushed aside and silenced by those who believed they had a greater claim to be heard.

'A duty under God,' Firth was saying. 'No one here is searching for vengeance or retribution, and certainly—'

Someone in the crowd called out to dispute this and there was laughter.

'Surely, no one here will demand that these innocent — for that is what they are in the eyes of our Lord — that these innocent children be punished. Rather, we ask that they be understood and forgiven and afterwards helped back on to the one true path ahead of them.'

'Would that be the Path of Righteousness, then?' someone else called out.

Merrit searched, but was too slow to see who had shouted.

The constable took a step towards the crowd and then a step back.

Firth faltered and then continued. 'Yes, yes,' he said. 'Of course it is the Path of Righteousness. There is no other path to follow. These lambs may have strayed, but the way ahead is still open to them, will yet become clear to them. And we – you, I, we here – we are the ones who are now being called upon to shepherd them back on to that path and into His waiting fold.'

Angelica Firth, Merrit saw, now sat with her mouth firmly closed, though with her eyes still fixed on her husband. He himself had clearly strayed from *her* path, unable to resist this extemporary preaching, unable to resist following one of these other, easier paths into one of his own exhausted sermons.

So the girls were sheep who had strayed from the Path of Righteousness, and who had then become prey to the Forces of Evil and Wrongdoing. It was all that simple.

Firth raised the Bible he held higher above his head, causing its trailing ribbon to hang against his face, a vivid red line over his forehead and cheek. He looked ridiculous. He clearly believed he had made his mark on the proceedings – done what his wife had wanted him to do – but instead he had succeeded only in making himself look ridiculous.

Merrit rose and thanked him.

At first, Firth was reluctant to sit down. He looked to his wife for her praise or acknowledgement, but the woman only lowered her face. Firth seemed to sag where he stood. Merrit repeated his thanks and the minister finally sat down. He put the Bible in front of him and wrapped the ribbon around it.

'Doctor Nash?' Merrit said.

Nash considered the offer before standing.

'I am Medicine,' he said. 'Reverend Firth is the Church, Alderman Webb is the Law, and I suppose Mister Merrit might be said to be a representative of the Greater State temporarily among us. Medicine, Church, Law and State. We are your so-called representatives, and these are the institutions we represent. You might consider that we are about to sit in judgement upon some of you, but it is equally the case that *you* might now sit in judgement upon us. We are a formidable force, the likes of which, perhaps, this place has not seen within the memory of anyone here. The four of us against these five young children. Are they to be broken by us? Are *we* to be challenged by them? All big questions. I have medical expertise. I shall bring no other judgement to these proceedings. I may have beliefs and opinions beyond this – who among us does not? – but I shall restrict myself to this expertise and its bearing on all that may be about to be revealed to us. I ask only that my fellow members do the same.'

Merrit nodded in agreement with the simple plea, surprised and pleased by Nash's concise and reassuring even-handedness. It was the speech he wished he himself had thought to make.

'I shall, of course,' Nash went on, 'also endeavour to ensure that there is no suffering – physical or mental – endured by either the girls or their families during these proceedings.'

He was talking about Agnes Foley, and Merrit understood this and signalled his agreement on the point.

No one in the audience contested the words, and as Nash sat down there was loud and prolonged applause for what he had said, and both Webb and Firth participated in this. But Webb, Merrit saw, managed to appear to be clapping without his palms actually making any sound.

At the rear of the room, Angelica Firth sat with her arms folded across her chest, her eyes still fixed on her husband, her pointed immobility cancelling out his own over-enthusiastic response to everything Nash had just achieved.

Rather than rise again, or strike his gavel to end the applause, Merrit waited a few moments longer for the clapping to fade of its own accord, and then he thanked the three men for their contribution.

His next duty was to call for Mary Cowan to come to the front of the room and to sit in the raised chair beside Webb and answer their questions.

He looked down at her. She seemed even more of a child than ever, and it suddenly struck Merrit that it was too much to ask of her. The journalists would already be sharpening their pencils. The girl continued to avoid his eyes. Her father's hand lay on her leg. The man sat close beside her, his face closer still as he whispered to his daughter.

The girl gave no response to this, and only then, as her father took away his hand and as she drew her leg further from his, did she look up at Merrit for the first time that morning. And perhaps she even smiled at him. It seemed a smile, but perhaps it was something else, perhaps merely a signal of recognition – of satisfaction almost – regarding what was about to take place between them. Or perhaps it was intended to suggest to him the strength of her own conviction in the power she possessed and was now about to exercise. She was an innocent, strayed child, and here he was, an instrument of the all-powerful, cumbersome and slowly turning machinery of the State.

And then, as quickly and as unexpectedly as it had come, this smile faded from her lips, and she sat upright and straightened her blouse. Her father looked at his daughter with something close to pride in his eyes. The girl's legs swung an inch clear of the floor. They would be even further from it once she was in the chair beside Webb and facing the room.

Merrit cleared his throat and raised his palm.

Mary Cowan lowered her toes to the floor.

'Please,' Merrit said.

And the girl steadied herself, ready to stand and walk to him.

Part Two

Part Two

9

'TELL US HONESTLY WHAT YOU TRULY BELIEVE YOU SAW,' Merrit said to the girl. He had left his seat beside the others and now stood close in front of her, his face level with hers. 'In the clearing in the woods.' And again it seemed to him to be the opening of a tale.

'What she *saw*,' Webb shouted from the table. 'What she *saw*. She must tell us what she *saw*. Not what she *believes* she saw. And then we must decide whether she is lying or not, or the nature of her lies, or the extent of her mendacity. Asking her what she *believes* or *imagines* she saw or didn't see will lead us nowhere and leave too much doubt. How will *that* allow us to progress? As the minister here has already pointed out to us, she now has a single path ahead of her – to tell us the truth. Or, if she chooses otherwise, to lie to us, and then for *us* to decide on the matter.'

And where, exactly, would that *lead us?* Merrit thought.

Webb, however, was pleased with the small, emphatic speech, and many in the watching crowd nodded their heads in agreement with him.

Merrit wanted to tell the man to shut up, to wait his turn, to let him finish his own opening remarks to the girl. Now, he knew, he would be unable to deny either Firth or Nash their own interventions.

And almost as though in response to this unspoken thought, Firth half-rose from his seat, sat back down and then half-raised his hand, lowering it to the solid, immovable block of the Bible still in front of him.

Merrit nodded to him, this half-measure man.

And again, Firth glanced at his wife as he started to speak. 'She must tell us what in her heart of hearts she believes she saw. She must know we are not here to judge or condemn her, merely to assess the events which have attached themselves to her.'

Merrit closed his eyes and then suppressed a groan at hearing this.

Firth went on: 'The child must know that God witnesses all, that He, and He alone, will be aware of all her subterfuges, evasions and lies, and that He alone shall be her one true judge in all of this.' His emphasis on every 'He' left no one in the room uncertain where the weight of his own appeal lay.

No, Merrit thought. *All this is happening now because* we – *and we alone – are her witnesses and judges.* He sensed that Webb was about to say exactly this and he held up his hand to stop the man.

'I'm sure she understands that,' Merrit said to Firth.

He turned back to Mary Cowan. He hoped to appear friendly to her, approachable. She was a child and he was a man. She possessed no true power or authority, and he possessed every power and authority required.

'Do you understand me, Mary?'

'Understand what?' she said to him. She looked directly at him. They were her first words to the inquiry.

'The difference between telling the truth and lying.'

'In my heart of hearts?' she said to him. 'That I must tell you what we saw and not what we only *believe* we saw?' She was mocking him.

'What you – and you alone – saw,' he said. 'We shall ask the same question of the others in due course.'

She looked from him to Firth.

'Answer my questions,' Merrit said softly. 'The others may follow me with questions of their own. Tell me honestly what you saw.'

'Everybody knows what I saw,' Mary Cowan said. 'But the more details I remember, the more likely there are to be differences between my story and the stories of the others.'

'"Stories"? Is that what they are?'

At the table, Webb slapped his hands hard on its surface.

'A story need not be a lie,' Merrit said to the girl. 'A recollection, a remembrance.'

'But that's what *he*'s saying.' She turned in her seat and pointed at Webb. 'That a story is not the truth, that I'm making it up, lying.'

He saw what a maze she was leading them into with this deliberate tangle of words and meaning. All he had wanted from the girl was for her to repeat in the court what she had already recounted a hundred times outside of it. He had seen the same few quotes in a dozen newspaper and magazine articles. All he wanted now was for her to say the same things here, for a proper record to be made of what she said, and for this to be their true beginning.

Tell us, he wanted to say to the girl. *Just tell us*. And even as he suppressed this sudden blister of impatience, he understood what she was doing: she was not allowing that simple and vital line to be drawn, that foundation to be laid. She would tell them a story containing unassailable truths, laughable lies and every variation in between. And then afterwards – upon her cross-examination, so to speak – she would reconfigure these truths, half-truths and lies, and the ensuing whispering and conjecturing would create countless other new shapes around her. Nothing of the case would be simple. The people who already scorned and denied everything the girl said would continue to scorn and deny her; and those who believed her, for whatever reasons, would have their own convictions strengthened by hearing her repeat everything here, in this courtroom, with its air of unassailable authority and endorsement. Everything here would be written down, nothing altered, nothing embellished or angled one way or another. The watching journalists might continue to do that, but the inquiry records would not.

A further few seconds of silence passed between Merrit and the girl.

'No one will think any the worse of you,' he said eventually.

'For what?' She seemed genuinely uncertain of what he was suggesting.

'For altering what you've already said. To admitting, perhaps, to not having been entirely truthful. I doubt if even—'

'He's calling her a liar.' This was the girl's father, who rose from his seat a few feet behind Merrit and turned to address the crowd.

'I am not calling her a liar,' Merrit said. 'We have not yet heard anything of what she might be about to tell us.'

Cowan faltered at this. 'You called her a liar,' he insisted. 'And if she's a liar, then you're calling me a bad father for making her a liar. Is *that* what you're saying?' He looked at the journalists as he made these unsupportable accusations.

Merrit, understanding the man's motives, waited without speaking.

'You'll be called to give your own testimony on the matter,' he said eventually.

'And for you to call *me* a liar, too?'

Someone shouted for Cowan to sit down, and he reluctantly did this, searching the crowd to see who had called.

'Thank you,' Merrit said to him, further defusing the small bomb the man seemed forever priming himself to be.

Then he turned back to the girl. He knew that he had taken a chance in putting her before them first, and he knew now that the balance had momentarily tipped against him because so far that gamble had failed.

It was time for the first cornerstone of the inquiry to be laid.

He went closer to her and she leaned slightly forward in her seat as though to confront him, or perhaps to brace herself against whatever he said next.

'We have all read the newspaper reports in which you and the other girls are repeatedly quoted – but mostly you – and we all know that what you said you saw in that clearing in the woods was a strange creature, neither truly animal nor properly a man. In some of the reports you called it a devil or a demon. In one or two of the articles this strange creature is referred to as *the* Devil.' He paused. 'Is that what you still believe – that *the* Devil appeared to you in the woods?' It was a ludicrous and excessive hammer-blow of a question to which there could be no single or convincing answer.

He waited. Mary Cowan was reluctant to answer him. She

closed her eyes briefly, though whether in confusion or calculation, he could not tell. He held his gaze on her.

After a moment, she opened her eyes and said, 'It was a creature half-man and half-animal. How would any of us know if it was *a* devil or *the* Devil? The Scriptures and other books talk of devils and they also talk of *the* Devil as a single man. How would we know which we saw? Some call him a man, some call him a creature. If there *is* only one, then perhaps that's what we saw. If there are hundreds, or even thousands of devils, then perhaps it was one of them. *I* never said it was *the* Devil.'

'Oh?' Merrit said, caught momentarily off-balance by the strength of this rebuttal, encouraged only by that solitary 'perhaps'. 'Why not?'

He struggled to remember which of the other girls might have called the creature the Devil. He felt she had set another small trap for him and that he had wandered blindly into it. The closely watching crowd would afford him only a few more seconds' grace.

'Then can you tell us why you made that distinction in the first instance? There must have been considerable uncertainty in your own mind for you not to be certain. I even wonder—'

'Because why would *the* Devil appear to us, here? Why would *the* Devil show himself to five young girls in this small place? If he is what they say he is' – and here she looked pointedly at Firth – 'then surely he would be somewhere else and doing something a lot worse. Why would he spend his time frightening girls gathering mushrooms in the woods?'

There was both laughter and murmured concurrence at the remark and Merrit saw precisely what the girl had done.

Mary Cowan allowed this laughter and murmuring to rise,

and only when it started to fade did she say, 'That's why *I* took it to be one of those lesser demons – because of who we were, and what we were doing. *I* never said it was *the* Devil, just a creature I'd never seen before, that *looked* like a demon.'

Everything she said continued to reveal to Merrit how greatly he had so far underestimated the girl. Even the names themselves – devil and demon – were starting to sound either ridiculous or meaningless.

'And how did you know that?' he asked her.

'Know what?'

'That this so-called creature even *looked* like a demon. Might it not merely have been a wild dog running through the undergrowth?'

There was a slight return of the laughter at this. 'Wild dog?' he heard several people say. 'What wild dog?' 'In those woods?'

'Or a deer, say, up on its hind legs to forage leaves off a low branch?' This seemed a much more credible explanation to Merrit, and the laughter behind him died.

'A deer?' Mary Cowan said.

'On its hind legs, against a tree to pull down food. Foraging.'

Mary Cowan smiled at this. 'I know what a deer looks like,' she said. 'I think most of us here do, some better than others.' She was playing to the crowd again and the laughter resumed.

Merrit looked at Nash, who mouthed the word 'poaching'.

'So it was definitely not a deer,' he said to her. 'At least we have established something solid amidst all this fog and diversion.'

But there was still some laughter in the room and his words went largely unheard.

The woman recording these proceedings – she sat at a separate table beyond Nash – gave him the 'repeat' signal – a single finger held in the air for a second and then lowered.

Merrit shook his head at the request and the woman waited for him to continue.

'Perhaps you were all already over-excited,' he said. 'Perhaps you then saw something or someone and it either frightened or surprised you and your imaginations did the rest.' He knew that he was stumbling, groping, that he was a long way from his intended course. All these paths, tracks and courses; it was as though they were all again wandering mapless amid the undergrowth and trees.

Mary Cowan waited without speaking.

'Why would we all separately say what we had seen?' she said eventually.

'You might have *spoken* separately, as individuals, *afterwards*,' Merrit said. 'But you were all together and closely attached when whatever this creature was first revealed itself to you.'

There was further murmuring at the phrase, at its darker implications, and Merrit, though having chosen it deliberately, regretted it. Everything now was a pointing finger, a suggestion or a breath of disbelief.

'Is that what it did – *reveal* itself to us?' Mary Cowan said. 'Did we not just *see* it? Are you saying it was waiting there for us, to *reveal* itself?' She again added a salacious edge to the word.

'It's what you yourself said,' Merrit said. 'You said the creature came out of the shadows and the undergrowth to reveal itself to be half-animal, half-man. The article is on that table.' He pointed to the table where his papers lay and wondered what he would do if the girl demanded to be shown the exact words. It was what she might have said, and what he vaguely remembered reading.

But the emphasis of his pointing finger and the mound of papers appeared to have worked, and it was a chance that Mary Cowan was not prepared to take.

'At first it was hidden,' she said. 'Or at least where we couldn't see it. Then it was revealed to us and we saw it. I didn't say it *hid* itself and then leaped out in front of us and surprised and scared us.'

'But it did that anyway?' Merrit said.

'Of course it did.' She paused. 'Would *you* not have been scared at seeing it?'

'I would have been absolutely terrified,' Merrit said. 'A demon? The Devil himself, even? Of course I would have been terrified.' He felt suddenly more certain of his way ahead, of this small, unexpected convergence. 'But perhaps all *I* would have seen after that moment of surprise and fear was a feeding deer. I asked you a moment ago how you knew the creature was a demon. Well?'

'Well what?'

'How did you know the creature was something as unmistakeable as a demon – something, surely, that hardly anyone else has ever seen – and not, say, merely a grazing animal?' He was going to add, 'Unless, of course, demons are a common occurrence hereabouts,' but he knew that this would be a misstep of his own.

'Because I've seen pictures,' Mary Cowan said. 'All five of us have. Everybody here has, even you.'

It had been a pointed question and her answer had quickly blunted it.

'Of course we have,' he conceded. 'And so the demon you saw in the woods was identified by you as such because you recognized it from the pictures you had all already seen. It was what any of us would have done. Is that right? Anyone who knew the first thing about devils and demons from the pictures they had seen would have known immediately what they were seeing in that clearing. Your individual descriptions certainly paint that same picture, would you not agree?'

Mary Cowan remained silent and composed in the face of this barrage, finally saying, 'Which question am I meant to answer?'

At the table, upon this repeated mention of devils, Firth again half-rose and lifted his Bible into the air.

Merrit saw what rings the girl would run around the man when he began his own questioning.

Firth's impotent and barely noticed protest complete, he sat back down without speaking.

Merrit pressed his point further. 'So – you knew it was a demon because it corresponded with the pictures you had seen – and here I must assume that we are talking about drawn or coloured illustrations and not actual photographs – because it corresponded to the pictures you and all the other girls were long familiar with. Perhaps in your illustrated Bibles or Sunday-School texts.'

He wanted the point clear. But before she could answer him, he said, 'Tell me, do you actually *believe* in the Devil, in demons?'

'Believe?'

'Do you believe in their existence, here on earth?'

'I believe in God, in His son and the Holy Ghost, so I suppose I must also believe in the Devil.' She smiled at Firth as she said all this, and the unsuspecting man smiled back at her and gently nodded his approval.

'And – or so the rest of us might now suppose – now that you have actually *seen* one of these demons, you believe even *more* firmly in their existence. You have the evidence of your own eyes, so to speak.'

'I know what I saw,' the girl asserted, a first note of uncontainable petulance in her voice. It was a considerably weaker rebuttal, but did not seem so in that court. 'Are you going to repeat *all* your other questions?' she said.

Merrit shook his head. Almost an hour had passed and it had seemed like only minutes. Next she might ask him if *he* did not believe in the Devil or in God, and his answer or the manner in which he gave it would reveal too much. His first assault on her, whatever its successes or confirmations in his own mind, had clearly failed in the eyes of the watching townspeople. He wished he'd brought a dozen pictures of the Devil into the court and given them to her, asking her which one resembled most closely the devil she had seen in the woods. Perhaps he should have asked her if she believed in fairies, in mermaids or in unicorns. But that, too, would have been too hard and too unfair a blow upon what might remain of her child's innocence in the eyes of the room. Many there would have known her as a baby and then as a small child, and some might still think of her as such. Besides, what children did *not* believe in those things? And what if she had then asked him if he himself had not once believed in the same? He could imagine the newspaper headlines.

Mary Cowan leaned forward again, affecting an air of uncertainty and looking from side to side, to the watching crowd, to her father, to the three other men at the table. Her ordeal was over and she knew this.

'I want to thank you for your honesty here today,' Merrit said to her.

She sat back, feigning surprise and disappointment. 'Is that it, then?'

He had hoped she might respond in some less predictable way to this final gentle prod.

'Is it the turn of the others?' she said, meaning Webb, Firth and Nash. She looked back to the table and smiled again at Firth.

'Not today,' Merrit said, and he took a step away from her and motioned for her to leave her seat and return to sit beside her father.

'I don't mind going on,' she said, seizing this final small advantage.

'Please, return to your father.' Where what little power she had exercised over the room would finally evaporate.

Mary Cowan rose from her seat and moved in slow, measured paces back to her father, who rose at her approach and put his arm firmly around her shoulders. And that, too, Merrit saw, was unwelcome to her. Perhaps, the thought suddenly occurred to him, he might capitalize on this understanding and announce to the girl and the court that her presence at the inquiry would thereafter no longer be required. But this, too, was beyond him, and so he said nothing and took his own slow, measured paces back to the table and the three waiting men.

10

Lᴀᴛᴇʀ ᴛʜᴀᴛ sᴀᴍᴇ ᴇᴠᴇɴɪɴɢ, Mᴇʀʀɪᴛ ᴡᴀs ɪɴᴛᴇʀʀᴜᴘᴛᴇᴅ ɪɴ his work by a sudden rapping at his door. Nash called in to him and then pushed the door open.

'Agnes Foley,' he said. 'She's had a seizure. Her father sent for me.' He took Merrit's coat from where it hung on the door and threw it to him where he sat.

'You want me to accompany you?'

But Nash was already back out in the hallway and descending the stairs.

Merrit put on his coat and went after him, following him through the lobby and out into the street.

'Is there a reason for wanting me there?' he called after Nash.

Ahead of him, Nash finally stopped and waited, turning to face Merrit only as he arrived beside him.

'You cannot do again what you did today,' he said.

The remark, and the undisguised anger with which it was made, surprised Merrit and for a moment he was uncertain how to respond.

It had been his intention, after the day's disappointing start, to avoid the other members of the tribunal. The inquiry had adjourned much sooner than expected, shortly after his preliminary questioning of Mary Cowan. None of the others had insisted on following his faltering lead. Of them all, he had hoped Nash would blame him the least for the confused and uneasy start.

'I don't understand,' he said, understanding perfectly what Nash was telling him.

'What you did with the Cowan girl. All this talk of devils. Everything you said gave further spurious credence to the tales she's telling.'

Merrit could not agree with this scatter shot of an accusation, but nor could he wholly deny what Nash was suggesting.

'Perhaps Webb and Firth will redress the balance,' Merrit said, and he saw by Nash's response to the remark that he had clearly heard the disdain it contained.

'And what will either of *them* achieve by trampling over that same flattened ground?' Nash said. 'The girl is lying through her teeth. She's a liar. Everything she says is a lie, a game. A game in which she alone understands the rules and the rewards. Everything we do in there indulges her in her lies. You – we – gain nothing, and yet stand to lose everything.'

'Whereas she, on the other hand, has everything to gain and nothing of any real consequence to lose?' Merrit said.

Nash resumed walking. 'I'm sorry,' he said after a moment. He looked at his watch. 'For my outburst. None of us could have avoided doing what you did.'

'Perhaps,' Merrit said.

Neither man spoke for a moment. Then Merrit said, 'Is Agnes Foley badly affected?'

'I've treated her for the same thing before.' There was

neither alarm nor urgency in Nash's voice. 'She always recovers, however dramatic the immediate effects of the seizure. In truth, there's little I can do for her.'

'Then why——?'

'Why did I want you to accompany me? Apart from feeling the need to criticize and harangue you, you mean? To see her, I suppose. To see her and to understand properly what you'd be dealing with in trying to do to her——'

'What I tried and failed to do to Mary Cowan?'

'It would never have come to public questioning with Agnes Foley,' Nash said.

It was what Merrit had already decided; but Nash was telling him more.

'Look at her, Agnes Foley, and see the others,' he said. 'Don't make the mistake of treating the rest of them as younger, more gullible or suggestible versions of Mary Cowan. They may indeed be all of those things, but——'

'But I might as well put them in that same chair and beat them with a stick in front of the watching town for all the good it will do me?'

Nash laughed at the remark. 'There would be plenty willing to take over from you when your arm grew tired.' He paused. 'You may not have realized it earlier – I doubt if any of us did – but Mary Cowan was your – our – one solid opportunity to cast any real light on this business. The others are nothing compared to her. Perhaps it would have been to all our benefit if you'd questioned *them* before you set her upon her pedestal and then bathed her in the warm glow of your attention and authority.'

'I thought that if she confessed, there would be no need for any of the others to come anywhere near the inquiry,' Merrit said. 'I was hoping to allow them to stay as far away from it and her as possible.'

'I know,' Nash said. 'But I doubt if either Webb or Firth would understand or applaud your motives.'

Merrit conceded this in silence. 'Then are they all lying?' he said eventually.

'Of course they are. And I hope you believe and accept that as completely and as strongly as I do. Their motives or under-standing of the matter might be different, but the end result will still be the same: lies, lies and more lies.'

'Perhaps they'll surprise us all,' Merrit said.

'Perhaps,' Nash said. 'I suppose my true point is that public opinion here will swing and turn on every contradictory wind, every gentle breeze and draught, even. You can tell them as often as you like that this is not a proper courtroom, that this is not a trial, that these girls are not the accused, that you are not their judge, that no one will be found innocent or guilty, that no one will be sentenced or set free and rewarded or—'

'But all *they* will see and hear is the power enshrined in me, a stranger, pitted against a girl?'

'You were pitted against the strongest, most determined of them this morning,' Nash said. 'Imagine walking towards that same chair with Agnes Foley sitting in it.'

Their pace slowed. Nash was not telling him anything he didn't already know. It felt colder than usual and their breath clouded in the evening air.

'And what about me?' Nash said unexpectedly as they entered an unlit alleyway.

'In what sense?'

Nash paused again before answering. 'I'm your medical authority, your expert. You surely know as well as I do –

and certainly as well as all those watchers and listeners do – that there is something of both an adolescent and a sexual nature connected to all these "happenings", all this so-called hysteria. Am I to stand in front of that girl and question her on that? On that, specifically. Am I seriously expected to ask her about, say, her menstruation, call it what you will, her "courses", her "terms", her – God help us – her "flowers"? Am I honestly expected to do that, openly, on your behalf? It wasn't all that long ago that doctors believed menstruation, especially at its onset, to be the primary cause of hysteria in young women. Fifty years ago, menstruating women were deemed to be unreliable witnesses in court.' He paused at Merrit's surprised response to all of this. 'What? It makes even *you* feel uncomfortable? Are you saying it wasn't another of those threads you anticipated tugging at and unravelling on your quest for the truth?'

'I imagine I hoped the subject would not arise, not be brought up or confronted directly,' Merrit said.

'You imagined. You hoped. My antediluvian predecessor here once told me that he ascribed melancholy in older women to accumulated menstrual discharge. Do you honestly expect *me* to stand in front of that girl – let alone any of the younger, more excitable ones – and God forbid that I should ever find myself putting these points to a child whom everyone knows is imbecilic – and raise all or any of these subjects?'

'I see your predicament,' Merrit said. It was clear to him by then that Nash had given considerable thought to everything he had just raised.

'You're aware of my predicament,' Nash said coldly. 'Force me to confront the Cowan girl, and all these points will rise to the surface just as swiftly and as unavoidably as your painted pictures of devils and demons rose to the surface. The moment I am called upon to attest to the physical or mental health of the girls, then all of this will come tumbling out, however much *you* might want to contain or suppress, dismiss or ignore it.'

'I see that now,' Merrit said.

'And even if *I* am able to avoid the issue, then who's to say another medical practitioner won't appear and insist on raising precisely those same points. It's an open inquiry; you wouldn't be able to prevent it.'

'No one has put their name down,' Merrit said.

'Yet,' Nash said. 'My predecessor still lives here.'

The suggestion alarmed Merrit and he was unable to conceal this fully.

'Don't worry,' Nash said. 'He's barely coherent at the best of times. Everyone hated and mistrusted him before he retired. It's why *I*'m so popular.' He waited for Merrit to laugh at the joke, and then laughed with him.

They walked further along the unlit alley, entering a warren of narrow streets and small, congested houses. In addition to their breath, smoke now hung in the cool air, and they could smell and taste this as they walked.

'Is this where she lives?' Merrit said, looking around them.

Nash pointed out the house. It looked even less well maintained than those which surrounded it. The paint on its door was flaked, damp patches stained its brickwork, and the solitary ground-floor window was covered over with card.

'That happened a few days ago,' Nash said. 'Someone thought that a brick through the glass might help matters along.'

'Was anyone hurt?'

'The father was cut. The girl was upstairs.'

'Have the police been told?'

Nash ignored the remark, and Merrit knew not to persist. 'I see,' he said eventually.

'So you keep saying,' Nash said an instant before knocking at the door.

It was opened by the man Merrit had seen in the small group standing behind Cowan during their confrontation in the square. Foley was clearly pleased and relieved at seeing Nash there, but then became wary at the appearance of Merrit immediately behind him.

'Why is he here?' he said to Nash.

'I was with him when I received your message,' Nash lied.

'I insisted,' Merrit said. 'Is your daughter—?'

'It's finished,' the man said. He led them along a narrow passageway into the scullery at the rear of the house. The room was dark, illuminated by a single lamp and by the glow of a low fire.

The girl lay on a table, her head flat to the boards, and with clothing piled on top of her.

'I laid her out and kept her warm,' Foley said, clearly following earlier instructions from Nash.

'How severe was it?' Nash asked him. He put a hand to the girl's wet forehead, drawing back her long hair.

Foley turned his back on them for a moment and Nash tapped Merrit's arm and surreptitiously revealed to him the indentation running diagonally across the girl's brow. He was quick to lay the hair back over this before her father turned.

'Five minutes?' Foley said. 'Everything – her whole body, head, arms, legs. I got her to the floor and held her the best I could until it started to slacken and then subside. I waited

123

until it was finished before lifting her on to the table and covering her.'

'The third seizure this month,' Nash said to Merrit.

'Third in twenty days,' her father said.

'Does anyone understand the cause of them?' Merrit said, immediately regretting the words.

'She's having them now because of all the worry connected to your trial,' her father said bluntly. 'Because of all the things she's being accused of.'

Merrit looked to Nash.

'It's a possibility,' Nash said. 'In this heightened condition . . .'

'My apologies,' Merrit said.

'For what *they*'re worth,' Foley said. But then he appeared to regret the remark and he bowed his head.

'You have every right to feel angry,' Merrit told him, uncertain what effect this might have on the man. 'And if Doctor Nash tells me that his services here are being engaged in connection with his work on the tribunal, then I'm certain that funds can be found to pay for those services.'

Nash and Foley shared a smile at this.

'He treats her and I pay him when I've got the money,' Foley said.

'And I know to the penny what I'm owed,' Nash said, causing the man to lay a hand briefly on his shoulder.

On the table, the girl started to mutter unintelligibly and then she opened her eyes and looked around her.

Nash spoke to her, repeating her name over and over until she understood who he was and what had happened to her.

She pushed herself up on to her elbows and looked around her, relieved when she saw her father. Her chin and neck and the material of her nightdress were wet with saliva. Her breath smelled of vomit.

'I cleaned her up,' Foley said.

'Was there much?' Nash asked him.

'The same as usual.' The man put a cup to his daughter's lips and poured water into her mouth, much of which only added to the dampness of her chin and chest. 'Open,' he said to her. 'Open, open, open.'

The girl finally understood him and opened her mouth wider.

'Swallow,' he said. 'Swallow, swallow, swallow.'

Nash listened to her heart and lungs, sitting her forward to tap up and down her back. She was skin and bone, her ribs and shoulder blades and vertebrae all clearly visible through her pale flesh. Her collarbones looked as though they might snap beneath one of Nash's misplaced taps. She submitted to all this, and to Nash raising and then lowering her nightdress, without complaint or even any noticeable response.

Nash looked in her mouth and her eyes. He held up her hands and tugged at each small finger, then did the same with her feet and toes.

'Are you here to question her?' Foley said to Merrit as the pair of them watched all this.

'Far from it,' Merrit said, but did little to either convince or reassure the man. 'You weren't at the inquest today,' he said.

'I had a day's work. I heard what happened. I heard you got no proper answers from the Cowan' – he hesitated, and then thought better of what he had been about to say – 'girl.'

'It seems I merely trod on a few toes and pointed a few fingers in completely the wrong direction,' Merrit said.

'Cowan accused him of calling his daughter a liar,' Nash said.

Foley considered this, and Merrit saw the quick, uncertain assessments he was making on his own daughter's behalf. Perhaps this had been Nash's purpose in making the remark.

'Your daughter, Agnes, need not appear before us,' Merrit said, wondering immediately if this was a rash promise to make.

And again the man looked unconvinced.

'On medical advice,' Nash told him. '*My* advice.' And he held the man's gaze until Foley finally nodded.

The promise, Merrit finally understood, was Nash's, and not his own, to make.

'Then will you try to talk to her in private?' Foley asked him.

'Perhaps there will be no need.'

'Meaning that one of the others will confess everything and then tell you how easily led Agnes is in all of this?'

'Perhaps she was just desperate to be included in what the other girls did,' Merrit said. He remembered the story of the girl's legs being beaten by Mary Cowan in an effort to drive her away.

'That's all she does,' Foley said. 'Follow, wait, repeat, wait, follow.'

At the table, Nash lowered the girl back down, making a pillow of the clothing for her head.

She lay without speaking, her eyes fixed on the ceiling, a bubble of saliva repeatedly forming and bursting at the corner of her mouth.

Nash took a bottle from his case and gave it to her father. 'It'll help her sleep,' he said to Merrit. 'The important thing is for the seizures to occur as widely spaced as possible, for her to recover fully from the previous one before suffering the next.'

'And is three in twenty days an excessive occurrence?'

Nash avoided answering him. 'What's important now is that she sleeps,' he said. He watched as Foley poured the medicine into his daughter's mouth. 'She can't use a spoon,' he said to Merrit.

'Of course,' Merrit said. 'I mean, I see.'

Nash stood and watched until the girl finally closed her eyes and her breathing grew calm.

A few minutes later, he and Merrit were back outside, having declined Foley's offer of a drink.

'Her forehead . . .' Merrit said as they began their journey back towards the centre of the town.

'My predecessor's inept delivery,' Nash said. 'Forceps. She was dragged out of her dying mother. She was fitting before she was an hour old.'

'And her mother died at the same time?'

'A week later. Blood poisoning.'

'And your predecessor?'

'My predecessor's proudest boast was that he'd spent six months working in the hospital at Scutari. Imagine that. I doubt if childbirth and post-natal nursing ever seemed particularly important or worthwhile to him after that.' Nash paused. 'At least you know now that she can never come into your court.' He waited for Merrit to nod his agreement.

'The others will exonerate her,' Merrit said.

'You seem very certain of that.'

'Or if not, then everyone will see that she was led by them, merely repeating whatever they said.'

'And what if either Webb or Firth calls for her to be questioned?'

'I still have *some* authority . . . surely?' This was intended by Merrit to be a small, self-deprecating joke, but if Nash understood this, then he didn't share in it.

They left the narrow streets and re-entered the road leading to the square.

After a further minute of walking, Merrit said to Nash, 'Are any of the other girls . . . I mean, are they . . . ?'

'Are they menstrual? Can you not even say it? Mary Cowan, certainly. Margaret Seaton – she of the unidentified bedroom assailant – very likely. She's fourteen. The others, unlikely.'

'Can you find out?'

Nash laughed at this. 'Why? Because it might become conclusive proof of something? You yourself have insisted often enough that they're not witches.'

'No, but if it helps account for anything . . .' Merrit said.

They arrived at the square and stopped short of its brighter lights.

'What will happen to her?' Merrit said, meaning Agnes Foley.

'There's every likelihood that she'll go back to an asylum. I advised her father against removing her in the first place. Ten years ago, the law would have prevented him.'

'Why did he do it?'

Nash considered this and shrugged. 'Because she's his daughter? Because he believed there might still be something worth salvaging from the nightmare his life had turned into? I'm only guessing. Perhaps you have some suggestions of your own as to why a man might cleave to his only child, his only

128

living relative, even one who's become what *she* has become.'

There was nothing Merrit could say to this. 'The other girls would never have wanted her as part of all this,' he said. 'Her unpredictability, the way she is already judged.'

'Or perhaps the exact opposite,' Nash said. 'Perhaps she is their one solitary, constantly glowing ember.'

'Ember?'

'Of true hysteria. Her condition. Perhaps there is something in her – and in her alone – something she cannot exercise solely at whim and which at the same time she cannot conceal to even the slightest degree. Perhaps her conviction is the strongest of them all. Perhaps *she*, and not Mary Cowan, is their true centre. Perhaps *she* is directing them.'

'You can't truly believe that,' Merrit said, unconvinced by all this speculation.

'No,' Nash said, 'I don't.' And then he yawned and wiped a hand over his face. 'Sorry – no, of course I don't believe it. But she's still a part of all this, and whatever role she fulfils in the eyes of the others, and of her accusers here, it's something *you* would do well to consider before dismissing her completely from the proceedings.' He held out his hand to Merrit.

Merrit suggested a drink at the hotel, but Nash declined.

'Will you say something to the others, to Webb and Firth?' Merrit said.

'About tonight, the girl? Of course. I can become every evasion and excuse you cannot bring yourself to become.'

The inquiry was not sitting the following day, after which it was the weekend.

The two men parted, and Merrit walked a full circuit of the empty, gaslit square before returning to his room and his interrupted work there.

11

THE THREE EMPTY DAYS PASSED, AND THEN THE INQUIRY
resumed. Everyone insisted on telling their own
particular tale. Little helped. Witnesses – though Merrit
came quickly to realize the invalidity of the title – were
offered the opportunity of speaking to either himself, Webb,
Firth or Nash. Most, not unexpectedly, insisted on talking
directly and privately to Merrit. They told him their stories,
added memories, revisited old histories; they shaded with
prejudice and self-regard. All of them, one way or another,
knew the girls concerned: some had known them since they
were newborn babies; others recited long and complicated
stories of involvement with the girls because they were their
relatives, however distant, their neighbours, their teachers,
because they were shopkeepers or tradesmen or friends of
friends. And some – too many, Merrit also quickly realized –
repeated only what they themselves had already heard from
others.

A mountain of extraneous material was collected and
sorted and filed. A mountain of common, hard-won, unpro-
ductive ore with its one buried vein of precious, unvarnished
truth running somewhere deep within it.

But it was all a necessary part of the process, and Merrit

understood that. He sat, he listened, he questioned, he nodded appreciatively; he kept all indication of scepticism, suspicion, disbelief and doubt from his voice and his eyes. He took notes, he kept records, he referenced and collated. And when he was finished with all these tale-tellers – or, more accurately, when they were finished with him – this rising mountain of paper was assessed and sorted and packed into tight folders and dark cases, and then seldom seen or consulted again. It was all, Merrit knew, a valuable collective letting out of breath, and that, too, he understood better than any of them.

He sat in the courtroom, at the same table, and listened. People came to him individually and in pairs, sometimes in small groups. Usually, Webb or Firth sat elsewhere in the room, listening to their own shorter queues of confessors. Nash came less often to these sessions; few indicated that they wished to tell their tales of the girls to him. He was still a doctor, still someone regarded by many with suspicion, mistrust or fear. Talking to Nash – or so it occurred to Merrit when he glanced at the man and his witnesses – seemed to many to be a kind of test or a tempting of fate which few were willing to undertake. It surprised him to see that people spoke more readily to both Webb and Firth. But perhaps, he reasoned, that was because those other two men represented a kind of higher, more detached and better understood authority in the place.

Merrit showed all three men which forms to complete when compiling this sudden leaf-fall of stories, what vital details to retrieve. He showed them how to annotate salient points for later cross-reference. Individual occurrences – the events of the clearing in the woodland, for instance, the smashed crockery, the painted wall, other lesser, though now rapidly

131

multiplying unexplained events attached to the girls – were collected on separate sheets.

A kind of order was imposed and then maintained. Procedures were made plain and straightforward. As far as possible, the chaff was separated from the grain, and the grain was then graded and sorted. It may have been a largely artificial order – another of Merrit's hard-learned lessons – but it was nevertheless a necessary one. Boundaries needed to be drawn, individual compartments established and kept separate.

Wives sat beside their husbands and repeated everything the men said. Husbands sat by their wives and echoed the closing words of every sentence. Truths and lies were plucked from the same twice-told tales; speculation settled in drifts; tiny, inconsequential-seeming remembrances and proven, verifiable facts were bound together, separated and then lost in the swirling confusion of all that was now being cast into that same rising wind.

Little surprised Merrit. He knew there was a discernible pattern to these things, and that soon that pattern would reveal itself to him here. He sensed who was a reliable witness and who was not. Ten times on that first morning he imagined picking up the written testimonies and then tearing these in half, then quarters, then even smaller pieces in front of the people who were still talking to him, and who were refusing, despite all his own signals and declarations, to fall silent.

Some witnesses told single tales of individual girls, but most told many, merging one with another and then another as, thus prompted, they remembered more. People guessed at what they could not possibly have known. They embellished and speculated, coloured, re-shaped and illuminated. They insisted on their own reliability, their trustworthiness, their honesty and their sincerity. Some, Merrit knew, spoke to him merely for the pleasure of being heard by him. Some came to the table in their best clothes. Some waited for hours for their moment in front of him. Some told him to expose and then to condemn the five girls for the malicious fraudsters they were, and others asked him to forgive them and to bring as quick and as resolute a conclusion as possible to the whole affair.

Some of them, Merrit imagined, were saying the same things to the ever-growing crowd of journalists – he had counted seven of the men that morning – who were forbidden entry into the building whenever the inquiry was not in public session. He occasionally asked people if they had spoken to the newspapermen, and most denied this; others told him indignantly that they had every right to talk to whoever they chose. He guessed that the men waiting outside were offering promises of payment or other bribes.

At one o'clock, he rose from his seat and told everyone still waiting that the inquiry was adjourning for lunch. He told people to mark their places and to leave. He listened to the few half-hearted complaints, but did not answer them. No more than an hour, he repeated. The sooner they went, the sooner the inquiry would resume, the sooner they would be given the opportunity to tell their own tales.

People rose and left the room. Merrit signalled to both Webb and Firth that he wished to speak to them. Nash, having exhausted his own short queue, had already returned to his work elsewhere.

Waiting until their audience had departed, the three men went into the room's small ante-chamber, where a lunch of tea and sandwiches had been set out for them by one of the clerks.

The three men sat and faced each other.

'Why was Nash allowed to leave?' Webb said bluntly. 'Very unprofessional.'

'Busy, I'm afraid,' Merrit told him. 'Besides—'

'While *we*, on the other hand, undertake our civic duty free of charge and at no inconsiderable expense to ourselves.'

Merrit remained silent. The man would be receiving his usual salary and a small supplement for the duration of the inquiry.

'Has anything yet come to light that might . . . you know?' Firth said hopefully.

Webb looked at him. 'Might what? Might what? Might give the lie to everything we've already heard from Mary Cowan or are yet to hear from her scheming cohorts?'

'We can expect little in the way of actual verification or confirmation of any of these events at this early stage,' Merrit said.

'Stories,' Webb said, his mouth full. 'Not "events", stories.'

'I believe most people are merely happy to be afforded the opportunity to play their own small part in all of this,' Firth said.

'Exactly,' Webb said. 'But only because they believe – as *I* believe – that we are all paying far too much unnecessary attention to the girls. And because this is what decent, honest people do at times like this – they talk, and then they talk some more, and then they talk some more still. No one wants to be excluded. I listened to a man who came from ten miles away, who knew none of the girls, who had never even heard of any of them before all this, and yet is now convinced that he, and he alone, possesses the one perfectly good explanation for everything that has happened. Knows the woods like he knows his own home, he said. Said he knows "what a place" it is for exactly "this kind of drama". And after him, I spoke to a neighbour of the Lisset girl, who had waited for three hours to impart the information that he could tell me nothing whatsoever about the child except that she had changed – Hallelujah – and that she seemed hardly to be the same small child she had once been.'

'She's twelve,' Merrit said.

'I spoke to her teacher,' Firth said.

'And?' Merrit asked him. He had hoped the woman would have chosen to speak directly to him. He guessed she was a member of Firth's congregation; it was clearly how the man had attracted most of his other witnesses.

The woman might not know any of the individual girls as well as their families knew them, but she almost certainly understood something of their changed nature when they acted as a group, when each of them was watched and encouraged and supported by the others.

'She said she was concerned,' Firth said hesitantly. 'She said the girls repeated their stories in the school. She said they clung to each other – not physically, necessarily, she made that much clear to me – but she said they were more and more dependent on each other.'

'In any specific way?' Merrit said.

'She said it was clear to her that Mary Cowan was firmly at their centre and that the others took their cues from her. She said the girl was manipulative and that—'

'What a surprise,' Webb said.

'And that she seemed to take no little pleasure in the power she now exercised. She said the other girls were happy to be led by her, to do her bidding. They looked up to her. Others tried to join the group but were pushed away.'

'Did she say anything of the nature of Agnes Foley's involvement?'

'She said the girl was a pathetic and easily led creature.'

'So was she not surprised that the others included her in the group?'

'A little. But she said it was perhaps just a consequence of the fact that she was with them in the woods on that day.'

'When the Devil jumped out and shouted "Boo" to them,' Webb said and laughed.

'Was she surprised that all this was happening now?' Merrit asked Firth.

'She said she was only surprised that it had been allowed to get so far out of hand, and so quickly.'

'At last,' Webb said. 'At last the woman begins to talk some sense.' Breadcrumbs fell from his lips and he caught these in his cupped hand.

'She said the girls in the school were always forming such associations and connections, that these small, shared fantasies weren't at all uncommon,' Firth said, increasingly uncomfortable with everything the remark suggested.

'But that usually such associations were either quickly forgotten or abandoned?' Merrit said.

Firth nodded. 'She said she blamed all this' – he waved his hand at the room around them – 'for turning this thing into what it has become.'

'Others said exactly the same to me,' Webb said. 'And *I* told *them* that it wasn't their place to speculate, that the business of the court was not for them to even consider, let alone approve or disapprove of.'

Merrit told them to be patient, that relatively little had so far been gathered. If witnesses were dismissed or challenged, then they would become resentful and their stories might change. Rocks of anger, mistrust and suspicion now hurled at the girls might easily find new targets.

'Everything is a rod for our own backs,' Webb said. 'I listened to another man who said we ought to take the girls back into the woods and question them there, that it would be a better place to force a confession from them.'

Next, Merrit knew, Webb would suggest this himself. It was something else he had considered during his three long days of preparation.

'Well?' Webb said.

'I suppose we might verify all the lesser points of their story if we were in the place with them,' Merrit said, but with little conviction.

'Someone suggested to me that I might hold a service in the place,' Firth said. And he too seemed hopeful of being able to do this.

'What sort of service?' Webb asked him. He grinned and then winked at Merrit. 'Dear God, don't tell me you intend to summon up the Devil and then do battle with him yourself, man.'

'Of course not. I merely—'

'Because if that *is* your intention, may I suggest you take your formidable lady wife along with you in case you yourself are either quickly defeated or won over by him.'

Firth turned and pointed at the magistrate. 'I take great offence at that suggestion,' he said. 'Great offence.'

'What suggestion?' Webb said, barely suppressing his laughter. 'I meant no offence. All I meant was that you ought not to be dabbling—'

'Dabbling? It is my vocation, my calling, my—'

'Not to be dabbling in something completely beyond your control or understanding. And what if you *were* to be consumed – destroyed, even – by these immeasurable and unquenchable forces of evil? Surely it would be better to have your wife beside you, adding her own pious ballast and thrust to the glorious battle.'

'And to be destroyed alongside me?' Firth said. 'Is that what you're suggesting?'

Merrit saw that the unconsidered mockery had run its short course. 'Whatever happened,' he said loudly, drawing the two men back to him, 'it isn't a good idea – the service in the woods. And certainly not while the inquiry is still in progress. Afterwards, perhaps, when everything is explained or admitted or forgiven. But not now or any time soon. Anything of that nature might only give support or credence to what has yet to be proved or disproved.'

'I understand that,' Firth said, but with an uncontainable note of disappointment in his voice. 'In fact, several of my parishioners said the same to me.'

'Then listen to them,' Merrit said.

'Of course. But I must have my part – my *spiritual* part – to play in all of this.'

'Of course,' Merrit said, surprised by the man's continued insistence.

Webb flicked his eyes to the ceiling. He took another sandwich and opened the pieces of bread to see what lay within.

'Of course you must play your part,' Merrit said. *Your wife will see to that.* 'But we must avoid anything inflammatory until everything here is completed.'

Firth nodded once, already calculating, Merrit guessed, how much of this to report to his wife.

Already there was kindling and there was fuel, blazing sparks and a fanning wind. Already there were people gathering at the waiting fire to watch and to warm themselves.

'What would you *do*, exactly?' Webb said to Firth.

'Do?'

'In the clearing. Regardless of Satan himself either putting in an appearance or knowing when he was beaten and staying well clear.'

'I imagine I might attempt—' Firth began to say.

'Perhaps something at the chapel might be more appropriate,' Merrit suggested.

'Less heathenish,' Webb said. 'Less . . . less . . .'

'More within the bounds of what others might want or expect of you,' Merrit said.

'Of course.' Firth picked up his first sandwich and bit into it.

'Everything must be tempered,' Merrit said. 'Everything fairly and evenly considered. They can tell us what they know or what they think they know. They can paint it one way or the other. And when all that is done, they can consider themselves to have performed their duty, played their part, and then they can forget about it all. This thing will soon be over. It may be a storm, but all storms blow themselves out and the clear blue sky returns.'

'"This too shall pass"?' Firth said.

'Precisely,' Merrit said.

'It's October,' Webb said. 'Our own particular calm and clear blue sky is still a long way off.'

'So you've weathered other such storms?' Firth said to Merrit. He chewed at the sandwich until it could have been little more than liquid in his mouth.

'Many,' Merrit told him.

'And the outcomes?'

'Panic always dies, controversy always settles,' he said. He looked from Firth to Webb, who, despite his own undisguised hostility and doubts concerning the inquiry, seemed to better understand and accept everything he was saying to them.

In turn, Webb put a hand on Firth's shoulder. 'You announce your service – out in the chapel yard if you like, out under that clear blue sky – and I'll bring the Chamber of Trade and the Lodge along and make it a proper sort of celebration.'

Firth flinched at both the man's touch and at the suggestion. 'Of course,' he said. 'A proper celebration.'

12

'YOU TOLD ME YOU SAW A MAN,' NASH SAID TO MARGARET Seaton.

'A man?'

'In your bedroom. You said he touched you and tried to climb into bed with you.'

'Into bed with me?' The girl sounded genuinely alarmed, as though she were hearing these things for the first time.

Nash glanced over his shoulder at Merrit and the others, none of whom made any response other than to remain watchful and silent.

'Seven weeks ago. I came to visit you – to ensure you had come to no harm,' Nash said. 'The doctor, you remember?'

From her seat, the girl looked out at her parents and then at the others around them – her brothers and neighbours and friends.

'I hadn't,' she said hesitantly, her eyes everywhere except on Nash.

'Hadn't what?' Nash said.

'Come to any harm. You looked.'

'So you do remember me coming to see you?'

'Of course I do.' She seemed suddenly more confident. She

sat upright and held back her shoulders, flattening her hands on the seat of the chair.

'I came because you said someone had come into your bedroom.'

'That's what I said,' she said.

From where he sat at the centre of the table, Merrit watched as people around the room started to speculate in whispers as to what the girl might now be suggesting.

'You told your parents—'

'I know what I *told* them,' Margaret Seaton said angrily. She rose in her seat briefly and then sat back down.

'Are you saying that that's all you did – *told* them that you made the man up?'

She seemed not to understand the question and all it implied.

Beside him, Merrit sensed Webb's impatience with Nash's gentle, oblique approach to the girl.

'No – I told them that because *that*'s what happened,' Margaret Seaton said eventually.

In the audience, the whispering rose to a murmur before dying.

'So there was definitely a man? Because when you repeated everything to the constable the next day, the word you used first was "figure". After that, you said "someone" several times, and even "something".'

'It was a man,' Margaret Seaton insisted. 'Of course it was a man. That's what I told them – a man.'

'Why "of course"?' Nash said.

She considered this. 'Of course it was a man,' she repeated. 'Who else would it be?'

It seemed to Merrit that the girl was now playing to her

audience. Several in the crowd laughed at her remark. She seemed suddenly much older than her fourteen years.

'But clearly not a man you recognized,' Nash said.

'I would have said.' She sounded petulant now.

'So perhaps it was a young man; a boy, perhaps?'

'It wasn't a boy. I didn't see his face, but it wasn't a boy. I said a man because it was a man.'

'A man as tall as me?' Nash asked her. 'Taller? Shorter?'

She looked at him. 'Shorter,' she said.

'I'm quite tall,' he said. 'Taller than most.'

'Then it definitely wasn't you, was it?' Margaret Seaton said sharply.

The remark caught Nash unawares and he took a step away from her. There was more laughter.

Merrit watched all this closely. He had agreed to Nash questioning the girl first because he had been the first person outside her family to visit her and talk to her following the incident, and because he had already asked her these same questions, which he might now usefully put to her again in an attempt to discover any telling discrepancies or shifts in emphasis. Apart from which, neither Webb nor Firth possessed either the delicacy or the expertise to examine the medical aspects of the girl's story.

'No, it definitely wasn't me,' Nash said to her. 'Are you surprised that people laughed at that? Or was that your intention?' There was a firmer edge to his voice.

'What?' Margaret Seaton said, still indignant.

Control, Merrit thought to himself. *Public opinion*.

Beside him, Webb leaned closer and said, 'This is more like it. He's going to push her back.'

Merrit doubted this, but nodded.

'He touched you – first your feet and then higher up your leg. And then he tried to get into your bed. He tried to get into bed with you. He didn't merely approach the bed, stand over you or sit on the bed beside you – he tried to get into bed with you. After touching you. He tried to get into bed with you because that's where you had been all the time this strange, unidentifiable, not-too-tall man was in your bedroom with you.'

There were a few insuppressible exclamations from the crowd at this.

Merrit tapped a finger on the table, attracting Nash's attention without revealing his intention to anyone else.

Nash signalled back that he understood. 'I'm sorry,' he said to the girl.

'Well . . .' she said.

'You didn't scream,' he said.

'I did scream. I screamed blue murder. I screamed at the top of my voice.'

'But that was after he'd gone,' Nash said. 'You remained silent while he was in your room and trying to get into bed with you – *beside* you – and then when he'd gone, you screamed to attract your parents' attention.'

The girl was briefly confused by what he was half-asking, half-telling her.

'So?' she said. 'So?' She looked back to her parents.

Nash held up his hands to her. 'No one doubts that,' he said. 'It's what both your mother and your father said happened.'

'Good. Because it's the truth. That's what did happen.'

Nash nodded slowly. 'I was merely wondering,' he said, 'why you didn't scream when you first knew the man was there – why, knowing he was there, you didn't scream to frighten him off, or at least to prevent him from trying to climb into bed with you.'

Margaret Seaton said nothing in response to this, looking directly at Nash and breathing hard.

The girl's father called out to Merrit, and Merrit raised his hand to the man. Acknowledging this, Seaton said nothing further.

When Merrit looked back to Nash, both the doctor and the girl were looking at him.

'Can you not answer Doctor Nash?' he asked her.

'I don't know what he's asking me,' she said unconvincingly. 'Why I screamed at one time and not another?'

'Yes,' Merrit said.

'I don't know,' she said. 'But I'm telling the truth when I say the man was there.'

Merrit waited without speaking, hoping she might add something to contradict herself. And then precisely what he had hoped would *not* happen, happened: another man in the crowd called out, 'Was it the Devil?' And the instant the question was asked of her, Merrit saw the look on the girl's face change from one of confusion and uncertainty to anger and scorn, which lasted at least ten seconds before she was able to regain her composure and then smile again.

'Who's to say?' she said loudly.

Nash turned to Merrit with his eyes closed. He shook his head once and held a hand to his brow.

There was nothing Merrit could do to intervene and quieten the rising uproar and laughter. He knew that Mary Cowan and her father were in the audience. He had seen the two girls exchange repeated glances. He regretted the older girl's presence and influence. In an ordinary court he would have kept her apart from these other witnesses, but here he was powerless to do that. He looked at her now and saw that she was smiling, laughing almost, and that she and Margaret Seaton were again holding each other's gaze.

'Shall I intervene?' Webb asked Merrit, indicating Nash, who was struggling to extricate himself.

Merrit told him to wait as the noise in the room slowly subsided.

Finally, Nash returned to his place directly in front of Margaret Seaton, deliberately breaking the connection between her and Mary Cowan.

'So,' he said, waiting for the silence which followed as people strained to hear what the girl might say next. 'Do you believe it *was* the Devil?'

The question sounded as preposterous and as disbelieving as he had intended it to sound.

'I suppose it . . . if it . . .' Margaret Seaton began, quickly faltering to silence.

'Because if it *was* the Devil – and no one here is calling you a liar, and you are still giving evidence, remember – then you are the only one of the five of you to have been approached on an individual basis. Quite a privilege, I would imagine.'

Margaret Seaton leaned sideways in her seat to look again at Mary Cowan, who fixed her own gaze on the back of Nash's head. Then she too shifted from side to side in an effort to see around him and back to Margaret Seaton.

Nash, Merrit saw, had guessed this and moved closer to Margaret Seaton than before.

Thus isolated, Margaret Seaton quickly felt the weight of her small defeat. 'It wasn't the Devil,' she said. 'I never said it was. *You* said it was, not me. I never said that, not once.'

'It was someone in the audience who offered up the suggestion,' Nash said calmly. 'I just thought that, having seen the Devil once, in the woods, he might have made this return visit to you, and that if it *was* him, then you would easily have recognized him such a short time after his first appearance to you in the company of the others.'

'I told you – it wasn't him,' Margaret Seaton shouted.

'And how can you be certain of that? Oh, that's right – because it was definitely the Devil or one of his minions in the woods, so of course you would recognize him, or it, if he, or it, came to you privately afterwards.'

Merrit knew from the girl's statement to the police that she had already agreed with Mary Cowan that the creature in the woods was at least *a* devil, of sorts.

'It was dark,' Margaret Seaton said weakly.

'In the woods or in your bedroom?' Nash said.

It occurred to Merrit that the girl had forgotten exactly what she'd already told the police and was now struggling to maintain her balance. She continued trying to regain her sight of Mary Cowan, and Nash continued to prevent this.

'In my bedroom,' she said eventually. 'But it wasn't all that light in the woods, either. I mean it wasn't sunny – it was the woods.'

Nash let the impact of all this sink in. Several in the room called for him to stop pushing the girl.

'He's putting words into the child's mouth,' one woman shouted.

Nash turned his back on the girl. 'No one here believes it was anything other than a shadowy figure in the room,' he said. 'Who knows, perhaps even someone in her own family looking in on her. Perhaps she was dreaming. Perhaps she was only half-awake. Perhaps something woke her and she was alarmed because she didn't know what it was. I could offer her a dozen such considerably more believable and acceptable explanations, a dozen such easy routes out of the predicament in which she now finds herself.' He looked at Mary Cowan and her father as he said all this. 'We all *know* it wasn't the Devil, perhaps not even *a* devil' – and if he had expected a whisper of appreciative laughter at this, then he was disappointed – 'but what we *don't* know is what *did* happen. Or perhaps it doesn't matter that we know. Perhaps all that matters now is for *all* the girls to find their own separate ways out of this shared predicament of their own making and—'

'Why does he keep calling it that?' Webb said to Merrit.

'And then afterwards to follow the usual, ordinary courses of their young lives.'

Several in the crowd applauded Nash at this, but only a few, and their applause turned quickly back to silence.

But it was something, a turning point perhaps, and Merrit noted this.

Nash finally stood aside from Margaret Seaton and the girl's gaze returned immediately to Mary Cowan.

But now, Merrit saw, Mary Cowan looked away from her, first at her father and then down into her lap, anywhere but at Margaret Seaton, deliberately avoiding the younger girl's silent plea.

'Are you looking for someone?' Nash asked Margaret Seaton.

'Looking for who?'

Nash shrugged. 'Mary Cowan, perhaps? Do you think

that once again she'll tell you what to say or do, make everything all right for you?'

'The man's a bloody barrister,' Webb said to Merrit, almost admiringly.

'Why should she do that?' Margaret Seaton said.

'Because I think it's clear to everyone by now that she's the one you and the others are following in all of this.'

'She was there, that's all,' Margaret Seaton said, but then regretted the remark and all it implied concerning Mary Cowan's status in the group. 'I mean, she was the eldest. She was the one – I mean – it wasn't the Devil in my room, just a man I didn't know.'

'So you keep telling us,' Nash said. 'I really don't think there's anything more to be gained by pursuing this, especially not here, now, in front of all these people, is there?'

'What have *they* got to do with it?' Margaret Seaton shouted, almost screamed. '*They* weren't there.'

'Are we back in the woods?' Nash said. 'Or still in your bedroom?'

'You know what I'm talking about,' Margaret Seaton said.

Merrit finally signalled to Nash that he should stop provoking the girl like this, that his point was made.

'You watch,' Webb said to Merrit. 'Next he'll say "No more questions".'

But Nash merely stood in front of the girl for a moment longer and then turned away from her and walked slowly back to his place at the table.

Beside Webb, Firth signalled to attract Merrit's attention. Merrit was in no position to refuse the man.

Caught unaware by the minister rising beside him, Webb started to protest, but Merrit ignored him.

'She's had enough,' someone shouted, and Merrit could only agree. Nothing more was likely to be gained by Firth's intervention, but perhaps the minister's remarks and questions might now calm the situation and, more importantly, allow the girl to calm herself. The man would certainly not wield the stick Nash had just wielded; at best he would place a calming hand on her.

Nash's questioning had revealed all he had intended it to reveal, and had been considerably more potent as a means of swaying public opinion than Merrit had expected. But now that same public would want to hear Firth's soothing platitudes. The fourteen-year-old girl could not be left so vulnerable and so exposed to doubt or ridicule or public opprobrium any longer.

'I know you,' Aubrey Firth said loudly to Margaret Seaton, approaching her with his hands together, his fingers locked.

'Is the man praying?' Webb asked Merrit.

'So?' Margaret Seaton said suspiciously.

After everything the girl had just endured, Firth had clearly expected a warmer response from her. 'In fact, I might with good cause say that I know you well,' he said.

'I come to chapel sometimes. I was in the Sunday School when I was a kid,' she said, already looking beyond the man to her wider audience.

'As a child, yes,' Firth said, unable to resist this small revision. Any other man might have read these warnings and left the girl alone. 'So you do indeed know the appearance of the Devil in all his vainglorious disguises.'

'His what?' Margaret Seaton said.

'His appearance. How he appears. What he looks like. His demonic features.'

Margaret Seaton shrugged.

'Ask her something she can answer,' someone called out. 'Stop talking in riddles.'

'You're not in chapel now,' someone else shouted.

The two remarks struck Merrit as the beginning and the end of Firth's misguided intervention.

Eventually, someone shouted for Firth to sit back down and to leave the child alone.

Angelica Firth, Merrit knew, was not in the room to prop up her husband's faltering efforts.

But instead of leaving the girl, Firth merely raised his Bible-less hand and waited for silence.

'What?' Margaret Seaton said to him after this had eventually fallen.

'You must *say*,' Firth said to her.

'Say what?'

'You must tell us the truth.'

'Oh, dear God, not all *this* again,' Webb said, this time loud enough for everyone to hear.

Beyond him, Nash sat and wiped his brow and face with a handkerchief. After this he dried his palms on his sleeve. He seemed to Merrit to have genuinely been shaken by his short encounter with the girl, relieved to be finished with her. Merrit wanted to say something reassuring to him, but was unable to do this while Webb sat between them.

The girl remained silent and unmoving in front of Firth.

'Can't we move on?' Webb said, distracting Firth.

And seizing this advantage, Margaret Seaton said, 'Have we finished, then?'

Others in the crowd continued to call out.

Merrit finally decided to intervene. Nash's small drama was over, and nothing Firth might now attempt would either match or revive it.

'Perhaps the child requires a break,' he suggested to Firth, hoping the man would take this opportunity to extricate himself from the hostile glare of his audience and return to the security of the table.

'Yes – sit down,' someone shouted, and others called the same, almost as though joining in a game.

But Firth hesitated where he stood, and it occurred only then to Merrit that even though the man's wife was not present, they were still her questions he was putting to the girl, prepared and rehearsed by the pair of them the previous evening.

'They want you to sit down,' Margaret Seaton said to Firth. She smiled coldly at the minister's obvious discomfort.

Caught like this, there was nothing Aubrey Firth could do except retreat the few steps back to his seat. He did this, and as he came, Merrit thanked him for whatever he had been about to attempt. But it was clearly no consolation to the humiliated Firth, who would now only be able to repeat to his wife everything that had just happened to him.

'What now?' someone called.

It was by now almost three in the afternoon and so the answer to this was clear.

Merrit looked at the girl still in her seat. She was smiling again, raising her hand to people in the crowd. 'You can go,' he said to her, but his words went unheard amid the rising noise as people sensed an end to the day's proceedings.

Beside him, Webb leaned to Firth and said, 'What did you think you were playing at, man?'

'Playing at?' Firth said.

'You heard me,' Webb said, and then he rose and started shuffling together his papers before Firth could answer him.

13

13

THE FOLLOWING DAY, MERRIT WALKED AGAIN INTO THE woodland. As before, he went alone. He was walking to clear his head, and to think, to consider the course they had all taken and its likely outcome.

Wherever he went in the town, people watched him. Many shunned him completely. Others, less reticent now that the inquiry was under way, made remarks within his hearing about the harm he was causing – both to the girls and to the place itself. Or they commented on his 'true' or 'hidden' or 'secret' purpose there; on his masters. There was little that Merrit had not heard countless times before, and he seldom responded to these provocations, answering questions only when they were put to him honestly and directly.

He crossed the river by the stone bridge and walked along the opposite shore to the empty warehouse. The daubings there had been scrubbed clean and existed now only as a succession of off-white circles. The trees on this side were thicker, and the land steeper, and his path followed the low, rising contour of the hillside.

This was not a return to the clearing. He and the others on the tribunal had now decided to visit the place in the near future. There had even been a suggestion that the girls and their families might accompany them on that occasion. This had been suggested by Firth, but had then been quickly rejected by the others. Nash, in truth, had shown little enthusiasm either way, but Webb, predictably, had argued fiercely that taking the girls and their eager audience back to this centre-point of all that was still unfolding around them would be seen by many – in the town and beyond – to be both indulgent and provocative.

The watching world, Webb now insisted, had come only to titillate itself, to point its fingers and to laugh at them for the gullible provincials they had all allowed themselves to become.

The complaints were as familiar to Merrit as those of the other townspeople, and he had countered by insisting to Webb that there was no longer any alternative except for the inquiry to complete its course and for his own report to be submitted. He flattered Webb by saying that surely he, a magistrate, understood the validity and force of this outcome – of the further line it would eventually draw – better than any of them.

It was in an effort to better plot and understand that course ahead of them that he was walking alone now. He continued up the hillside, following a path which repeatedly turned as it rose through the trees. Little of the town was visible beneath him – only the same tall chimneys and rising smoke he had previously seen along the path leading to the clearing.

In the distance, to the south and the west, he could also see where small fields lay amid the thinner stands of trees. He had learned from a farmer that rye and barley had recently supplanted corn in the district because of the price of corn and its falling market. He had also learned that the rye harvest had been poor in recent years, and that latterly two whole crops had been lost to blight. In addition, with the recent closure of the tanneries and their associated trades, cattle and their hides had also lost much of their former value in the place.

He looked down on these fields and saw where the sparse crop had not even been worth the effort of harvesting that year. Elsewhere, the ground had already been burned, leaving patches of black amid the abandoned crops and the turning colours of the trees.

After half a mile, the path turned more sharply than usual and he arrived at a recently felled tree which lay across it. The trunk had been sawn through and a mound of sawdust lay around the stump. Merrit sat down and lit a cigarette.

In addition to excluding Agnes Foley from the public sessions, and following the counter-productive appearances of both Mary Cowan and Margaret Seaton, he had decided not to interview the youngest of the girls – Maud Venn, aged nine – there either. So far, Maud Venn had done little except repeat to the police what the two older girls had already said. He decided that he would visit the child at her home, away from the scrutiny and the whispering of the court.

From the start, they had been a divided panel. It was a common enough occurrence – on occasion Merrit had found himself in conflict with *all* the other members – and even though he understood and accepted this, it was still something he regretted.

As he considered all this, he heard sounds in the trees close by: the noise of men's voices and laughter, of chopping and sawing.

There was a fork in the path ahead of him, a narrower course leading further up the hillside. The main path was rutted and marked by lines of water where heavy carts had passed along it.

Having decided to follow the path towards the working men, Merrit had just arrived at this fork when he saw a figure coming out of the trees ahead of him. A woman wearing a long coat, and a bonnet which hid her face. She walked with her eyes to the ground, stepping over and around the obstacles at her feet, and it was not until she was almost at the junction that Merrit recognized Angelica Firth. At that same moment, perhaps seeing movement ahead of her, she looked up and saw him watching her. She stopped walking for a moment, pushed her bonnet back from her brow and then continued towards him.

Merrit raised his hand and called to her, but other than go on walking towards him, she made no return gesture. She looked behind her, and then all around Merrit, as though expecting to see others there.

She expects to see her husband, Merrit thought. Perhaps Firth had already told her of Merrit's dismissal of his proposal to visit the clearing and hold a service there.

Eventually, the woman took off her bonnet and came to him.

'I was walking,' Merrit said. 'Clearing my head.'

The sound of the woodcutters could still be heard behind her and she again looked briefly over her shoulder. 'They've started cutting,' she said. 'For the kilns.'

'Kilns?'

'Charcoal. They come every year at this time for a few months and set up a camp here while the burning lasts. I visit their wives and children.'

'Are they not local men?' he asked her.

She shook her head. 'They move from place to place, wood to wood. Each year they mark out a different part of the woodland here and make arrangements with the landowners to fell the trees and set up their kilns.'

'Do they come into the town?'

'Sometimes. Though I doubt—' She stopped abruptly, suddenly unwilling, or so it seemed to Merrit, to continue talking to him.

'Do you know them well?' he asked her.

She hesitated before answering him. 'My husband always extends an invitation to them to attend his services. He's behind in his pastoral work because of your inquiry. I was visiting them on his behalf.'

Merrit wondered if her own appearance had been any more or less welcome than the reception he imagined Aubrey Firth would get from the men. He wondered what they had said to her, what she had achieved.

'Are they far?' he asked her.

'Half a mile or so. Coppicing. Most of the wood they burn, but some they sell to the timber merchants for hurdles and whatever else they make from it.'

'Tell your husband he needn't attend all the public sessions. If he prefers to—'

'He told me what happened,' she said abruptly.

'Oh?' He was uncertain what she meant.

'His public humiliation in front of the Seaton child.'

'It was regrettable,' Merrit said, conceding nothing.

'He still believes there is a dimension to this whole ridiculous affair that he thinks you are deliberately ignoring.'

'A spiritual dimension?' What did it serve Firth to make the same tired complaint to his wife?

'It's what we both believe,' she said. 'But you, Webb and Nash have clearly decided among yourselves that it is of little consequence or value.' Like her husband, everything the woman said continued to sound prepared and rehearsed.

Merrit knew that whatever he might say to deny this would not convince her, would only be further fuel to her fire.

'Why do you say "ridiculous"?' he asked her.

She shrugged. 'Because it's the word used in most of the newspaper articles that have already been written.'

'Meaning because the girls are lying and everyone knows it?'

'Because they're lying and playing games with you.' She smiled briefly. 'What on Earth did you imagine or hope you'd find here, Mister Merrit – our own innocent little Hamadryas or Oxylus?'

Merrit didn't understand her and waited for her to explain.

'Wood nymphs,' she said. 'A long, long time ago I studied the Classics. Or at least it *seems* a long, long time ago now.'

'I see,' Merrit said.

She shook her head at the remark.

'As I say, if your husband wants to—'

'You deny my husband his own true part in this thing, and yet you give the girls themselves every opportunity imaginable.' She unfastened the button at her throat and Merrit saw the smear of black along her sleeve. Had one of the burners grabbed her, manhandled her away from them? She too saw this and brushed at it with her hand, succeeding only in extending the stain and blackening her palm. She took out a handkerchief, licked it and cleaned herself.

'I admit that yesterday was unfortunate,' Merrit said.

'Regrettable *and* unfortunate? Whatever next?'

159

'Margaret Seaton had said everything she was ever going to say long before your husband rose to question her.'

'He should have been given the opportunity from the start. Perhaps she would have felt less threatened by him.'

But it was clear to Merrit that she herself did not truly believe this and it would have been unfair of him to contest the point.

'Perhaps,' he said. 'But Doctor Nash—'

'Doctor Nash frightens them,' she said.

'In what way?'

'In the way all doctors frighten all people. They're adolescent girls. They imagine he knows things about them that others are only too willing to ignore.'

After this, neither of them spoke for a moment. The smell of wood smoke came through the trees to them and they both turned to watch it filtering upwards through the canopy of high branches.

'Have you heard anything more about your husband's possible appointment?' Merrit said eventually.

She bowed her head briefly. 'It's unlikely that any decision will be made while all this is happening,' she said.

Another source of her continued hostility.

They were interrupted a moment later by the voices of the woodcutters, much closer now, and Merrit looked beyond Angelica Firth and saw several of the men coming towards them through the trunks, the smoke drifting at their feet in the damp air.

Seeing them approach, Angelica Firth told Merrit that she was already late for another appointment, and she left him and continued walking along the downhill path without any other farewell.

Merrit watched her go for a moment before turning his attention to the approaching men.

There were five of them, all carrying either a saw or a long-handled axe, and with trestles balanced on their shoulders.

Merrit called to them and they came to him, unconcerned by his unexpected presence there. They gathered around him and put down their trestles and tools. An older man explained to Merrit that they were on their way to saw up the felled tree he had passed. The others sat on the trestles and took the cigarettes Merrit offered them.

They all wore rough leather aprons or jerkins and had billhooks pushed into their belts. With the exception of the older man, they all had blackened faces and hands.

Merrit asked them about their work and they told him they'd started the first of the burns and that they were now cutting and gathering and stacking timber to keep them busy for the next two months or so.

One of them asked him who he was and he told them. They had heard of him and his work there, and they all listened closely to what he said.

'Do you know the clearing?' he asked them.

'Know it? We made it. Last year.' This was the older man, whom the others were happy to allow to be their spokesman. 'We cut most of it for poles and rind. The rest we either cleared out or coppiced.'

'Rind?' Merrit said.

'Bark. The copse-ware merchant takes it along with the shroud-cuts and spar gads.'

Not only was the place a different world, it even had its own language.

161

'Did you ever see the girls in the woods?' Merrit asked the man.

'There were always children in there. They used to come and watch us. We never knew their names. We were bogey-men to most, I imagine.'

The others laughed at this.

'We used to let them take whatever spray – kindling – they could carry,' the man said.

'Do you think they knew the woods well?'

The man shrugged. 'There are plenty of paths. The trees might be thick in places, but not everywhere.'

One of the other men whispered something to him and the man grinned.

'He said to tell you that nothing ever showed itself to *us* in all the time we've been working here. Not here, not any-where. And certainly not Old Nick.'

There was further laughter at this.

'Have you been coming here long?' Merrit asked him.

'Forty years in my case. Started when I was ten.'

The others told Merrit how long they had been working in the woods.

'We have a camp and we spend the nights out here when the kilns need tending,' the older man said. 'You can imagine all sorts in here at night.'

'Even the Devil?'

The man shook his head. 'I know that's what they're saying. Does the place believe them?'

'Some, perhaps,' Merrit said.

'Then more fool them.'

The others laughed again at this and Merrit laughed with them.

'At one time, they were so scared of us they used to try and keep us out of the town. They told us to stay in our caravans and tents and to keep our women and children with us. We were thieves, molesters and worse. Anything that went wrong, they always knew where to look. And then soon after that some of them started coming to us for remedies and charms.'

'Remedies?'

'Medicines. Stuff we've always used. Some of our younger children attend the school here. Perhaps *they* know the girls you're looking at. Perhaps it was one of *us* they saw.' He turned and asked the others if any of them had been back to the clearing since the previous year. None of them had.

It was clear to Merrit that any of the men, with their blackened faces and hands and their vividly white eyes and teeth, appearing out of the gloom of the trees and perhaps wreathed in the smoke of their kilns, would certainly have frightened a child. But if it had been one of the woodcutters, this would surely have been established by now. The girls were long familiar with the men and their work in the place. Besides, the man himself would have come forward and everything would have been explained.

'Time for us to get on,' the older man said. He held out his palm, feeling for the light rain that had started to fall. They picked up their trestles and saws and walked to the felled tree. Merrit accompanied them and then watched them for a while as they worked, surprised by the speed with which they stripped the tree of its branches and bark, leaving the trunk smooth and pale and shining in the falling light.

14

THE FOLLOWING MORNING, IT WAS THE TURN OF EDITH Lisset to be questioned.

This time, Webb insisted on approaching the girl first, and though unwilling to agree to this, Merrit was unable to refuse him. Merrit saw more clearly than ever where the seeds of their collective failure now lay, and he knew Webb's manner would only further alienate the watching crowd. The girl was twelve – two years younger than Margaret Seaton and nearly four years younger than Mary Cowan, and while those two might certainly be considered as much young women as grown girls, Edith Lisset was all too plainly still a child.

To Merrit's mind, it had still not yet been clearly established whether Edith Lisset had received her injuries on the night of the broken crockery from wandering barefoot in her nightdress through the room of scattered shards, or whether, as Nash suspected, she had deliberately inflicted these upon herself.

The four men met an hour before the public was admitted. More journalists than ever had recently appeared in the town, and more of the mezzanine seating had been opened up and made available to these newcomers.

'More paintings have appeared,' Nash said matter-of-factly as the four of them gathered. 'Obscenities, this time. Accusations.'

'Saying what?' Merrit asked him. 'Where?'

'The door of Agnes Foley's home. Her father came to see me last night. He said he heard the men doing the painting, said he heard their laughter when he called out to them through the locked door.'

'What did he do?'

'What *could* he do? He was alone with his daughter in the house. After a few minutes, he heard them running away. Later he went out and tried to wash the words off. They called his daughter a whore and a liar.'

The choice of words surprised Merrit.

'A whore?' Webb said. 'The child's an im—'

'She's ten,' Nash said. 'Her father thinks the men might have targeted the wrong house. Mary Cowan lives only fifty yards away.'

'Still . . .' Webb said. '"Whore". It's a bit . . .'

'Strong?' Nash said.

'I was going to say excessive. I have daughters of my own, remember.'

'Of course you do,' Firth said. 'It's a terrible accusation to make of any man's daughter, whatever her disposition.'

'It's just anger,' Nash said. 'Frustration.'

'Frustration at what?' Merrit said, already knowing what Nash would tell him.

'At how long all this is taking? At how little has so far been achieved? At the lack of revelation or resolution? At the contempt, mockery and ridicule that floods in here every time we open the doors? Take your pick.'

165

'The inquiry is only ten days old,' Merrit said. He had conducted others lasting up to three months.

'It's two *months* since everything started,' Nash said. '*You* may only have been involved for a matter of days, but the rest of us . . .' He signalled his apology to Merrit.

'Gentlemen,' Webb said, 'might we turn our attention to today's proceedings?'

'In which you are our chief prosecutor,' Nash said.

'Hardly that,' Webb said. 'Hardly that.' But it was clear to them all that he took no small pleasure in the title and the power it bestowed upon him.

Merrit shared a glance with Nash. Only he, Merrit, it seemed, had heard the veiled criticism in Nash's remark.

'Do you have your questions prepared for the girl?' Merrit asked Webb.

'Questions? I'm a magistrate, man. Of course I have my questions prepared. Preparation is the key to all this. And, if you will forgive me the observation, it is precisely the *lack* of proper preparation thus far that has led us to where we are today, with so much lost and so many squandered opportunities behind us.' He avoided looking at any of them as he said all this. 'Let us hope that with the proper preparation and approach nothing else is to be denied us.'

Merrit regretted this melodrama. 'Of course,' he said. 'How long will you need?'

'How long?'

'With Edith Lisset.'

'As long as it takes for her to understand what a mistake she will be making if she chooses to follow in the footsteps of her co-conspirators. As long as it takes for her to accept that she has nothing to gain by continuing to tell her lies and make up her tales. As long as it takes for her to realize that the time has come for the application of some firmness in the matter.'

'So you'll keep an open mind, then?' Nash said, sharing a further glance with Merrit.

'Her parents will be present, remember,' Merrit said, hoping to temper Webb's ambition.

'Then all the more reason to pull up the solitary root of truth from the mulch of scheming and deceit in which it has become so firmly embedded, and in which it is growing ever deeper,' Webb said.

Merrit flinched at the words.

Webb formed his hand into a fist, then pushed out a rigid forefinger and pointed at each of them in turn. None of them was clear what he intended by the gesture and so all three remained silent.

'Quite,' Firth said eventually.

Webb relaxed his fist and lowered his arm. After that, he said little to any of them, anxious only to assume his place at their centre.

As they eventually left to take their places in the courtroom, Nash, walking behind Merrit, whispered, 'Watch him,' and Merrit nodded once without turning or breaking his stride.

The room was again full. Edith Lisset and her father sat at the front waiting to be called. It surprised Merrit to see that the girl's mother was not present, but then he remembered all Nash had told him about the woman's ailments and infirmities. He saw that Mary Cowan and her father sat close behind Edith, just as the pair of them had sat close behind Margaret Seaton when she had been giving her testimony.

Further along the same bench, Agnes Foley's father sat alone, an empty space beside him marking the absence of his own daughter.

Merrit acknowledged this audience and made his usual opening remarks. He told them what they hoped to achieve that day and asked for their patience. The court had grown considerably more restless and less restrained since its opening sessions, and Merrit knew that there were times now when it came close to disorder. He would put it no more strongly than that in any of his daily written summaries.

He then addressed the watching journalists, saying he hoped they were there in the interests of openness, fairness, even-handedness and justice. Most nodded obediently at the words, but some, he saw, sat without responding to this plea, and a few quietly laughed at him behind their hands. It was no more or less than he expected of them.

At ten, he fell silent and the whole room listened to the chiming of the clock which signalled their start.

After a few more seconds of settling and adjustment, Webb rose to his feet and leaned forward over the table. He then surprised the others alongside him by pointing directly at Edith Lisset and her father where they sat and telling them to stay where they were.

'She needs to face the room to give her testimony,' Merrit said to him.

But Webb ignored him, his finger still aimed at the girl and the man as though it were a pistol, just as it had earlier been pointed at the three of them in the ante-chamber.

'Yes, you,' he shouted at the pair. 'Both of you.'

People shifted in their seats to look.

The man rose and pulled up his daughter beside him.

'I did not ask you to rise,' Webb said firmly.

They sat back down.

'And why did I not ask you to rise and for the girl to take her place in front of us all?'

'This is irregular,' Merrit hissed at Webb, and again Webb ignored him.

'I did not ask you to rise and for the child to stand before us because, firstly, I have no intention of letting her return so swiftly to the centre of all this unnecessary upheaval. And because, secondly, as is my right – and, I would suggest, my *duty* – I have a few words I wish to address to the people here on my own behalf – words to my colleagues, to my neighbours, to my friends; to the tradesmen with whom I undertake transactions daily; to those who encounter me in my official capacity – not, perhaps, always under the happiest or most congenial of circumstances, but who encounter me in that capacity knowing that I can be trusted to act fairly and firmly and justly in all our shared interests. *These* are the people I stand here, today, to address.'

A few in the crowd made derisory noises at the end of this small, clumsy punch of a speech, but most remained silent, slowly nodding their heads in vague agreement with everything Webb had just said.

Beside Merrit, Firth too seemed to be in agreement with the man. But beyond him, Nash sat with his eyes averted as though to distance himself from Webb and every threatening, self-serving or coercive remark he now made.

'*Honest* people, I might add,' Webb went on before Merrit could intervene. 'Decent people, law-abiding, Church-going, tax-paying people. *We*, *you* – you and I together – *we* do not find ourselves at the centre of all this unwelcome attention.

We do not find ourselves twisting and turning these strings of decency, truth and legality into ever more convoluted knots. *We* do not make our pleas for understanding and sympathy. *We* do not crave attention and special accordance. No, not us, not us.' He moved his pointing finger from the girl and her father around the crowd. 'Not you, not you, not you. I know you all. And what of the dozens of *other* children – other girls – in this small place? Where are *they*, with their own array of perverse and self-regarding demands?'

'Irregular,' Merrit repeated, more loudly this time, so that Webb could not again completely ignore him.

Webb paused briefly and glanced at Merrit.

'I am being instructed to fall silent and to sit down,' he announced. 'I am being *commanded*. First I am assured that I might say a few words – words of reason, words of explanation – that I might speak on behalf of, if you will, the ordinary men and women of this place – and now I am being told to hold my tongue.' He threw up his hands, soliciting several cries of support from the crowd. He waited for these to increase in number before turning fully to Merrit and saying, 'See?'

Merrit shook his head and looked back to Edith Lisset and her father, who was now looking hard at Merrit, clearly wanting him to intervene on his daughter's behalf.

Behind them, Merrit saw Mary Cowan and her father laughing together.

He looked from the audience back to Nash, but Nash showed little surprise at what Webb was doing, and gave no indication of being about to support Merrit in silencing the man.

Beside him, Firth sat watching Webb with a look now close to admiration on his face.

It was only then that Merrit saw Webb's wife and two grown daughters in the crowd, and seeing the women there, he immediately understood the magistrate's true purpose in everything he was saying. He searched for Angelica Firth but could not see her.

Finally, sensing that a point had passed, that the clamour was dying and that Webb had perfectly achieved his aims, Merrit rose from his seat and struck his gavel on the table.

Silence fell haltingly, a succession of reluctant, faltering echoes.

'Thank you,' he shouted. 'And thank you, too, to Alderman Webb for making himself so completely clear to us all. If that was his intent, then you have your champion. If you demand a public mouthpiece, then you are indeed fortunate in having him step forward on your behalf.'

As intended, the remarks unsettled as many in the crowd as they reassured. Webb himself, Merrit saw, stood for a moment with his eyes closed and a satisfied smile on his lips, as though basking in the warm sun.

Merrit then gestured for Lisset and his daughter to rise, and for the girl to take her place at the front of the room.

Lisset was clearly reluctant for her to do this after all that had just happened, but Merrit assured him that once Edith was being properly questioned, these outbursts would be at an end and protocol would be observed. He looked directly at Webb as he said this, but the man remained untouchable behind his supercilious grin.

Edith Lisset came from beside her father and sat in the chair. Her father then followed her and sat a short distance away. In rising and walking away from him, the girl had looked even younger than her twelve years.

Webb left his place beside Merrit and took up position directly in front of Edith.

'Tell him to step back,' her father said to Merrit.

'What?' Webb seemed to stagger back a pace, as though he'd been pushed.

'Please, step back slightly,' Merrit said. 'The room can't see her.'

Webb took several paces further away from the girl. 'Is this far enough?' He looked at Edith Lisset's father.

'Is it?' the man asked his daughter.

'Further,' the girl said, barely audibly, and the man repeated the word to Webb.

'One more step and no further,' Merrit suggested to Webb, sensing the magistrate's growing impatience at the way he was being treated in his own court. He now stood six feet from Edith Lisset, holding himself as though he were standing close to the edge of a sheer drop. Nothing of this further small, exaggerated drama was lost on Merrit.

Waiting a moment, Webb then spun on his heels to face the crowd. 'See?' he said, mock-disbelievingly. 'Everything, all the smallest details. They exercise this power and they take a perverse and immature delight in doing so. Do you see now how so . . . how so *unnecessary* much of this is?'

'Please,' Merrit said to him. 'Address the witness.'

'I'm addressing the court,' Webb said bluntly. 'I'm speaking to my friends and neighbours.'

'So you have already made perfectly clear to us.' It would have served no purpose for Merrit to have reminded Webb that this was not a true court.

'I have every right,' Webb said.

And again, any refutation of this would only have played into the man's hands.

Then Webb, perhaps realizing that he had drawn out these entwined threads of outrage and common sense far enough, bowed slightly to Merrit and took a further step away from the girl. 'My apologies to you both,' he said, turning from her to her father. 'It was not my intention to frighten, embarrass or humiliate you in front of your own friends and neighbours.' And once again, his intention was perfectly clear.

'Oh, really?' Nash said in a loud whisper to Merrit, who raised a finger to his lips.

'And if I have inadvertently done so, then I apologize. I have daughters of my own. Grown now, but daughters all the same. Daughters who were once as old as Edith is now' – he said the girl's name as though the two of them were well acquainted and he thought fondly of her – 'and who themselves once possessed the same childish beliefs and dreams and fancies.'

Many in the crowd knew the spoilt, pampered women and some smiled at hearing Webb say all this. It was not a plea to a common, shared history and it would fail him completely if pushed any further.

At the table, Merrit signalled to Webb and then tapped his watch to suggest a degree of urgency. It was almost ten thirty.

'Our judge asks me to continue with the matter at hand,' Webb announced. 'And I must obey him.' He bowed again to Merrit, who looked away at the gesture.

'Poltergeists,' Webb said loudly. He then looked in a full circle around him, a surprised and puzzled look on his face as though the word had come from elsewhere. 'That's right – poltergeists.' He fluttered his hands in front of him. 'Things

173

that go bump in the night. Bump, creak, groan, knock, rattle, whisper, moan. Or' – and here he turned sharply back to Edith Lisset – 'in your case, things that smash up whole dinner services of best and not inexpensive Staffordshire pottery, and which then attack you with the shards of that pottery and cut your feet and arms. I assume you do still bear something of the scars of this assault after so short a time.'

Uncertain what was being asked of her, Edith Lisset held up one of her sleeved arms and her father immediately went to her and pushed it back into her lap.

'Commendable, sir,' Webb said to him. 'No one likes to see one's own child make a mockery of herself like this. Whatever next – an exhibit in a travelling fair? The Child who Conjures up Restless Spirits? Roll up, roll up, watch her perform, see those spirits materialize before your very eyes?'

The man looked at Webb with hatred in his eyes, and Webb saw that this time he had gone too far.

'Please,' he said. 'I was merely hoping to establish the facts of your own daughter's involvement. She smashed all her mother's best crockery and then she somehow managed to repeatedly cut herself using a piece of that crockery as a blade. Is that not correct? Are these not the facts of the matter as more or less established?'

'She never . . .' Lisset began to say, already stumbling.

'And is it not likewise established that when the constable came to write up his report of the affair, the word "poltergeist" was most certainly used?'

'Not by—'

'And used not only once, not twice, not even three times. Do you know how many times the word was used?'

'We only told him what he asked us,' Lisset said, again looking to Merrit for his intervention.

But Merrit knew that the safest thing now was for Webb's questioning to run its course. There would be no new revelations, no unexpected disclosures or confessions. The small maelstrom was turning, gathering and then losing momentum occasionally, but it was still turning, and both its centre and its racing currents remained clearly visible to Merrit. The only thing uncertain to him now was the distance yet to be travelled into the surrounding expanse of calm, clear water.

He was distracted from these thoughts by Webb shouting the word 'Eleven.'

The magistrate repeated this a further three times.

'Eleven what?' Lisset said.

'Eleven times,' Webb said, gripping his lapels and drawing back his shoulders. 'The mention of poltergeists. Eleven times. It seems such a strange word for such a young girl to either know or to employ. For people such as you and your wife to know, even. Eleven times. Tell me, does it crop up often in your usual daily conversations?'

As intended, there was laughter at this.

'Poltergeist,' Webb went on. 'Let me enlighten our audience further: a disturbed spirit, all too often called into its malicious and restless existence by the unsettled minds of disturbed young women.' He paused, turning back to Lisset. 'Is that your own understanding of the term?'

'Yes,' Lisset said, the word drying in his mouth.

'Sorry?' Webb said.

'Yes,' Lisset repeated.

Beside him, his daughter, who had so far said nothing,

reached out a hand to him. At first the man seemed about to take this, but then he drew away from her and folded his arms across his chest.

'You don't sound very convinced,' Webb said to him.

'I know what it means, what it is, what it—'

'And so, following on from that – from your *expertise* on the matter – would I also be right in thinking that you and your wife have already made all the logical and not unreasonable connections there are to be made between this malign spirit and your daughter's – what? – unsettled, uncertain nature?'

'I don't understand what you're saying to me,' Lisset said.

It was unlikely, Merrit considered, that anyone in the room fully understood what Webb was either asking of, or suggesting to, the man.

'Oh, really?' Webb said, feigning surprise. 'Then are we to understand that you merely *assumed* that some spirit from the Netherworld had come into your home, summoned by her for the sole purpose of smashing your wife's best cups and saucers and dinner plates and giving your daughter those scratches on her arms? After all, what *else* could possibly explain all this strange activity?'

At the table, Nash leaned to Merrit and said, 'Stop him. He's putting words into the man's mouth. It's the girl he's supposed to be questioning.'

Merrit agreed with this and struck his gavel on its block. But Webb pretended not to hear this.

'Well?' he said to Lisset. 'Well?'

'We didn't hear the word until afterwards,' Lisset said, his words again barely audible above the laughter.

Merrit resisted striking the block a second time; it was a father's instinct and duty to protect and defend his child.

'*Of course* you learned of it afterwards,' Webb went on. '*That's my whole point.* It's the whole point of *all* of this. Everything is explained away *afterwards*, everything is given a considerably more elaborate and exciting cause than it warrants or deserves. These are not unquiet spirits and disturbed emotions we are dealing with here, merely the devious minds of a group of plotters determined to hold themselves at our centre and to continue exercising this small, illusory power over us. We suffer here – we are mocked and judged here – on a capricious whim. Not because of any true force of nature or mankind – on a whim.'

There was an unexpected outburst of applause at the words, and Webb capitalized on this and turned and bowed slightly to his audience.

Afterwards, perhaps realizing that nothing he would go on to say would achieve the same impact, he signalled to Merrit that he had finished with the girl.

In the ante-chamber, the clock chimed again. Half an hour had passed.

But she hasn't even spoken, Merrit wanted to shout at Webb before Nash did.

Finished with the girl and her pathetic father. Finished with the others on the panel. Finished with them all. Webb stood with his hands still clasped to his lapels and looked at his wife and daughters, all three of whom were also vigorously applauding him. By now his cheeks and forehead were slick with sweat, and the rim of his tight collar was damp with the same.

Merrit finally rose from his seat and gestured to Edith Lisset and her father, and the man immediately seized this opportunity and pulled his daughter from her chair and led her through the noisy crowd and out of the room. The girl and Mary Cowan, Merrit saw, held each other's eyes for the duration of the short, uncomfortable journey. Mary Cowan slowly applauded her. And as Edith Lisset passed close by her, she closed her eyes briefly, in what seemed to Merrit to be an act of acknowledgement or confirmation, or perhaps even one of contrition.

He held up his hand and called for silence, waiting until Edith Lisset and her father were out of the room and the door had swung loudly shut behind them.

Only when the applause finally died did Webb return to his seat.

Up in the mezzanine, Merrit saw journalists start to leave, probably in the hope of catching the man and his daughter outside. Others were already writing in their notebooks, talking excitedly among themselves as they began to give shape and colour to the morning's wasted proceedings.

15

IT WAS AN HOUR PAST DUSK WHEN MERRIT REACHED THE home of Agnes Foley to see for himself what had been painted there. The window remained boarded to the street. Everything he saw, everything that had a bearing, would find a place in one or other of his reports; or if not the reports themselves, then in their footnotes and appendices. He well understood what layers, what priorities existed in the minds of his masters. A smashed window, a defiled door and a captive, intimidated, imbecilic child and her powerless father would all rate low, if at all, amid their own considerations.

Even as he walked, slowing as he approached the house, Merrit was already considering where best to fit the report of this damage and these acts of intimidation into his own overall record of events in the place.

He was relieved to find the street empty, having come there via a succession of back alleys and side streets. The house was in darkness, not even the glow of a lamp inside. On the wall, the painted words had been scrubbed out but not completely removed, and their obvious threat and warning remained. In addition to the writing, there were symbols similar to those Merrit had seen on the empty warehouse. He felt a great deal of sympathy for the man and his daughter, but it was becoming increasingly apparent to him that he was in no real position to help them; perhaps only the opposite.

He waited a moment on the far side of the narrow, unlit street, and then he continued to its end, turning back towards the town centre along another alleyway unfamiliar to him. He emerged into a broader lane, and was briefly uncertain which way to turn, choosing left simply because this would not bring him back too close or too soon to the brightly lit centre of the place.

It was as he followed this lane that a figure stepped out in front of him, watching him as though attempting to identify him in the darkness. It was a man, and he held out an arm to half-block Merrit's way. Merrit's first thought was that it was Cowan, and that he had been followed in the darkness. But then a match was struck and in the brief flaring of the flame Merrit recognized the journalist he and Nash had encountered outside the hotel a week earlier.

The two men considered each other for a moment.

Then the journalist said, 'Come to look at the – what shall we call them – runic symbols? His Satanic Majesty's some-what obvious etchings?'

Merrit went closer to him. 'Whatever they are, they look remarkably similar to the daubings on the empty warehouse,' he said.

'Oh, identical, I'd say. But perhaps better targeted.' And then, to Merrit's surprise, the man held out a hand to him. 'Stannard,' he said. '*London Illustrated.*'

It was one of the papers Merrit received at home, and he stood for a moment with his hand clasped in Stannard's, assessing the man.

'Is your photographer not with you?'

'For the scrubbed-out words? Hardly seemed worth his while. I'll sketch them, add one or two embellishments. The odd goat's skull or pair of horns over the word "whore" might not go amiss. As they stand, they display a considerable lack of imagination.'

'Or demonstrate precisely the imagination of the man who wrote them?'

'Cowan, probably,' Stannard said.

Merrit resisted showing surprise at the name. 'And the brick through the poor girl's window?'

Stannard shrugged. 'The same. Why "poor girl"? Because she's an imbecile? Because the other girls are somehow taking advantage of that? Or because, being what she is, she is all the more natural and obvious a target for that brick? Either way, I don't see any shattered windows or dirty words on Cowan's house.' He offered Merrit a cigarette and Merrit took it. Then the man indicated a walkway which left the alley via a flight of steps. 'It leads down to the railway station,' he said.

Merrit followed him and the two men walked the short distance to the small, empty station and sat together on a bench beneath a wooden awning.

'Are you here for the duration?' Merrit asked him.

Stannard leaned forward and shook his head. 'If it hadn't been for this morning's very newsworthy little outburst by your tin-pot judge, I would have gone back to London on the four o'clock train.' He looked along the tracks, which curved into a high, impenetrably dark tunnel.

'Do you wish you were back there?' Merrit said.

'Naturally. As do you, I imagine.'

'Oh?'

Stannard turned to him. 'Sorry. I just imagined that you,

of all people, understood better than any of us how far out of hand all this now was.'

'Perhaps if everyone allowed—'

'I was sent to cover the inquiry you undertook at Hanford Hall,' Stannard said. 'Remember?'

'Eight years ago,' Merrit said. He remembered perfectly.

'Almost nine now. "The Evil Serving Girls." That was me.'

'That's what they were – girls.'

'I know. Girls just like these. They destroyed flower beds, smashed the glass in greenhouses and mutilated and killed animals.'

'Chickens,' Merrit said, smiling at the memory. 'They killed half a dozen chickens, that's all.'

'Ah, yes. And why do you suppose the perpetrators of supposedly unbound and bottomless evil always pick on the poor old chicken as their first victim?'

Both men laughed at the remark.

Merrit remembered more of the case. 'A gardener's boy spurned one of the girls for her arch-rival and she decided to get her revenge on him.'

'You were there and then home in six days,' Stannard said. 'I doubt if this Assistant Chief Constable is going to be so easily or speedily satisfied.'

'It looks that way,' Merrit admitted.

'But you remain convinced that the cause of all this will prove to be something equally banal and down to earth?'

'As opposed to what?'

Stannard conceded the point. 'I personally endeavour to use the word "Supernatural" at least once in each paragraph. It's a good headline word.'

'Along with "Devil" and "Evil"?' Merrit said.

'Perhaps. But with Magistrate Webb pontificating on the stump, I don't have too much to do by the way of titillating or salacious embellishment. And, as I may have mentioned to you previously, it certainly sells papers.'

'And it sells them best of all in London,' Merrit said. 'Is everybody there having a good laugh at everything that's happening here? All safe at home and confident that this place is an uncivilized hole and its inhabitants all survivors of another age struggling through harder times than they themselves will ever be forced to endure?'

The outburst revealed a great deal, and Stannard considered this before answering. 'I won't repeat anything you say,' he said. 'One of my competitors wrote that the girls were no better than superstitious heathens practising black magic.'

'Only because it's an easy accusation to make,' Merrit said. 'And because it's what a lot of those distant readers already half-believe anyway. Or perhaps you're lying to me; perhaps *you* wrote it.'

'I believe my own imperfect judgement on the situation was to suggest that these were unsettling times we were *all* living through – the new century, the new king, the new world forever with its eye on the future and never the past – all that more widely applicable mumbo-jumbo.'

'And is that what you genuinely believe?'

Stannard shrugged. 'It's an easy and convenient assumption to make. This place certainly wasn't made any *more* settled by *Alderman* Webb's little outburst, whatever he hoped to achieve by it. I saw him outside, afterwards. Him and his wife and daughters in their pearls and fur coats. They had a crowd around them. He wanted my photographer to take their photograph.'

'And did you oblige him?'

'Of course I did. A picture of him in all his bloated pomp and self-appointed glory alongside the scrawny, barefoot girl he'd just publicly attacked and ridiculed.'

'She wasn't barefoot,' Merrit said.

Stannard smiled. 'She was after I'd slipped a few coins into her father's hand and he told her to take her shoes off.'

'Webb shouldn't have used the court like that,' Merrit said.

'Like what?'

'To his own ends.'

'He took advantage of it not being a proper court, that's all. In all likelihood, it's the kind of thing he does every week. His grandfather probably worked up the same self-righteous lather in sending turnip-stealers to the Antipodes.'

'And you probably commended Webb on everything he'd said,' Merrit said.

'"Commended" might be putting it a little strongly. But he certainly caught today's draught of public opinion. And "Poltergeist" — we've all been waiting for days for that one to come up. What a godsend the man is. There are only so many "Ghostly"s and "Supernatural"s a man can decently use in a single piece.'

'Is it really all so much of a game to you?' Merrit said.

Stannard considered this. 'Do you think instead that I should believe everything the girls say? Are you telling me that you yourself aren't already convinced beyond all doubt that they're all liars? *Has* the Devil appeared to them in the woods, then? *Is* he attacking girls in their bedrooms and smashing up dinner services? *Is* he stalking the town with a brick in his hand and a bucket of whitewash?'

'You know that isn't what I meant. But there is still some serious and malicious *intent* here.'

'Of course there is – intent. At Hanford, remember, you found a toad with its mouth stitched up in your desk drawer.'

'A warning to informants,' Merrit said, and smiled again at the memory. 'They also said the estate dogs were driven mad by the girls pricking their own fingers and dripping blood into the animals' food.'

'I wrote about it,' Stannard said. 'After which the girls were blamed for a fortnight's bad weather which led to apple blight in the surrounding orchards.'

And is this the same? Merrit thought, but said nothing. *Is this the same?*

They were distracted by the arrival of a small engine, which came noisily and slowly out of the tunnel, belching steam and smoke in a high plume. The engine pulled no carriages and came through the station at the same slow pace. The man at its controls looked down at them as he passed by. He took off his cap and used this to wipe his face.

'I do understand your predicament,' Stannard said as the noise began to fade.

'And know perfectly well how to turn it to your own ends,' Merrit said, regretting the remark immediately.

'Naturally,' Stannard said. 'You do what you do and I do what I do. We're probably not as dissimilar as you'd prefer to believe.'

'Doctor Nash believes that the girl we saw today cuts herself deliberately,' Merrit said. It was an apology of sorts, and Stannard understood this.

'It's common knowledge,' he said. 'She cut herself on the night in question, and she's cut herself since, keeping the wounds fresh. You can touch them for a price. I have photographs if you'd like to see them. There's even a whisper that one or two of the others are involved in the same thing.'

The suggestion alarmed Merrit, but again he said nothing.

'I thought at one point that Webb was actually going to strike her,' Stannard said. 'Edith Lisset. I thought he was going to taunt her for half an hour, listen to all her refutations and small mockeries, and that he was then going to slap her across her face, tell her to come to her senses, to remember where she was, and to insist that she start telling us all the truth. You get the picture – *he* – man of the people and bringer of common sense – would succeed where *you* – interfering outsider with all your protocols and regulations – had only ever failed.'

Merrit already understood this. 'And is that what you'll write in your report – that Webb came close to striking the girl?'

'My article's already written and sent – at least something got back to civilization on the four o'clock train. Don't worry; I stuck to the facts, for what they're worth.' He laughed at the words, and then added, 'What *you* might like to consider is that Webb also looks to me like a man who knows how to cover his own back.'

Stannard held his gaze until Merrit nodded his acknowledgement of this.

'All I needed from today,' Stannard said, 'was the picture of him and his wife and daughters.'

'He'll probably want copies,' Merrit said.

'He's already ordered them. Seriously, you should——' He stopped abruptly.

'I should what? Take a leaf out of his own book?'

'You should be careful of him.'

'In what way? I imagine I already—'

'That draught of public opinion I mentioned – Webb keeps his own close eye on it. He wasn't the only one in there who wanted – figuratively or otherwise – to slap some sense into the girl.'

'People are bound to be divided,' Merrit said, and again it sounded like nothing more than the excuse it was.

Stannard took a piece of paper from his pocket and gave it to Merrit. It contained sketches of the warehouse drawings and the words painted on Agnes Foley's door.

'So?' Merrit said.

'What you might also now like to consider is how much more or less seriously you would be forced to take these things if the same symbols or words turned up on Magistrate Webb's own highly polished front door. He has some powerful friends and acquaintances in the county.'

'Including the Assistant Chief Constable?'

'Oh, undoubtedly. If not higher.' Stannard held out his hand and made a convoluted gesture with it to remind Merrit of Webb's involvement with the town's Masonic Lodge. 'And what if the same paintings and words appeared on the walls of your own court?'

'Unlikely,' Merrit said.

'But not impossible. It would certainly attract *my* interest. Besides, I'm a journalist – *everything*'s a possibility. Possibility is the air I breathe. But perhaps you're right – perhaps tomorrow that wind of public opinion will fade from a blast to a gasp and everything will turn into one big joke, something to laugh at instead of to fear.'

'There have already been cartoons,' Merrit said eventually. 'In the papers.'

'I know. Even one of you.'

'I hope it did my noble brow and determined gaze full justice,' Merrit said.

'And tomorrow you might be drawn with horns, cloven hooves and a pointed tail, and with egg all over that same noble brow.'

Merrit acknowledged this. It had happened before.

'Did you manage to speak to Webb?' Stannard said. 'Afterwards.'

'About his behaviour? I thought it best not to prolong whatever uproar he was intent on causing.'

'I see.' He offered Merrit another cigarette. 'You may have plenty of other uproars yet to endure or subdue.'

A second small engine came in the opposite direction from the first, moving out of the trees towards the tunnel. This one pulled two dark, empty carriages, and again the driver stood and watched them as he passed.

'He wants to shout and tell us that there's no point waiting,' Stannard said. 'Or perhaps this is his only appearance of the day – out of the trees and into the tunnel and then back again.'

There was now something in Stannard's voice that made Merrit believe he was saying all this to avoid disclosing something more directly to him.

He turned to the man and held his gaze. 'Do you know something?' he said.

'About what?' Stannard turned away from him and cleared his throat.

'Those other uproars?' Merrit said, waiting.

'A colleague of mine on *The Times*,' Stannard said. 'That's what we are, we gentlemen of the press – colleagues.'

Merrit prepared himself. 'What did he tell you?'

'The Cowan girl. Four years ago. A baby went missing. The mother insisted Mary Cowan was supposed to be looking after the child, but the girl said she'd returned it to the mother hours earlier and left it with her.'

'There was none of this in any of the reports,' Merrit said. He tried hard to remember. He felt sudden alarm at the revelation.

'There wouldn't be,' Stannard said. 'There was a search, of sorts, but never an official inquiry or any charges laid. The suspicion at the time was that the baby – already known to be sickly – had died in the care of the already less-than-capable mother and that she'd cast around for someone to blame.'

'I ought at least to talk to her,' Merrit said. 'What's her address?' He tapped his pockets for his notepad and pen.

'Woman called Wilson,' Stannard said. 'Derby Asylum. She was committed a month afterwards.'

Merrit stopped searching. He took a deep breath of the cold night air. 'Why so far away?'

Stannard shrugged. 'To get rid of the source of contagion? She'd been committed there before, a year before the baby was born. According to the *Times* man, her mind was more and more unbalanced after the birth. Everyone said the baby had been too much for her. There was never any indication of the father.'

'But someone here, presumably?'

'Presumably. Mary Cowan swore her innocence – she was only eleven or twelve at the time – and everyone believed her. Whereas the mother condemned herself with everything she did and said, everyone she went on to accuse. I think in the end, after she'd been committed, she even confessed to smothering the baby herself and then of burying it out in the woods somewhere.'

'Inadmissible evidence,' Merrit said. 'Was the body found and examined?'

'Apparently she couldn't remember where she'd buried it. There were a few searches, but nothing of a systematic nature, and nothing was ever found. I can get you the articles, if you like.'

'Please,' Merrit said. 'Did you write anything on the case yourself?'

Stannard shook his head. 'I only worked in London then.'

'So, did Webb, Nash and Firth all know about the dead child?'

Stannard was reluctant to speak.

'Of course they did,' Merrit said. 'And, presumably, of Mary Cowan's alleged involvement in it all.'

'Except she swore she never was involved, and everyone believed her. And afterwards, after the woman had been committed and then made her confession, there was no reason for Cowan *not* to be believed.' Stannard put a hand on Merrit's arm. 'You might be doing a lot more harm than good if you drag any of this back up to the surface now.'

'Harm? Another uproar, you mean?'

'I mean harm to yourself, to your inquiry. The two events are unconnected. It was a long time ago, four years, perhaps five. The Cowan girl – whatever she's become since – was no more than a child herself. Besides, how can the alleged murder of a baby – infanticide – compare to what's happening now? All we have today are stories, tales, fabrications, lies, call them what you like. Stories, lies – theirs and ours – and a few unexplained ghostly occurrences thrown into the mixture for good and sensational measure. Not that unusual, surely? And certainly nothing you yourself haven't already encountered and then either exposed, disentangled or smoothed out in the past.'

Everything Stannard said continued to sound unconvincing. How could the two events *not* be connected in some way, even if only because the recent events were, to Mary Cowan, a happy echo and memory of the power she had once exercised and the punishment she had earlier avoided. All this was surely as plain to Stannard as it was to Merrit?

But the man had told him all this, and perhaps it was enough.

'Thank you,' Merrit said.

'I doubt I've done you any favours. I'm only surprised you didn't know of it already.'

'Is that what you thought – that I knew – that we *all* knew – and that everyone was deliberately keeping silent?'

Stannard shrugged.

It started to rain, and Stannard rose from the seat and pulled up his collar. He walked several paces away from Merrit and then returned.

'Give her – give them all – enough rope,' he said. 'Remember Hanford Hall. Once the jealousy over the spurned girl came to light, the ghosts soon stopped rattling their chains, trampling flowers and pulling the heads off chickens. Ghosts, devils, poltergeists.' He smiled again at the word. 'Perhaps Blood-and-Thunder Webb even did you all a favour today. Perhaps the girls *have* been given their chances and have refused to seize them; or perhaps they've so far been too stupid or too blind to see what was on offer to them.'

'Or perhaps Mary Cowan—'

'Or perhaps Mary Cowan made everything clear to them from the very start,' Stannard said, his patience at an end. 'Yes, perhaps.'

The rain started to fall more heavily, and both men finally left the seat, running from beneath the awning to the lesser shelter of the high siding wall which curved like a black cliff away from the station and into the even greater darkness of the tunnel beyond.

16

Two days passed before Merrit visited Maud Venn, the fifth and youngest of the girls. He went in the company of Nash, who was not the girl's doctor, but who knew her parents socially, and who had guaranteed them his presence alongside Merrit.

Their home was on the southern outskirts of the town, close by the railway track, which crossed the lane a short distance ahead of the detached house.

As they approached, Nash held Merrit's arm and pointed to something through the thin stand of trees which lined the embankment there.

Merrit followed him to one side, and together they watched the girl herself, sitting alone on a fallen tree and holding an imaginary conversation with invisible friends.

The first thing that struck Merrit about Maud Venn was that she looked considerably younger than any of the others, and seemed a baby compared to the two older girls. She was now nine, but had been only eight at the time of the initial uproar.

The two men crouched behind a woven hedge to avoid being seen by the child.

'She's a baby,' Merrit said.

'It's certainly what her father thinks,' Nash said.

'Meaning *he* doesn't see her – doesn't want *me* – to see her as a part—'

'Of that little gang. No.' Nash was adamant on the point, and Merrit heard the warning note in his voice.

They continued watching the child for a few minutes longer, until Merrit became aware that they in turn were being watched, and he shielded his eyes to look at a man further along the road.

'Her father,' Nash said. He rose from where he crouched and signalled to the man, who came to them.

'I was watching her from the house,' Venn said, briefly taking Merrit's hand, his attention still fixed on his daughter, who remained oblivious to their presence.

'She seems happy enough,' Merrit said.

The remark seemed to offend Venn. 'What do you mean by that?' he said abruptly.

Merrit looked to Nash for his intervention.

'She's had nothing whatsoever to do with any of the others since all this got out of control,' Venn said.

Nash put a hand on the man's shoulder.

'My wife says I'm over-protective,' Venn said to Merrit.

'It's understandable,' Merrit said. He had been told of the man's objections to even this private interview, and he was conscious now of the need not to upset either him or his wife and thus risk being kept away from the girl completely. There were powers he might invoke were this to happen, but he knew from experience that the use of those powers seldom led to a happy outcome.

'You can see for yourself,' Venn said, absently motioning to his daughter.

194

It was unclear to Merrit what he meant by this. 'Do you believe the other girls led her astray?' he said.

Venn turned to him. 'You know that I'm a solicitor, Mr Merrit. I won't make any accusations or allegations that I am unable to substantiate. My living here is a precarious one at best. I trained in Manchester and was articled in Chester.'

'Before washing up in this backwater along with the rest of us,' Nash said, but failing in his attempt to put the man at ease.

'And your wife is a schoolteacher,' Merrit said.

'Part-time.'

'So she knows the other girls.'

'She does,' Venn said coldly and turned away from them, causing Merrit and Nash to exchange a glance.

'I do understand your concerns,' Merrit said to Venn, but again the man was little convinced by this.

Without warning, Venn then called loudly to his daughter, who rose from where she sat and looked around her. Seeing her father at the hedge, she called out his name, held out her arms and ran to him. She reached him and hugged his legs and the man picked her up and held her face to his.

Merrit had already learned from Nash that the man and his wife had lost two younger children to a fever two years previously, both dead within a month of each other. He knew therefore what a precious thing this surviving child was.

The girl went on talking, babbling into her father's ear and casting glances at both Merrit and Nash, who waited to be introduced to her.

But instead of doing this, the man started walking towards their home, carrying his daughter so that she hung over his shoulder, still watching Merrit and Nash as they followed a few paces behind.

As they approached the gate to the small garden, a woman appeared and came out to meet them. She took the girl from Venn's arms and clutched her to her own chest. She, too, looked warily at both Merrit and Nash.

Nash introduced Merrit to her – her name was Aline – but this did little to allay her suspicious manner. She stood to one side, her hand cupped to her daughter's head as the three men went into the house ahead of her.

Merrit noticed she slid both the latches on the gate before following them. She did the same with the bolts on the door.

Venn led them into a small parlour, a large part of which was taken up by a piano, over which a damask cloth had been draped, and upon which stood a succession of framed photographs of the two lost children. The room was a shrine, and though Merrit understood that he was being honoured by being allowed into it, everything about the place made him feel uncomfortable. Nash, too, seemed unsettled by the array of small, watching faces.

'Doctor Nash told me of your loss,' Merrit said, motioning to the photographs.

'Daniel and Rachel,' Venn said quickly. 'It was God's will. They suffered – I can't deny that – but they're at peace now.'

Aline Venn looked more closely at the pictures as her husband said this. Perhaps it was a small routine to be endured by everyone who entered the room. 'In His company,' she said. 'At peace in His company.' She left them to prepare tea, taking her daughter with her, and the cool silence of the room was broken only by the sounds of a distantly whistling kettle and rattled crockery.

The three men made small talk. Nash asked Venn about business but there was no enthusiasm in the man's answers. They spoke of others they knew, and of the local societies of which they were both members. But it was talk only to fill the silence of the room and to avoid any premature mention of Merrit's purpose there.

Eventually, the woman rejoined them and the tea was served. The crockery in her hand betrayed her slight but constant tremor, and after a few seconds of this her husband took the spoon from her saucer and then gently prised her hands apart until the cup and saucer were also separated. She apologized for this, adding a further awkward note to the room's tensions.

During this time, Maud Venn had been apart from them. They could hear her in the kitchen – the door was kept open for that purpose – and whenever she was silent for more than a minute, one or other of her parents called to ask her what she was doing. On one occasion, they received no answer, and Aline Venn went immediately to investigate.

'She won't have heard us calling,' Venn said nervously, watching the door for his wife's return.

When she came, she explained breathlessly and at great length that the girl had wandered outside to water the vegetables they grew there.

If he had not fully understood it before, Merrit certainly knew now that to have insisted on questioning the child in front of an audience would have been tantamount in her parents' eyes to damning and then crucifying her. It was why he began by reassuring them both that this would never happen, quickly adding that, in all likelihood, this would be his only encounter – he called it an 'interview' – with the girl, with them all.

'A newspaperman came,' Aline Venn said. 'Questions, questions. I asked him if he didn't think we'd suffered enough.'

'She was innocent of his intentions,' Venn said. He smiled thinly at his wife, but made no other gesture of reassurance.

Merrit was struck by the strangeness of the remark. He wondered if the journalist had been Stannard.

'Do you wish to speak to Maud alone?' Venn then asked him.

'Perhaps after we three have spoken,' Merrit suggested, as though this interview with the parents had not been his true reason for coming.

'Is this for your official record, to be included in the inquiry transcript?'

Merrit shook his head. 'I have no reliable means of keeping an accurate record outside the courtroom. I'll make notes of my findings and, if you require, you'll be able to verify that they accurately represent whatever you might tell me today, whatever might be revealed.'

The man and woman shared a nervous glance at the words.

Seizing this opportunity, Merrit said, 'Is it your opinion – your *belief* – that your daughter is being led astray, misled by the older girls?'

'Of course she is – was,' Aline Venn said immediately. '*Of course* they're leading her on. They're *all* being led on. Maud's a baby – you've seen her, a baby. Mary Cowan and Margaret Seaton, they're closer to grown young women. Or if not women, exactly – though they certainly like to present themselves as innocents to the world, to this place – then they're neither of them the child that Maud certainly still is.'

'Do you have good *cause* to believe that any of these others is leading your daughter on?' Merrit said this to Venn, knowing his own response would be more measured.

The man considered his answer and then delivered it like the solicitor he was. 'It has been clear to us for some time now that the older girls – Mary Cowan in particular – are directing every move. We've told Maud not to associate with them. Why would they want someone who is still a baby to accompany them everywhere? To say nothing of Agnes Foley. Why?'

'I don't know,' Merrit said. 'Perhaps simply because they appreciate having an audience, followers?'

'They have their all too willing and gullible audience in the rest of us,' Aline Venn said. 'In everyone here, and now in you and your panel.'

'It's our job to consider everything that's come to light here, and afterwards to—'

'And afterwards to forgive them their outrages and slanders, and for things then to proceed as though none of this had ever happened,' Aline Venn said. 'They claim to have seen the Devil – the *Devil*, Mister Merrit – here, in our woods. We've raised Maud as a God-fearing lamb. Her brother and sister are already in His tender care. And here is *she* – their living sister – wandering around the town, innocently repeating what she's been told to say and telling everyone that she has seen the Devil.'

'She was with them, that's all,' Venn said. He raised a hand to his wife in a placatory gesture, but the woman pulled herself out of his reach.

'It's what she's still *saying*, the terrible lie she's supporting,' Aline Venn said.

'Perhaps they allow her to be part of their group precisely

because she is more likely to be believed than some of them,' Merrit suggested. 'Less likely to be challenged or dismissed out of hand. People will know – see – that she comes from a good, stable home, see that she has loving and God-fearing parents who—'

'Which is more than most of them have,' Aline Venn said sourly.

Merrit waited for her to go on, but she was silenced by her husband's waiting hand, which she finally took and held.

'Forgive me,' she said. 'It wasn't my intention to speak ill of them.'

'Nothing you say will be repeated,' Merrit said. 'Presumably, you know the other girls better than most because of your position in the school.'

'She hasn't worked there for the past month,' Venn said. 'We thought it best. She stopped the day your inquiry was announced.'

'But before that?'

'Of course I knew them. It's why I know they're lying now. Mary Cowan especially.'

And perhaps the pair of them also knew about the baby which had died while allegedly being cared for by Mary Cowan. And perhaps this, under the gaze of their own dead children, coloured everything they were now telling him. He waited for Aline Venn to go on. Venn released his grip on his wife and took back his hand.

'The Cowan girl . . .' Merrit prompted.

'She was always excitable, even as a young girl,' Aline Venn said. 'Always craving the attention and praise of others. First it was the attention of the other girls in her class, then the improper attention and admiration of the boys. She was – is – always showing herself off to them.'

'Leading them on, like she leads your daughter on?'

'To different ends, perhaps, but yes. Everything's a competition to her, a race, and she is only ever truly content when she's in the lead. She wants everything to be exciting, always to be at the centre of things.'

'And you see this invented tale of the Devil in the woods to be merely a continuation – the culmination, perhaps – of that same need, that same desire?'

'I do,' Aline Venn said firmly. 'And I can tell by your tone that you share something of that conviction.'

'I only know what I've seen and heard and been told of the girl since my arrival,' Merrit said.

Aline Venn shook her head at this unconvincing half-denial. 'But you've heard tales, no doubt. You've spoken to her. You've seen how she twists things, turns one way and then another in front of you to suit her own ends and to make you look foolish.'

'And all the time getting the attention of the audience she insists upon?'

'The audience she craves, yes.' The woman looked triumphantly at her husband.

Venn, in turn, looked at both Merrit and Nash, clearly surprised by the force of his wife's conviction in all she had just said.

'Do you share these views?' Merrit asked him, taking advantage of this small imbalance between the couple.

'She is my wife,' Venn said. 'Of course I share them. I might not have expressed myself in so particular a manner, but, in the spirit of the thing, my wife and I are in complete accordance on the matter.'

'So you are convinced that the older girls are fabricating all these tales among themselves, and that both your own daughter and, say, Agnes Foley are being somehow *used* by them?'

'I would prefer it if Maud were not spoken of as though she were party to these events in a similar fashion to the Foley child,' Venn said.

'Because she is retarded in her manner?' Nash asked him, surprised by the man's remark.

'Because she is retarded, yes.'

'But no less innocent than your daughter in all of this, surely?'

'Perhaps. But I would prefer to think of my own daughter's innocence as being born of her trust and her immaturity rather than – well . . .'

'Rather than because she is considered an imbecile and cannot be expected to know her own mind?' Nash said. 'And because she might yet be returned to the asylum as she grows into an adult?'

But if the words were intended as a rebuke to Venn, then the man did not hear this.

'If that is what must happen to her, then yes,' he said.

Merrit signalled to Nash not to pursue the point and perhaps reduce even further the man's rapidly dwindling goodwill.

There was a brief, awkward silence after this, during which the passing of a train could be heard. Another cup rattled in its saucer on a low table.

'Does your daughter repeat the stories to you when you are alone with her?' Merrit asked Aline Venn when the noise and slight tremor had passed.

'The lies,' Aline Venn said. 'Yes.'

'To what purpose, do you think?'

'I don't understand you.' She looked nervously at her husband.

'I mean, why does she repeat them when there is no one new to hear or impress or convince? She must surely know your own feelings on the matter by now.'

'She does,' Aline Venn said.

'So why does she persist, I wonder?'

'Because – because *they* told her to,' Venn said.

Merrit knew it was no more than an angry guess. 'Not through any true sense of conviction, then?' he said.

'She's nine. Barely nine. What conviction?' Venn rose in his seat and then sat back down.

'So you're angry because you believe she's continuing to tell lies?' Merrit said. It was a clumsy but effective jab at the man.

'I'm angry – I'm concerned, alarmed – because she knows the difference between telling the truth and lying – we've taught her that difference – and because she shows no shame when she repeats those lies – no shame whatsoever; no doubt, even.'

'And, presumably, because she's lying, you also believe that she is showing some malicious intent in persisting with those lies?'

'I would have thought the two things inseparable, the one evidence of the other,' Venn said.

'I doubt if she truly—' Merrit began.

'And *I* doubt you would be so calm if it were your own daughter,' Aline Venn said. 'Telling all *your* friends, neighbours and colleagues that she had seen the Devil so close to all *their* homes and *their* livelihoods.'

Merrit conceded the point.

'Nor if it were your own daughter supporting the tale of a girl insisting that a grown man had tried to climb into bed with her. Maud has asked me many times *why* a man would want to do such a thing to a girl. What would you tell your own daughter, Mister Merrit?'

And to that, too, Merrit could offer no answer. 'Do you have any theories of your own regarding that particular story?' he said.

Aline Venn answered him, but only obliquely. 'You need to look harder at them – those three, the older ones,' she said.

'Meaning that boys, young men are already a part of their attention-seeking ways?' Merrit said.

'Meaning they know well enough how to turn themselves from children into young women when it suits them to do so. All evasion and innocence one minute, then all fluttering eyes and furtive glances the next.'

Venn was again anxious at hearing his wife make these accusations. 'Perhaps we ought to confine ourselves to what the girls themselves claim to have seen,' he said.

Aline Venn fell silent at the pointed remark, and Merrit said quickly, 'So do you not concur with your wife's suggestions?'

Venn took a deep breath. 'You have seen the girls for yourself, Mister Merrit. And from what I – we – hear, you have been as deceived and as thwarted by them as we here have been deceived and made fools of by them. I daresay you understand as well as any of us what things they are capable of.'

'Of course,' Merrit said. To Aline Venn, he said, 'I take it from all of this that you no longer allow Maud to associate with any of the others.'

'Of course not,' she said. 'We keep a close eye on her. It was one of the reasons why I finished my work at the school.' She glanced at her husband. 'And it is the reason why Maud herself has not been back there to sit among them while all this is happening.'

'Because you believe she would continue to want their friendship, to remain at the centre of all this?'

'She's a child,' Venn said, his patience with all these probing remarks finally at an end. 'She hardly knows *what* she wants. And she certainly has no true idea of the *harm* those others are causing with their tales, and causing to her.'

Merrit heard the criticism directed at himself in all of this, and said, 'I doubt if anything would be served by my talking to your daughter now, here.' The child, he imagined, would have overheard much of what had just passed between himself and her parents. The girls' tales all followed parallel courses, they had the same shape and repeated the same few details. Everything he had so far gained from talking to Maud Venn's parents would only be squandered upon hearing her own rote-like and predictable recital later.

'Would you at least like to see her again?' Aline Venn asked him unexpectedly as he signalled his intention to leave.

'Of course,' he said, unable to refuse her. Another small ritual to be observed in that shrine.

The woman left briefly and returned with the child. The girl wore a different dress and had washed her face and brushed her hair.

'Maud, this is Mister Merrit,' her father said, taking the girl's hand from his wife.

'I know,' she said. She avoided looking directly at Merrit, turning instead to the photographs on the covered piano.

'And do you know why I'm here, in the town?' Merrit said to her.

She turned to him. 'I know who you are and I know that you've come to punish us and take us away from our parents and to lock us up somewhere they can never come and see us again and that when we die we'll all go to Hell and I'll never see my baby brother or sister again and play with them.'

None of them was prepared for this evenly spoken barrage of accusation, and they all stood and looked down at the girl as they struggled to frame their impossible responses to her.

'What?' Maud Venn said when none of them answered her. She went to the piano and held up her fingers to the smallest of the photographs.

17

MAUD VENN'S OUTBURST AND THE SPEECHLESS SHOCK OF her parents at hearing it stayed with Merrit for long afterwards, and even as he and Nash walked away from the house, he understood that a turning point had been reached and that a crucial part of his work in the place had now been completed and left irretrievably behind him.

The next three days of the inquiry were filled with taking and filing the final testimonies of all those who had registered a wish to contribute.

Merrit, Webb, Nash and Firth sat in separate parts of the courtroom and each man continued to attract his own small queue of confessors.

By now, following his performance in front of Edith Lisset, Webb had come to attract considerably more tale-tellers and gossip-mongers than the others, and the man revelled in this, often addressing those who waited to speak to him *en masse*. It was another irregularity, but again one that Merrit could do little to prevent.

The members of Firth's congregation continued to present themselves to him, often approaching the man where he sat as though they were approaching him at his pulpit.

Nash, Merrit saw, still drew the shortest queues, and when

he attempted to redirect some of his own waiting witnesses to Nash, they insisted on remaining with him. Again, there was little he could do about this. Some even began their short journeys across the courtroom in Nash's queue and then diverted to Webb's growing audience. As with the events at the Venn house, Merrit sensed that here, too, the balance had shifted.

Webb indulged his close acquaintances, affording them longer than the majority of those who spoke to him, and allowing their testimony to spill over the single sheet Merrit had suggested to them all. Only Nash was firm with his interviewees, telling them before they started that they would be allowed only ten minutes, and then stopping them abruptly, whatever stage their tales were at, when this time was up. It was another reason for the defections to Webb.

On the third morning of this tedious and time-consuming work, and unexpectedly finding himself at the end of his own list of applicants, Merrit seized the opportunity and left the court and walked back along the road he had first taken into the woodland.

His head was filled — as it seemed always to be filled these days — with the facts and figures, sworn statements and obvious fictions of a hundred dates and names and places. Connections were established and verified only then to be severed, proved false and cast back into the rising wind. For every story confirming what he had already been told concerning the girls, there were half a dozen others which contested or contradicted that story. He had thought to sow a field of perfectly spaced and evenly growing corn, but instead he had created a tangled undergrowth of docks, weeds, brambles, rotten trunks and ever-encroaching bindweed and convolvulus into which little light or air was able to penetrate, and which grew darker and ranker and denser the longer this seemingly unstoppable process lasted.

As he walked, he began to consider what few as yet indiscernible ways out of this tangled mess might remain open to him. But little suggested itself other than to complete all this gathering-in and then to withdraw in the hope that his departure and absence would create its own ending or resolution of sorts.

As often happened, the investigation had created and then maintained its own growing momentum. And in truth, he now knew, it had been beyond his control within days of its beginning – ever since the history and geography of the town had been called upon, questioned, examined, taken apart and then rewoven into all these strange and unsettling new shapes. It was a vague and imperfect conclusion to draw after so long in the place, but it was one which served him better now than a more precise understanding of what he had so far failed to achieve there.

And the investigation had also moved beyond his control in the more obvious sense that the wider world was now show-ing an ever increasing interest in the place, and certainly more interest, via the newspapers, than Merrit had anticipated or had experienced elsewhere during similar inquiries.

One of Webb's associates, an ex-mayor of the town, had complained to Merrit that the newspapers had put a bell jar over the town, encouraging their readers to crowd round and peer in at the poor, simple, stupid folk inside. It was a common enough complaint, but the man had a point. He had then demanded to know what Merrit was going to do to ensure that this glass dome was taken away from them when all this was over and he himself had departed. They would all suffocate if it stayed in place, the man insisted. Suffocate, and then burn under the heated gaze of all those ever-hungry and demanding watchers.

Merrit had been able to do little to placate or reassure the man, who had gone immediately to Webb to repeat his melodramatic complaints. It was by then common knowledge in the place that Webb hoped to follow in the man's footsteps and become the new mayor at the following year's elections, and this was something else Merrit now needed to consider each time Webb was afforded the public platform of the inquiry.

Entering the woodland, Merrit knew that the chief part of the investigation – all this evidence-taking – had now passed, and that, in the absence of any late confessions from any of the girls, all that remained for him to do was to submit his report and then await whatever further action might be deemed necessary by either his own superiors or the Assistant Chief Constable. In all likelihood, he knew, the heat and glare of all this outside interest would quickly fade, and the embers of the fire that now burned would darken and cool and then be extinguished in the cold air of returning indifference. Another sensation or novelty would arise and faces would turn away. Hopefully, the girls would sooner or later understand that they had come closer to the edge of the abyss than any of them had ever realized or intended, and they would afterwards be grateful at having been allowed to move away from that edge and back into the anonymity of their ordinary young lives. And when the investigation was finally over – however disappointing, unrevealing or inconclusive it might prove to be – then all of this outside attention would cease and a new equilibrium would be sought and gained, cherished and guarded.

Merrit knew better than most that the world contained a multitude of natural checks and balances, and that these were always in play. He knew that a pendulum never stopped mid-swing; he knew that energy was never completely lost; he knew that tremors and echoes would continue to be felt and heard for long afterwards. But above all, he knew that everything changed with time, and that it was impossible for those checks and balances *not* to come into operation.

'"And This Too Shall Pass",' he said to himself, remembering Firth's remark of ten days previously. And then, looking quickly around himself into the surrounding trees, he repeated the words more loudly, over and over, until he was shouting them, and their subdued and overlapping echo came back to him where he stood.

'Talking to yourself. That's not a good sign.'

The man was close behind him, hidden by a thicker trunk, and the words gave Merrit a start.

He turned to see who had spoken, stumbling as a piece of rotten wood snapped beneath his foot.

Cowan stood only a few feet from him. It had clearly been his intention to surprise Merrit like this, and he took undisguised pleasure in Merrit's response. He affected nonchalance by rolling a cigarette and watching as Merrit regained his balance.

'Touchwood,' he said, nodding to the rotten wood at Merrit's feet. 'Fungus. Rots the wood from one end to the other, starting from the middle. Looks sound, but it eats up all the strength of the stuff. Then it turns white and crumbles away to nothing. Just crumbles up and blows away to infect another piece of sound timber. You'd never even know it had been there.'

'You were watching me,' Merrit said. 'Following me.'

'I saw you,' Cowan said, still grinning. 'Is that the same thing? I imagine that's the kind of thing an educated man like yourself would pick the bones out of.' He bowed his head and smiled, rolling saliva on his lips as he licked the cigarette paper to seal it.

'*Were* you following me?' Merrit said.

'Don't flatter yourself. I've got as much right as anyone – more than most, in fact – to be in these woods.'

'Why "more than most"?'

'What?'

Merrit waited. The man had understood perfectly what he was being asked.

'Do you have no answer?'

'More than most because I was born and raised here, as was my father before me.'

'And his father before him? Probably a few others before that, eh?'

Cowan scowled at the remark and the insult it contained. 'That's right,' he said. 'Exactly right.'

Merrit looked around them. 'Your daughter not with you today?'

'Why should *she* be here?'

Merrit shrugged, as though the question had been of no consequence. He knew that the man used the child as both a sword and a shield. He knew that the pair of them rehearsed and then recited the details of everything she claimed to have seen to the clamouring journalists in exchange for payment – payment which grew correspondingly larger with the addition of each 'exclusive' and increasingly lascivious detail. He knew that the man and his daughter had told five times more to the paying newspapermen than they had ever declared to the inquiry. And Merrit had heard in the course of his testimony-taking that Cowan now sold and resold his tales in the town's public houses for drink, often taking his daughter along with him to increase his appeal and his earnings.

'Why?' Cowan said to him. 'You want to see her again?'

'Not particularly,' Merrit said, turning away from the man and resuming his walk through the trees.

'What's that supposed to mean?' Cowan came after him, all but grabbing Merrit's arm to stop him walking. 'I asked you a question.'

Merrit finally stopped. 'It means there's nothing more to be gained by listening to her over-elaborate and ever-expanding tales. The inquiry can give little credence to stories created by her solely for profit.' He looked hard at the man as he said this.

'So you *are* calling her a liar,' Cowan said.

'I'd hardly be the only one.'

'And what about the others? What does that make *them*? You calling that Seaton girl the same? What about the retard, what about her? You call my own girl a liar, then you're saying it of them all.'

Merrit saw immediately why the man was accusing him of all this. 'More tales for you to tell?' he said, rubbing his fingers and thumb together.

'It's what you're saying,' Cowan said.

'Your daughter's at their centre,' Merrit said dismissively. 'That's all. She's at their centre — you're surely not denying that? — and her being at their centre is proving profitable for you. But, be that as it may, I suspect there are others in the group who might now wish to distance themselves from your daughter – your "girl" – and all that she continues to insist upon.'

'Why's that, then?' Cowan was suspicious now. He drew on his thin cigarette in long draws, burning it swiftly along its full length.

Merrit remained silent.

'I asked you a question.'

'Because if there are consequences' – Merrit gave the word an unmistakeable edge – 'then I daresay some of the other girls might consider themselves very much less deserving than your daughter of censure or even—'

'What sort of consequences? What are you talking about? Do you mean the police, what? She's a kid. Nobody's going to touch her.' Cowan seemed more confident now.

'Why? Because nothing she says can be either properly proved or disproved? Because it will all be one day put down to the overactive imagination of a child, to childish excess? She's no small or innocent child, and both you and I know that.'

Cowan smiled at the words, already assessing what they might be worth to him when repeated later. He feigned surprise. 'Do we? Do I? My own daughter, and *I* don't know what she is? Or perhaps only *you* see something different, Judge. Perhaps you've lived too long in London and places like it and seen too much of this kind of thing there. Perhaps they turn faster into scheming women in big cities. Who knows? Perhaps because you see it there, you see it everywhere else you look. Or perhaps it's just what you *want* to see.'

Merrit felt uncomfortable with this turn in the man's

accusations. He knew how these same remarks might sound when repeated to others.

'You understand me perfectly,' he said eventually.

'So you keep telling me,' Cowan said. 'But by which I take you to mean that *you*'re the only one who thinks he understands everything, and I'm just the poor, ignorant, un-educated man who——'

'No one's accused you of those things.'

'I could swear you just said exactly that.'

'You know she leads them on,' Merrit said, tired of allow-ing the man to twist and turn ahead of him like this. 'You know that she instructs and guides them, and then that she ensures they back up everything she herself goes on to con-coct. You've only got to watch the way they behave in front of her, listen to the language they repeat, to know all that.'

But Cowan went on grinning at him. 'You talk as though you've got proof of all this. If you've got it – if one or other of them *has* confessed all this to you, if one or other of them has come crying to you begging to be protected from my girl – then let me see it.' He knew there was no such testimony and it was why he pushed his advantage now.

Tired of the man's continued provocation, Merrit said, 'What do you want?'

The question surprised Cowan. 'Want?' he said.

'Of me.'

'Why should I want anything of you?'

'Then why not simply hide behind your tree and let me pass?'

'Who said anything about hiding? I was just standing there minding my own business.'

'You were hiding,' Merrit said. 'Otherwise I would have

215

seen you. And if I'd seen you, then you wouldn't have come as such an unwelcome surprise to me.'

'"Unwelcome"?' Cowan said. Now he pretended to be offended. 'You do seem to be dead set against me. Me *and* my poor innocent child, who has been exposed to such terrible things for one so young.'

'You're not talking to the journalists now, Cowan,' Merrit said, causing the man to laugh.

'Of course I'm not – they'd have had their hands in their pockets long since. *They*'d be showing a little more interest and respect for what I was saying – what I might *still* be saying to them later.'

Then Merrit took a chance. 'Was it you who put a brick through the Foleys' window? Was it you who painted on their wall?'

Cowan's laughter became forced and Merrit knew he was right.

'I don't know what you're talking about,' Cowan said. 'Only what I read in the papers.'

'What were they – warnings to Agnes Foley's father to keep his mouth shut, not to act or to speak out in his *own* daughter's best interests, but to pay every regard to yours?'

'The girl's got no more sense than a rabbit. You've seen her. Your heart must have sunk in your chest when you realized you had *her* as one of your chief witnesses. I can see in your face now that I'm right. Why, *has* the man said anything, pointed any fingers?'

'Of course he hasn't,' Merrit said.

'So, yet again, all you're doing is throwing around empty accusations, and mostly at the people who are already suffering the most in all of this.' He paused. 'Perhaps I ought to make a few official complaints of my own. Perhaps *you*'re the one getting a bit too involved for his own good. Perhaps hearing all those girls' stories has turned your head? Perhaps you *enjoy* listening to them tell their dirty little tales to you in private.' The man savoured the power of these dangerous accusations and the thought of all they might lead to were he ever to make them publicly.

'Whatever you see fit to believe . . .' Merrit said to him, and then he turned and started walking back in the direction of the town.

Cowan came after him, but this time Merrit kept walking.

'Running away?' the man called after him. 'Come too close to the truth of it all, did I?'

Eventually, approaching the edge of the trees, the outer buildings of the town visible to them, Cowan started to fall back. He raised his voice and went on shouting at Merrit, attracting the attention of the few people there.

Merrit finally slowed his own pace, not wanting to appear to be running away from the man. He nodded at the people who greeted him, most of whom were considerably more interested in Cowan, who had by then stopped at the edge of the trees, but who continued shouting his accusations as Merrit carried on walking.

18

THE FOLLOWING DAY, ALERTED BY THIS ENCOUNTER WITH Cowan and all the man had half-suggested, half-threatened, Merrit compiled an interim report and posted this to his superiors. He had been there eighteen days, over half his allocated time, and he was already uncertain what more there was to be achieved by dragging out these proceedings any longer.

He sent a telegram suggesting that the inquiry be brought to a close, and a reply was delivered to him an hour later insisting that the work continue and that he remain. An hour – long enough for his own superiors and the Assistant Chief Constable to have communicated and for all thoughts of an abbreviated investigation – and what this might imply in the eyes of the townspeople and the watching world – to be cast aside. He understood these politics, and he understood better than ever the exact and carefully regulated nature of his own role within them.

He acceded to this demand by return of post.

The telegram had been brought to him by the hotel clerk on a silver tray as though it were something precious. The boy had then stepped back and bowed slightly when relieved of this great weight.

The interim report consisted – as these things always consisted – mostly of lists of witnesses and the more general aspects of the testimony so far collected. There was no room for either assessment or judgement. It was Merrit's opinion that anyone reading even a small part of that testimony could do no other than conclude that the girls had created a conspiracy among themselves, and that, whatever talk there might be of ghosts, devils and poltergeists, nothing existed beyond their own colourful and over-excited imaginations.

It was not Merrit's place – and certainly not in this interim report – to speculate on the causes of, or reasons for, that conspiracy. Later, when the affair was ended, there would be opportunity for more informed and relaxed speculation. But until then, he was constrained to steer the inquiry along its own increasingly predictable course.

An hour after sending his confirmation, there was a knock at his door. His first thought was that it was Nash come to discuss what had happened at the Venns' house four days earlier. He had not seen the man outside of the public court since then.

But it was not Nash who entered at his shout. Instead, a short and excessively overweight younger man presented himself in the doorway, half-turning to edge himself sideways into the room. He wore a tight-fitting black suit and a bowler, which he removed and held to his chest as he came in. He carried a heavy wooden case, which knocked against the door frame as he struggled through.

Merrit rose from his desk and ensured that nothing of his work was visible there.

'I'm Pye,' the man said breathlessly. 'Oswald Vernon Pye.'

He spoke as though Merrit might already know of him, as though he might even be expecting him. He held out his arm, putting down his case. 'And you're Merrit.'

'The public inquiry will resume tomorrow,' Merrit said. 'No journalist can be—'

'You misunderstand me,' Pye said. 'I'm Pye – from the Psychic Research Society. Pye from *The Psychic*.' He took a card from his pocket and held it out to Merrit.

But Merrit refused to take this. 'I have nothing to say to you,' he said.

'Oh?'

'And especially not while my investigation remains under way.'

'You've already met our Mister Hale,' Pye said, again as though hopeful of a more positive response from Merrit. 'At Hanford Hall. And again at Loxley House. The hanged butler?'

Merrit remembered the man. 'He interfered with my work,' he said flatly.

Pye put the card back in his pocket, took out a handkerchief and wiped his shining brow and cheeks.

'And at Letchworth, I believe? The farmer. Bad business, I understand.'

Letchworth. Where a tenant farmer had been illegally slaughtering and selling his landlord's cattle and sheep and who, when caught bloody-handed, had insisted he had found a solitary carcass left by someone – or some*thing* – else. There had been a fight between the man and his landlord and the landlord had been left blind in one eye. At one point in the investigation, a ghostly nocturnal 'beast' had been blamed for the missing animals, and this man Hale had arrived and insisted on providing – 'creating' would be nearer the mark – proof of this beast's existence.

'A man lost the sight of his eye,' Merrit said.

'Like I said,' Pye said, 'a bad business.'

'Made all the worse by the interference of Hale and his ridiculous contraptions.'

'A single photographed sighting of the beast – supernatural or otherwise – and your inquiry would have followed a different course entirely.'

'The tenant farmer was found guilty along with a local meat-canner of killing and butchering the animals,' Merrit said.

'Ah, yes, *eventually*. Eventually, he was found guilty. But that ought not to have blinded *you* to all other possible explanations.'

Merrit shook his head at the all too familiar remark, unhappy that the conversation had come so swiftly on to this course. He had yet to meet anyone from the Psychic Research Society who was less than evangelical in promoting its aims.

'There was a single explanation,' he said. 'And a simple and obvious one at that. It's usually the way in these things. Please, I must ask you to leave. I can have no part in whatever it is you delude yourself you're here to achieve.'

Pye held up his palms at the remark. 'What I do *not* delude myself in believing is that I am able to keep an open mind on the matter.'

Whatever Merrit said in answer to this would only have encouraged the man further.

Pye wiped his face again and then nodded to the jug of water on Merrit's desk. 'May I?'

Merrit poured him a glass and, as though this were an

invitation, Pye came into the centre of the room and sat in the chair opposite Merrit's own. He emptied the glass in a swallow and held it out for more. Seated, the man's jacket and waistcoat stretched themselves even more tightly across the compressed globe of his stomach.

'I'm busy, as you can see,' Merrit said. He motioned to the files and papers beside the jug.

'Please, a few moments,' Pye said. He held up the spread fingers of his hand. 'Five minutes. At least allow me to explain why I'm here.'

'I imagine—'

'Poltergeist activity has been announced.'

'Not by me,' Merrit said.

'By others. It was in all the papers. Are they *all* wrong?'

'They follow one another like sheep,' Merrit said.

But again the man wasn't listening to him. 'No real surprise there, of course – the poltergeists, I mean – not where young girls are involved, and especially girls of that transitional, intermediary age.' He raised his eyebrows and then winked at Merrit as though the two of them were sharing a joke.

'Tell me what you want,' Merrit said, unhappy at indulging the man to even this slight degree, but curious to learn what further disruptive or inflammatory part he might now insist on playing as the inquiry moved towards its end.

'Good,' Pye said. 'I admire your forthrightness.'

My what? Merrit thought, but said nothing.

Pye closed his eyes briefly and then, opening them, said, 'A spirit photograph.' He held out his hands in a frame.

'Of the poltergeist?' *Why not the Devil himself?*

'Of the poltergeist. Or if not the thing itself, then of the results of its activity the instant this occurs.'

222

'Broken crockery, scattered bedclothes, scraped leaves, snapped twigs, all too human daubings and smashed windows?' Merrit said.

'Every one of them classic and well-documented manifestations,' Pye said. He had become more, and not less excited at everything Merrit had listed in an effort to deflate him.

'And all of it done by the girls themselves,' Merrit said.

Pye ignored this. 'I have other photographs,' he said. He tapped the wooden case with his foot.

'Is that your camera?'

'My psychic camera, yes.'

'How does it differ from an ordinary camera?'

'Ah.' Pye tapped the side of his nose. 'May I show you the fruits of my earlier endeavours?' He was already opening the case.

'The fruits of your earlier endeavours?' Merrit said.

'Exactly.' He took a large envelope from the case and immediately closed it again.

Merrit caught a glimpse of the ordinary-looking camera it held. He took the envelope from Pye and slid out its contents.

The first photograph showed a woman in a chair, gripping its arms, her eyes closed, and with a strip of silk or some other diaphanous material rising above her head.

'Ectoplasm,' Pye said.

'Silk or muslin?' Merrit said.

Pye swapped photographs. A child standing on the steps of what looked like an altar with the ghostly impression of a similar-looking child a few steps below.

'The Herriot twins. One five years dead, one living,' Pye said. 'I took that photograph in Saint Nicholas's church, where the unfortunate child is buried. Seven years ago. Nineteen hundred and three.'

'You double exposed the film,' Merrit said. He had seen both pictures many times before, but had never known the actual photographer.

The third photograph, however, was new to him, and at first he could not see what it showed. It looked like a drawing room, over-furnished and over-decorated.

'The vase,' Pye said excitedly.

Merrit looked closer. 'What of it?'

'What of it? It is suspended in the air. A second later it was violently and unstoppably smashed into a thousand pieces.'

Merrit looked again. It was difficult to see where the vase stood, but there was nothing to suggest that it was floating in mid air. 'You counted them?'

'Smashed beyond all repair,' Pye said. 'The Buxton poltergeist. Four sisters, two of them identical twins. Eighteen separate panes of broken glass and dozens of pieces of crockery. Just like your situation here. Identical, in fact.'

'We've had no floating vases so far,' Merrit said. 'The Devil and his slapdash art, but no lost vases. A dinner service, but not a particularly decorative or valuable one.'

Pye ignored all this. 'I was in the room when two of the children made the vase rise from the table entirely of its own accord, and then I continued watching as it flung itself against the wall. Luckily, I had the presence of mind to take the picture the instant before that happened.'

'Where are the girls?' Merrit said.

'Out of shot. It was a great pity. I have them in other photographs, their eyes turned to points of light.'

'Possibly the chemicals of your flashlight,' Merrit said.

Pye took the envelope from him and returned it to his case. 'Hale warned me of your own unbounded scepticism,' he said.

'Oh? And did he show you *his* photographs of the ghostly creature that had killed all those cattle and sheep and which had then conveniently jointed them and packed them in butchers' bags?'

'He captured the outline of a distant creature in the act of stalking its prey.'

'He showed you the outline of a cow.'

Pye wiped his brow again. 'Are you saying that you forbid me to be here, forbid me to attempt what I hope to attempt?'

'You are presumably well aware that I am in no position to do that,' Merrit said. 'The place is already awash with journalists and other photographers, though most of them are happy enough to turn their talents—'

Pye made a disparaging noise at the word and Merrit stopped talking.

Besides the growing numbers of journalists and photographers, there had also been a rumour that a well-known author, a man born less than twenty miles away and currently living in Paris, had shown an interest in the present 'affair' and was considering a return to the place to write about everything that was happening there, first for the press, and then in a book of his own.

In the past, Merrit had usually departed ahead of all these camp-followers and gleaners. They were heat and wind and noise to his silence and probing light; they were treasure seekers to his own careful and precise archaeological scraping.

'I can't forbid you,' he said to Pye. 'But I do possess certain powers with regard to you obstructing my own work here.'

'Your "own work here"?' Pye said. 'You make it all sound so . . . so . . .' He trailed off, his meaning clear.

'I make it all sound exactly like it is,' Merrit said. 'These are children. When all this is over and finished, they will remain here, live out their lives here. If you had your way, you'd turn them into freaks, curiosities to be stared at, animals that must forever perform.' He understood perfectly how pompous and condemnatory he sounded.

'Something they seem perfectly happy to be doing in front of you and your makeshift court,' Pye said. 'Something *you* seem perfectly content to observe and note down.'

'All I note down are the facts of the matter,' Merrit said.

Pye laughed at this. 'Along with the worthless opinions of anyone prepared to sit and talk to you. Do you honestly believe that a single undeniable photograph – of the poltergeist, or of evidence of its destructive energy, say – is worth less than all the contentious drivel you and your recorders have so far indiscriminately gathered up and packed away in your files?'

Merrit looked at his watch. Twenty minutes had passed. 'What do you propose doing?' he said. He wondered how many times he had had the same argument with all the other men like Pye, and how steadily and predictably the two opposing arguments had followed their parallel courses.

'Do I need your permission?' Pye asked him.

Merrit waited.

'I've already approached the Lisset girl's parents,' Pye said. 'They were only too happy for me to set up my equipment in their home.'

'And photograph what?'

'Whatever exists to be revealed there.'

'A sleepwalking child?'

'If that is all it is. Or perhaps a child commanded by spirits while she sleeps. Perhaps a child through whom the spirits have chosen to exercise their own malign intent.'

The same few revealing phrases. Like the cold shadows of clouds over a smooth hillside on an otherwise warm and sunny day.

'Of course,' Merrit said. 'If they've given you their permission, then—'

'They have,' Pye said.

'Then I acknowledge and appreciate your courtesy in informing me. When will you attempt it, the photograph?'

'As soon as possible, while the activity is at its height.' Pye was quickly back into his routine. 'As you may already be aware, these things come in cycles – periodic absences interspersed with bouts of intense activity. I hope at the very least to determine the true nature of the force driving the girl.'

'And what if the child herself, and not some external, controlling presence, was the source of that malicious intent?'

'Child? How old is she? The Buxton twins were sixteen.'

'Twelve,' Merrit said.

'Oh. I thought she might be older.' Pye seemed suddenly concerned by this. After a moment of silent consideration, he said, 'The surviving Herriot boy wept at the sight of his long-dead brother. Along with his mother and father. They held my photograph and wept for an hour. And when they were finally able to talk, they thanked me profusely for the picture and said they were convinced it was how their other child would have looked had he survived.'

'What killed him?' Merrit said, unwilling to counter with the truth everything Pye was telling him.

'Scarlet fever. He was four years old. The picture was a great comfort and reassurance to them all.'

'And if your camera – your psychic camera – does manage to capture a malign spirit sitting on the shoulders of Edith Lisset, leering over her forehead with its claws tangled in her hair and its tail playing back and forth across her thin chest?'

The remark caught Pye unawares. 'I don't understand you,' he said.

'What comfort and reassurance will *that* particular picture be to any of *them*?'

Pye shook his head at the remark. 'You surprise me,' he said. 'You imagine that any poltergeist will adopt such a form?'

'I don't know what rules or laws they follow,' Merrit said.

Pye rose from his chair, picked up his case and went to the door, looking back at Merrit as he went with something close to both pity and contempt on his face.

19

He encountered Nash later in the day as he walked in the square before dinner. It had become his habit to do this, and after a day in the confines of the court and his room, he was grateful for this brief time alone, now largely unapproached and mostly ignored.

Nash called to him and came across the open space to where Merrit stood at one of the shops. 'Are you on your way out?' he asked.

Merrit explained what he'd been doing. At first, something in Nash's manner made him cautious. It was the first time the two men had been alone since their visit to the Venn house, and Merrit imagined that Nash, having persuaded the Venns to talk to him, now considered himself to be responsible for what had happened there. He had hoped to talk to the man sooner than this, and was pleased to see him now. He also wanted to ask him about the dead baby, and why he and the others had remained silent on this.

'I've just come from the Lissets,' Nash said, his voice low, looking around them as he spoke.

'Something to do with the girl?' *Something to do with Pye and his psychic camera?*

'Will you come to my surgery?' Nash said, and, conscious

229

of the man's reluctance to go on speaking in such a public place, Merrit agreed.

Having arrived at his home, Nash led Merrit to his small dispensing room, where he poured them both a drink from a bottle marked with a skull and crossbones. He saw Merrit looking at this. 'My own warning to myself,' he said, and laughed. He seemed uncertain of how to continue.

'What's happened?' Merrit prompted him. 'More unexplained happenings in the middle of the night?' The flippant evasion felt sour in his mouth.

Nash drained his glass and took a folded sheet from his pocket and gave it to him.

It was a simple diagram of two parallel lines, between which five crosses and a succession of other, less obvious marks had been drawn.

'I don't see what it is,' Merrit said. 'More painting?'

Nash poured himself another drink. 'It's her arm, Edith Lisset's arm.' He drew his thumb and forefinger along the parallel lines. 'That's her arm and these are the marks on it.'

'Marks?'

'Cuts. Further cuts have been inflicted.' He added more drink to Merrit's glass.

Merrit considered what he was being told for a moment. 'Similar to the cuts she supposedly received from the broken crockery?'

'Different arm,' Nash said. 'And deeper.'

'Did she tell you how?'

'She told me a fanciful tale about fighting through brambles in the wood. Her parents called me to see her when they saw blood on her sheets.'

'And she was lying to you?'

'They're deep cuts. Not scratches. You can see for yourself – crosses. They've been deliberately made. Some of them were still bleeding when I cleaned and bandaged them. According to her father, she came home and went straight to her bed. It wasn't until an hour later that her mother looked in on her and sent for me.'

'Do *they* believe what she's saying?'

Nash shook his head. He flicked the sheet of paper Merrit held. 'Imagine that drawing in red, in blood, and with blood smeared the full length of those two lines. Whatever – *who*ever – cut her, it wasn't brambles. Something sharp and clean. There were also small bruises at her wrist and close to her elbow.'

'You think she'd been held?'

'Restrained.'

'Against her will?'

Nash shrugged, unwilling to speculate. 'As you know, I never believed from the start that she'd been accidentally cut by the crockery she'd brushed away.'

'What did the girl herself have to say?'

'That she'd been in the woods with Mary Cowan and Margaret Seaton, just the three of them, and that they'd wandered into the brambles and then panicked when—'

'When they saw something else?' Merrit said, half-hoping for the obvious lie.

'She said they were all frightened because Mary said she thought they were being followed, and then Margaret said the same. She became agitated telling me all this. There were no cuts or abrasions anywhere else on her – none on her legs, for instance, only her arm.'

'So if they're not self-inflicted, the others did them and she's now covering for them?'

'It's her right arm,' Nash said. 'She's right-handed. The original cuts were on her left arm and hand. When I asked her if someone else had done it to her, she became hysterical and started screaming and thrashing around in her bed, shouting for her father to get me out of the house. She tried to tear off the bandage I'd put on. It took both of her parents to calm her down.'

'*Do* you believe there was someone else in the woods with them?'

Nash shook his head. 'Five crosses. Five girls,' he said.

The same thought had already occurred to Merrit.

'My guess is that one of the older girls – Cowan or Seaton – made her prove herself to them.'

'Cowan,' Merrit said.

'Some kind of initiation ritual or pact, perhaps,' Nash said.

'Something to attach her to them and perhaps to draw her away from the younger girls?'

'From the baby and the imbecile, yes. Will you be the one to suggest that to the journalists, or shall I?'

'My apologies,' Merrit said. 'Did she say what happened to whoever might have been following them?'

'According to her, he – *he*, note – ran off as soon as they started screaming for help when they allegedly found themselves amid the brambles.'

'If it *was* one of the other two doing the cutting,' Merrit said, thinking as he spoke, 'then she must have let them do it for however long it took, regardless of being held.'

'I know. They were neat cuts, all five crosses near identical.'

'But why now, I wonder?' Merrit said. 'When all this is almost over.'

'Perhaps because she'd seen how it had all turned out and she'd threatened to say something, to break ranks?'

'Or perhaps it was what Cowan suspected, and this was *her* way of keeping the girl in line so close to the end,' Merrit said. 'Were you able to speak to her parents privately?'

'It's my understanding that they believe everything we believe, but that it was neither the time nor the place for them to admit it or discuss it openly. She was still bleeding and screaming where she lay, remember? And she's still their daughter. If they believe her capable of allowing someone to inflict this degree of harm on her – let alone what she may be capable of inflicting herself – then what *else* might they also start to imagine? They certainly didn't want *me* forcing the issue.'

'Because you're her—'

Nash slapped his palm on the arm of his chair. 'Because I'm *your* lapdog. Because everything I see and hear, everything I know of the place, I no doubt repeat in endless detail to you.'

The remark caught Merrit by surprise and he struggled for his response. 'I didn't mean . . .' he began.

'No,' Nash said. 'My apologies. What I said – being your lapdog – it was what Cowan shouted at me earlier as I was on my way to the Lissets' house.'

'In front of an audience, no doubt.'

'A dozen of his tap-room cronies.'

'And all of whom then added to the slander?'

'They were insults, that's all,' Nash said. 'It isn't just you who believes that everything here is drawing to its disappointing close.'

Merrit considered the remark and all it implied. He also

233

wondered how Cowan had learned of Nash's errand, but said nothing.

Nash refilled their glasses and the two men went from the dispensary into Nash's drawing room. Nash took back the simple drawing, tore it to pieces and threw these on to the fire, where they burned immediately, several of the scraps floating free of the low blaze and settling in the hearth, where they burned to small black outlines.

'Will you see her again?' Merrit asked him. It was beyond him to ask if he might accompany him and speak to Edith Lisset and her parents.

'I've said I'll return tomorrow. They made me promise not to tell you what had happened.'

'Did they believe you wouldn't?' It was a clumsy question.

'They said it in front of the girl to help calm her down. She was insisting by then that neither of the other two girls had had anything whatsoever to do with her cuts, that it was her own stupid fault for having wandered so deep into the brambles despite their warnings.'

'They were all three of them caught there a moment ago.'

'I know. It's a story we should be used to hearing by now. When I was back downstairs with her parents they asked me to be discreet.'

'Which is what you've been,' Merrit said, and again it felt the wrong thing to say.

'Then good for me,' Nash said, and drained his glass.

Neither man spoke for a moment, and then Nash said, 'The mother said a curious thing.'

Merrit waited.

'She asked me if all this self-inflicted and endured harm wasn't some kind of – she couldn't bring herself to say the word – she was asking me if it wasn't some kind of precursor to or indication of . . .'

'Madness? Insanity?'

Nash nodded. 'They were afraid that if I told others – they meant you – what had happened, then things might move beyond their control.'

'Unlikely,' Merrit said.

'That's what I told them, but I doubt if I sounded very convincing.'

'I understand you,' Merrit said.

'They look at Agnes Foley and imagine the same thing happening to their own daughter.'

'That's ridiculous.'

'You may know that and I may know that,' Nash said, 'but they don't know *what* to believe or to think. Their whole existence has been turned upside down by all of this.' He rubbed a hand over his face. 'Speaking of Agnes Foley, I heard from an acquaintance of her father's that he'd been contacted by the Health Commissioners to determine the effect of all that's been happening here on his daughter's health.'

'The Commissioners?' Merrit said. 'No one's contacted me. Someone may have spoken to the Assistant Chief Constable, but that aspect of things has nothing to do with what *I* might or might not . . .'

Nash started shaking his head at the words. '*Everything*'s to do with you,' he said as Merrit fell silent. 'Everything, one way or another. The only person who doesn't see and understand that—'

'Is me,' Merrit said.

Neither man spoke for a moment, and then Merrit said,

'Are they talking about returning Agnes Foley to the asylum, do you think?'

'I don't know. I'll have to speak to Foley.'

'Do you still believe he would have been wiser not to have insisted on bringing her home in the first place?'

'Of course,' Nash said. 'And certainly not for her to land at the centre of all this so soon after her return.'

A thought occurred to Merrit. 'Do you think Edith Lisset's parents believe *I* might possess the power to recommend her removal from them?'

Nash shrugged. 'Perhaps. Neither of them knows for certain *what* you're capable of, what powers you possess.' Then he smiled. 'To them, you're probably worse than the Devil putting in his shady, sulphurous appearance. At least with him, they can *choose* whether or not to laugh at him, ridicule him or take him seriously. But with you . . .'

Merrit considered all this. He was hearing nothing he might not be told by a hundred others. He also knew what an asset Edith Lisset's parents would now be to him while they were so confused and apprehensive about what might happen next to their daughter.

Nash guessed what he was thinking. 'You think that now she'll become the key to all this?' he said, his own lack of conviction clear.

'It's a possibility,' Merrit said. 'It's unlikely to be either Mary Cowan or Margaret Seaton, and definitely not Agnes Foley or the Venn child.'

Nash shook his head at the suggestion. 'It's too late,' he said.

'Then why all this now? *Some*thing's happening, but we don't know what.'

But again Nash was not convinced by this.

After a further few minutes' small talk, Merrit told Nash that he'd applied to bring the inquiry to an early close, and that this had been denied him.

'The powers that be?' Nash said.

'And the powers above them. Those men who need and crave their neat and packaged answers and solutions, a plan of action and a proper, satisfactory conclusion to everything. A place for everything in this perfectly ordered world, and everything in its place.'

'Satisfactory to whom?' Nash said. 'Besides, what did you expect? It's what you do for them; it's why they send you.'

Merrit held out his glass to be filled again.

'Perhaps all this,' Nash said, 'the scarring of Edith Lisset, perhaps it's simply the girls' way – Mary Cowan's way – of impressing your defeat upon you?'

'My defeat?'

'Perhaps they imagine they entered into a contest with you, and that they've now won. Not all of them, perhaps, but certainly Cowan. Perhaps she still imagines she's pulling the strings. Perhaps she wants to send a message to you, to humiliate you. Perhaps she thinks this is another way of somehow exonerating herself and justifying – to herself at least – everything she's done – achieved – here.'

'Then I wish *she* showed that same faith in those neat, clean endings that my masters insist upon,' Merrit said. He tried to remember how many glasses of whisky he'd drunk. 'Because if what you suggest is true, or even half true, then there's nothing more to be gained here by dragging this out any further. Even the scandal-mongering press and its starving readers will lose interest eventually.' He told Nash of his encounters with both Stannard and Pye.

'It's all a game to them,' Nash said.

'It's what they do when they've got nothing better to report on. Everything these days is novelty. Worth and value and true public interest count for nothing any longer.'

'You're wrong,' Nash said. 'It's all about money. Income – that's all they're interested in.' He, too, was starting to slur his words.

'They turn everything into something it isn't,' Merrit said. 'Suddenly *everything*'s a sensation, something to be built up, ridiculed, knocked down and then picked apart. Perhaps Webb was right from the very start – perhaps I *have* done more harm than good by coming here and seeming to sanction and endorse all this excited interest. Perhaps he alone – alderman and magistrate and mayor-to-be Webb – should have interrogated the girls, told them all that they were lying, told the town that they were lying, and then told everyone to forget everything that had ever happened here and to get on with their lives.'

Nash shook his head at the remark. 'It's this new century,' he said. 'We're all encouraged to behave differently, to think and to see things differently. People feel unsettled, forever anticipating change, forever waiting for whatever improve-ments and benefits they feel certain are coming their way.'

'And now, here, instead of all that, they suddenly find themselves in the middle of something more akin to an out-break of – what? – witchcraft? Pictures move on a screen, people talk through wires, fly through the air like effortless birds, know all the secrets of the human body and mind, and then this – the Devil appears, demonic symbols bloom like mortuary flowers, and markings appear in blood on the arms of young girls. All heresy and cant and turmoil.'

'You sound as though you regret ever having heard of this place,' Nash said, smiling again.

'Do I? Perhaps because I already know what little true or lasting good will come of whatever I might actually achieve here. This affair will leave its mark, that's all, a bad taste, a stain, something people will either try hard to forget, or which they'll speak of only in whispers for decades to come.'

'You've seen it all elsewhere,' Nash said.

'In one form or another. But perhaps you're right – perhaps it is all part of this new age you talk about. Perhaps now *everything* will have to be investigated, explained, picked apart, understood. Perhaps there will soon be an even greater demand to be endlessly informed, endlessly entertained and, supposedly, enlightened.'

'No more blissful ignorance, then?' Nash said.

'It was only ever bliss for those people determined to live in the dark and to ensure that everything stayed exactly as it always had been,' Merrit said.

'Your masters?' Nash said.

'My masters.'

The two men touched glasses.

After that, Merrit rose and said it was time for him to leave. He felt momentarily unsteady on his feet. Only then did he realize that he hadn't raised the subject of the Wilson baby, but he knew that now was not the time to turn back along that particular path into the cloudy history of the place.

Outside, it had grown much darker and colder, and Merrit wrapped the scarf he wore around his mouth and nose. His breath feathered in the air ahead of him as he walked. He considered the implications of all he had just learned – the same few ever-fracturing and re-forming thoughts – until it seemed to him that his mind and his ability to reason had become as numb to him as his forehead and his cheeks had become in the cold night air.

Part Three

20

ANGELICA FIRTH ATTRACTED MERRIT'S ATTENTION AS HE left the court. A motor car stood between him and the woman, its bonnet folded open, with a small crowd of men and boys gathered around its exposed and rattling engine. A pall of blue smoke hung over the machine. Merrit had been about to join this audience when he spotted Angelica Firth, her arm already raised to him.

He went to her. He had spent the morning with her husband and Webb, helping the men to sort the material they had gathered. An air of cold purposelessness now hung over this tail end of the proceedings, and though Webb showed little enthusiasm for the perfunctory and repetitive work, Firth remained as naively optimistic about the benefits of their labours as on the day it had all started over three weeks earlier.

He took Angelica Firth's gloved hand. 'Are you waiting for your husband?' he asked her.

The woman looked at the court door and then back at him. 'Is he still in there?'

'With Webb.'

'Still stacking up all the evasive and contradictory answers to your pointless and divisive questions?'

Merrit wondered for a moment if the remark was meant

as a joke, but then saw by Angelica Firth's expression that it wasn't. 'It is sometimes the testimony which seems the most inconsequential and innocuous at the time which later turns out to be of the most value,' he said.

'I'm sure it is,' she said.

He waited for her to reveal her purpose to him.

'Aubrey was passed over for the position he applied for,' she said. 'It was in Leicester.' She turned away from him as she said it.

'I'm sorry to hear that,' Merrit said.

'But I daresay not too surprised.'

'He seems a very capable and compassionate man.'

She shook her head at the words. 'A capable and compassionate man whom you allowed – perhaps "encouraged" would be a better word – to make a fool of himself by participating in your – in this ridiculous *fiasco* of spoilt, mendacious and manipulative children.'

'Do you know that?' Merrit said, his patience with the woman at an end.

'Know what? I know that the Church Appointments Panel had before them a pile of newspaper articles concerning this affair in which my husband's name was prominently and repeatedly mentioned. I believe one even referred to him as "God's Emissary on Earth".'

'Is it not how he sees himself?' Merrit said, knowing how provocative the remark would now seem to her.

'Not in *this* way. "Emissary"?' She lowered her voice. 'Here, in all of this, as embroiled as you have allowed him to become, he is nothing but a figure of fun, someone whose beliefs and concerns are found to be wanting, and who is then mocked and scorned for those beliefs.'

Like much of what the woman said, it was a practised speech.

'And so you believe that *I* am responsible for that mockery and scorn, for the failure of his application?'

'In large part, yes.'

'Your husband has made no such accusation. In fact, he hasn't even suggested to me that he—'

'It isn't his way.'

They were interrupted by the sudden, much louder rattle of the motor engine, and by the shouts and laughter of the men and boys around it. A thicker plume of smoke rose into the air above them.

Merrit watched all this for a moment, trying to determine if the woman didn't harbour some even greater resentment against him. Her husband's failure was his own, and she surely understood that as clearly as Firth himself did.

'You expected the inquiry here to perhaps follow a different course?' he said. 'To arrive at a more satisfactory – a more conclusive – resolution?'

She considered her answer. 'I believed you might maintain a firmer hold on the course of events, yes – that you would perhaps not seek to include every single piece of hearsay and gossip from every person inclined to utter it within a ten-mile radius. And I doubt if I – if *any* of us – understood the credence you would continue to accord those malicious little schemers.'

Many others had already said or suggested the same to him.

'So you believe the inquiry has only prolonged—'

'Our unnecessary and undeserved suffering at their hands, yes.'

'I was going to suggest that the inquiry had prolonged the uncertainty and mistrust surrounding these events.'

She said nothing after this, eventually taking an envelope from her pocket, tapping it against her collar and then returning it.

'The notification from the Church?' Merrit said.

'They consider my husband to have made "unfortunate" choices and decisions in involving himself with you. They consider his zealous pursuit of fairness and truth to have got the better of him. These were the same men who suggested to him in the first instance that it was his duty to participate in your work here – before, presumably, they too better understood the direction it would take.'

'He didn't participate unwillingly,' Merrit said.

'No. But alongside yourself, Nash and that overblown windbag Webb, what did he truly contribute other than to provide some kind of spurious moral authority or blessing to the proceedings? You used him, Mister Merrit – and, yes, perhaps he himself was only too willing to be used, to assume his rightful place on your panel – but you used him all the same.'

Her argument was not intended to be contested, and Merrit could offer no rebuttal or reassurance that she herself had not already considered a dozen times over. She was as lost, adrift and as abandoned in the place as her ineffectual husband was, and he, Merrit, an outsider, had come there and seen and understood this as clearly and as precisely as she herself had long since been forced to understand it.

'Is there anything I can do?' he said eventually. 'With regard to your husband's selection board, I mean.'

'His own judges. I doubt it. They seldom leave any room

for doubt or reassessment, these men. They themselves are invariably firm in their convictions, whatever the cost to others.'

Just like you are, Merrit imagined the woman adding, but the words remained unspoken.

'Another post may become available,' Merrit said, knowing how glib and unfeeling this sounded.

'What, and the memory of all this – of this farce – will quickly fade away and everything be forgotten? I doubt if even you are that deluded or foolish, Mister Merrit. This thing will leave behind it a stink for years to come.'

'You speak as though people won't now make every effort to move on,' Merrit said. 'Surely, the majority here already see this affair for what it was.' He waited to see what she might say next, what more she might be unable to resist revealing to him.

She, too, seemed to consider this for a moment, and then she said, 'You'll have heard by now about the Wilson baby.'

'Of course.'

'It was more or less common knowledge at the time that the Cowan child had killed it – accidentally or otherwise – and then that the mother was driven mad with grief. I imagine "deranged" was the word.'

'Deranged enough to confess to killing the child herself while the balance of her mind was upset?'

Angelica Firth laughed at the phrase. 'Mary Cowan was only believed because the baby's mother already had a reputation for waywardness and instability. She was at home for a week before she was finally arrested and committed, and she spent every waking hour of that time searching the woods for her lost baby, and then afterwards pulling out every last strand of her own hair. She dug everywhere she looked and found nothing.'

'And you know all this for certain because it—'

'Because I was with her for most of that time. She was a member of my husband's congregation. Everyone who knew her was afraid for her.'

'She confessed to killing the baby,' Merrit said. 'Or at least to finding it dead, burying it in a fit of grief or remorse and then afterwards having no memory of where the grave lay.' Whatever his thoughts on Mary Cowan, he was now convinced that this version of those distant events lay closer to the truth of the matter.

But Angelica Firth only smiled. 'It all seems very straightforward and believable – understandable, almost – when you say it as quickly as that.'

'The girl was never—' Merrit began.

'The girl was never forced to face up to what she'd done,' Angelica Firth shouted angrily, immediately lowering her voice. 'Excuses were made for her age and her supposedly innocent nature.'

'There was never any suggestion *after* the mother was committed to the asylum that it was for anything except her own good,' Merrit said. 'I checked – she hasn't recovered to even the slightest degree, and there is no suggestion whatsoever that she is ever likely to be released.'

'So?' Angelica Firth said. 'Her mind collapsed completely. Perhaps she merely submitted to what everyone repeatedly told her, and then afterwards convinced herself that she had indeed killed her own child.'

'It was over five years ago,' Merrit said as the woman finally

248

fell silent. 'Whatever happened then, it can have no bearing on what we are investigating today.'

'Why? Because those are the rules you insist on following? Because those few short years have passed? Because any mention of the killing might prejudice opinion against the girl now?' It seemed a clumsy attack after all she had just said, but because Merrit understood the true source of her anger, he said nothing to prolong her distress.

'I made wider inquiries,' he said eventually. 'No charges were ever laid. The body was never recovered, and the woman in—'

'Her name was Rebecca Wilson.'

'And Rebecca Wilson was quickly beyond all reach.'

'I know all that,' Angelica Firth said. 'Another book carefully closed and put back in its place on the shelf.' She again turned from Merrit briefly, wiping her face with her fingers, and when she looked back she signalled to someone over his shoulder.

Merrit looked and saw Aubrey Firth leaving the court and coming towards them.

'Does he know?' he said to her. 'About the lost position.'

'Since yesterday morning.' The three words seemed a final, uncrossable boundary to her disappointment.

The man had said nothing to him during their time together earlier.

Firth joined them and kissed his wife on the cheek.

'I told Mister Merrit of the panel's decision,' she said to him.

'Oh, yes, right,' Firth said.

'Please,' Angelica Firth said, 'whatever you do, don't say again that it's God's will.'

It seemed to Merrit that there was no limit to the woman's small cruelties, intentional and otherwise. But then it also occurred to him that this was not how she herself would regard these remarks. She was her husband's tether and his guide, and the man was only too happy both to fasten himself to her and to be led by her.

'I'm sorry if the panel believe you have somehow misspent your time at the inquiry,' Merrit said to him. 'Or if they consider me to have taken advantage of your expertise or sense of duty.'

'Not at all, not at all,' Firth said, watching his wife as he spoke.

Merrit was glad of the interruption, uncertain of what he might have said next.

Angelica Firth, too, seemed uncomfortable in her husband's sudden presence. She watched the men and boys still gathered around the motor car.

'At one time I thought I might acquire one myself,' Firth said to Merrit.

'I am grateful,' Merrit said unexpectedly.

Both Firth and his wife looked at him.

'For all your help. For what you represent here, for your support. For everything you've done to help me get at the truth of the matter.'

'Of course,' Firth said. 'Of course.'

Angelica Firth took several paces away from the two men, a clear signal for her husband to follow her, which Aubrey Firth did, never once looking back at Merrit as he went.

And watching them go like this, seeing Firth fall into step

alongside his wife, Merrit saw that their departure was both an act of deliberate severance and a loss – both to himself and to his purpose there – and he was surprised by how swiftly and keenly he felt that loss.

21

MERRIT SPENT THE NEXT TWO DAYS IN NEAR ISOLATION. Following the completion of his interim assessment, he started work on preparing the full report he would only properly begin writing when the inquiry was formally concluded. He listed the headings he would employ – there was seldom any variation in these – and then began to make notes on the information each would contain.

A further month would pass before this was laid on the Assistant Chief Constable's desk, and longer still – in some previous instances, this had taken up to a year – before any recommendations for further action were returned from his office to either the local police or other relevant authorities. As ever, as always, the storm would pass, the wind would die and the dust would settle. It was what everyone expected; it was what everyone wanted. Merrit's inquiry would be seen to have served its necessary and vital purpose, and then afterwards most of those briefly swallowed up in that storm would be able to return to their disturbed and diverted lives. In short, History would resume its slow, measured and predictable pace towards whatever lay ahead.

It was as he worked at this report on the second day that there was a sudden rapping at his door, and before he could call out, both the hotel clerk and one of the court's young constables appeared there.

'The girl's gone missing – wandered off – last night perhaps, no one knows – her father's frantic, he's downstairs now,' the constable said breathlessly to Merrit.

'In the lobby,' the clerk added. 'Doctor's with him. Doctor brought him here.'

Merrit laid heavy files over the scattered papers on his desk. 'Which girl?'

Neither boy could recall her name.

'The idiot,' the constable said. 'One of your suspects.'

Merrit ushered them out of the room ahead of him.

Downstairs, Nash and Foley stood together by the small fire.

Foley came immediately to Merrit. 'They're already out looking for her. I saw her last night, early, seven-ish. Not after that. When I looked in this morning, she was gone.'

'Perhaps she'd only just left,' Merrit suggested. He looked to Nash for whatever reason or stability he might bring to the man's panic.

'Those other two were round,' Foley said. 'Wanting me to let them in to see her. Banging on the door and shouting in at me.'

'Two of the other girls?'

'Mary Cowan and Margaret Seaton. Shouting and screaming that they wanted to see Agnes. Shouting at the tops of their voices. Language. Accusing Agnes of all sorts. Threatening her with what they'd do to her if the police came for *them* on account of what she'd told you.'

'But she hasn't said—'

'Said they knew you'd been to see her, said she must have

253

said *something* to you, said you must have got *something* out of her behind their backs. The Cowan girl shouted that she'd been watching outside all the time you and Doctor Nash were in the house.'

Merrit pulled the constable to him. 'Have there been any sightings?' he asked him.

The boy shook his head. 'Not that I know of,' he said.

Foley went on. 'They shouted in that she'd been blabbing her mouth off to you, laying all the blame on them. Said they weren't going to let her get away with it. They said I was making her talk to you in an attempt to keep her at home with me, that we'd made a bargain with each other. They were there for an hour, screaming and shouting all the time. They threw stones at the door and dirt at the window. Put the fear of God into us. Agnes was terrified. It was all I could do to get her into bed when they finally went.'

'But they went without gaining entry or actually seeing your daughter?' Merrit said.

'I made sure of that. The child was in a state, lying on the floor with her hands over her head, crying and screaming and kicking her legs. I was worried she was going to have another of her fits. I did my best to calm her – I lay on the floor with her and wrapped myself around her – but nothing I said or did had much effect while the pair of *them* were still out there shouting and screaming and throwing stones.'

'And all this lasted an hour?' Nash said, looking pointedly at the constable, who misunderstood him and merely shrugged.

'At least,' Foley said.

'And afterwards?'

254

'Another hour to calm her down, and then I carried her to her bed and sat with her until she finally fell asleep.'

'You should have sent for me then,' Nash said. 'I could have given her something.'

'They threatened to come back,' Foley said. 'The Cowan girl said she'd be back with her father and that the man would break down the door. She said it was clear I was lying to her and that Agnes had already confessed everything to you. She said she'd wait until I was asleep and get into the house then.'

'Was that the word she used, "confessed"?' Merrit said.

'Among others.'

'*Has* Agnes said anything to you?'

Both Foley and Nash looked at Merrit as though they couldn't believe what he'd just asked them.

'All *she* does – all she *ever* does – is repeat *their* stupid stories,' Foley said angrily.

'Satisfied?' Nash said.

By now, a small crowd had gathered at the hotel door, and Merrit sent the constable to keep people back. The boy warmed to the task, waving his truncheon at the onlookers and causing those closest to the door to complain at his actions.

Merrit then took Nash to one side. 'Do *you* think she left the house last night?'

Nash shrugged. 'It's possible that she fell asleep briefly and then woke in the same blind panic fully believing that the girls' return was imminent. I've just come from the house. Her bed was cold and her window open. Her father told me she often used to come and go through it – it opens on to the scullery roof. The two doors were locked from inside. The word "Liar" had been painted again.'

'And the two girls never returned?'

255

'It doesn't seem so. It was cold and dark by then. Their threats would have been empty. It's certainly unlikely that Cowan would have dragged himself away from the fire or bar to make good his daughter's threat.'

Merrit called the constable back to them.

'What are the police doing?'

'Organizing a search?' he said uncertainly. 'We've put out word that she's probably in the woods somewhere.'

'Is that likely?'

'It's where she'd go,' her father said. 'She was never bothered by the place. She knew her way around. She had dens there. They all did.' He smiled as he said it, already imagining his daughter found and safe. 'Perhaps she took herself off to get away from those two little bitches and then fell asleep hidden away somewhere after the disturbed night she'd had.'

'It seems the most likely thing,' Merrit said, doing nothing to betray his own lack of conviction. 'Do you remember where these dens are?'

The man looked suddenly disappointed. 'I never knew where they were, just that she had them. In the woods somewhere – that's all I know.'

'She won't have gone far,' the constable said. 'There's already a dozen men volunteered to look. They know that she's—' He stopped abruptly and looked at Foley. 'That she's, you know, a bit . . .'

'We know,' Merrit said. He turned the boy back to the door. 'We should join in the search,' he said to Nash and Foley.

Nash agreed, telling Foley to return home and wait there.

The man was reluctant to do this, but was quickly persuaded by Nash.

'What will it mean?' he asked Nash.

'Mean?'

'For her? All this. Running off.'

'It hardly—'

'They'll say I'm not fit to take care of her and protect her. They're saying it already. None of this was my doing.'

'I know that,' Nash said. He told him again to go home, promising to come there himself when the girl was found and returned to him.

'If that's where they bring her,' Foley said.

'I'll make sure of that, too,' Nash said, casting a glance at Merrit as he spoke.

'Can you do that?' Foley said.

'Of course,' Nash said, the words drying in his throat.

The constable cleared a way through the crowd for the three men, following them out into the square and calling for other volunteers. There were few offers. Several men stepped forward, but then withdrew when they learned who they were to be looking for. This change of heart surprised Merrit, and he himself asked them to join in the search. But the men were adamant that they had other business to attend to. They were convinced the girl would be quickly found and brought back home. One man expressed the opinion that they'd all done enough running around after the girls over the previous weeks and that it was time to stop. Most in the small crowd concurred with this. Foley shouted at them, but to little effect other than to alienate them even further.

Merrit and Nash went together to the edge of the woodland beyond the railway tracks. The trees here were close to Agnes Foley's home, and if she *had* run into them, this was the direction she would most likely have taken.

They met a second constable standing on the path. He told

them where men had already searched, and then directed Merrit and Nash up the hill to their right. They could hear the distant voices of the searchers calling to each other. Dogs barked occasionally, their noise echoing and amplified beneath the thinning canopy.

Merrit and Nash climbed the slope, levelling out fifty yards above the path and following a narrow, less well-defined track into the thicker growth ahead.

'There are small disused quarries up here,' Nash told Merrit. It was a popular place for the children to play.

'*Could* she have had another seizure?' Merrit asked him. 'Out here, alone? As a result of all the turmoil at home?'

'It's a possibility,' Nash said. 'Anything that upsets her can trigger the things.'

'Perhaps it's what the girls intended by their visit,' Merrit said, but he saw that Nash was not convinced by this.

They followed the path towards the quarries until the trees thinned and the workings became evident in walls and floors of shaped rock. There were men there ahead of them, and Merrit recognized the charcoal burners he had encountered a week earlier.

Several of these came to him. They had been searching for over an hour and had so far found nothing. Tracks had been found leading through the woods – most made by the children in twos and threes – but it was hard to say how recent these were. It had rained throughout the previous night and this would have destroyed a good deal of evidence.

'We've looked at the bottom of all the faces,' the oldest of the burners told them, his voice low. 'But it's unlikely she'd fall by accident. Kids have been playing up here for years.'

The others continued to wander in uneven lines through

the surrounding trees, thrashing the undergrowth with sticks. They too had their dogs with them and they directed the animals back and forth ahead of them in a calculated order.

'They're poachers,' the man said to Merrit, smiling, a black hand over his mouth. 'They know what they're doing.' He motioned down the hillside. 'Not like that lot.'

Merrit smelled burning in the air.

'We fired our kilns last night,' the burner said. 'They'll last for a couple of days yet. We can spare the time to help in the search. She's the idiot child, right? She used to stand and watch us work, stacking and sealing the kilns. Never a word or a sign. She'd just stand there watching. Hours, sometimes. And then she'd be gone just as fast and as quiet as she'd come.'

'Might she be there now, at the kilns?' Merrit asked him.

'There's always someone keeping an eye on the things. If she turns up, we'll know.'

They were interrupted by a call from one of the others and the three men went to him, leaving the track and pushing a way through the undergrowth.

But upon approaching the man, he waved them back. He came to them and showed them the small, dirty piece of cloth his dog had found and brought to him from somewhere further ahead. It looked to Merrit as though it had been on the ground for some considerable time. It was indeterminate in colour, frayed at its edges, and as much soil as material. He took it from the man, brushed it clear of debris and put it in his pocket.

Returning to the track, Merrit, Nash and the burner then walked from the disused quarry towards the smoking kilns.

Others were already gathered there, including the constable who had come to the hotel.

'Any news?' Merrit asked him.

He shook his head. He had a map of the woods with him and he showed them where the search had already taken place.

A whistle would be blown three times every thirty seconds when the girl was found. He was unsure if any parts of the woodland had been excluded from the plan, or if other parts had been searched more than once.

Despite the map and the seeming order, it was clear to both Merrit and Nash that a hidden, silent child might easily be completely missed in those parts where there were no dogs searching. The old burner understood this, too, and he told the men with the dogs where to search next. They went without questioning his orders. And if Merrit had been surprised by the reluctance of the men in the town square to help in the search, he was surprised now by the willingness of these outsiders and strangers to the place to play their own part.

The old man took Merrit and Nash to the kilns, and they felt the radiated heat of the mounds from twenty feet away. Men shovelled soil on to the smouldering heaps, keeping the heat buried and the flames subdued. Thin columns of pale smoke rose from the stacks into the branches above. Occasionally, when the overheated surface cracked, one of the men shovelled wet earth on to the mound to dampen and re-seal it.

Elsewhere, the old man showed them their iron burners — giant circular canisters twelve feet in diameter and eight high, filled with smouldering wood and capped with lids like giant saucepans. He pointed out where the girl had last stood and watched them, and the three of them went closer, searching through the flattened undergrowth for any sign of her now.

'It would be a good place to come,' Nash said. 'The warmth of the kilns. If she slept and woke she might not even remember that she'd run away in fear, and she might easily reveal herself.'

After this, Merrit and Nash left the clearing and continued their search on the slope leading back down to the river, neither of them knowing if they were the first to look in that direction, or if they were simply following in the footsteps of unsuccessful others.

22

THEY RETURNED TO THE TOWN IN THE LATE AFTERNOON, just as the light began to fail and as the woodland floor beneath the trees grew impenetrably dark. There had been no sign whatsoever of Agnes Foley, and Merrit and Nash went first to her father to tell him this. Foley's earlier anxiety had abated, and it surprised both Merrit and Nash to see how resigned he now appeared to be to the fact that his daughter, one way or another, was lost to him.

They did their best to reassure him, but Foley remained listless and distant in their company. Perhaps the girl had already wandered beyond the limits of the search; perhaps someone had already found her and was even now attempting to return her home; perhaps she had fallen asleep after her ordeal and was still sleeping; perhaps she'd had another of her seizures and this time had not recovered from it.

Foley said that it was likely to be another cold, wet night, and they told him that the charcoal burners had volunteered to keep calling for the girl while they tended their kilns. There was still some distant hope that she might find her own way to their fires and voices in the woodland.

Foley then insisted on listing for them all the people who had been to see him during the day, and in everything he said, Merrit heard the man's unshakeable conviction that *he* was the one most likely to be judged and found wanting for having allowed his daughter to run off like that. He remained convinced, too, that Agnes would again be taken away from him upon her return.

'Were either Mary Cowan or Margaret Seaton back here?' Merrit asked him.

Foley hesitated before answering. 'Mary Cowan came and stood and watched the house for a few minutes while everybody else was out searching. That was all. She made no attempt to get in or to shout her usual abuse at me.'

Merrit had already checked with a police sergeant: neither of the girls' families had helped in the search.

'How many were looking?' Foley asked Nash.

'Ninety, perhaps a hundred,' Nash told him. There had been twenty searchers, thirty at most. Many had searched until mid afternoon, or until they had reached the outer roads and paths in the woods with which they were familiar before turning back. It was difficult to see how the broader area could now be searched without any proper organization or overall control. It had already been agreed by the police that the same ground would be more thoroughly searched the following day. There was little true planning beyond that.

After an hour, Merrit and Nash left the house and walked to the centre of the town. People were gathered in groups around the square, all of them discussing the day's events. Speculation was rife, and as far as possible both men avoided adding to this as they were approached and questioned.

Arriving at the hotel, Merrit was surprised to see Webb waiting in the lobby. The man raised a hand to him as he and Nash went in. Webb seemed about to click his fingers, but then thought better of the gesture and lowered his arm. He motioned to the solitary chair opposite him and said to Nash that he wished to speak privately to Merrit.

'Privately?' Nash said to Merrit behind his hand. 'In the hotel lobby with everyone outside knowing he's here?' His warning was clear.

Merrit had already invited Nash to dinner at the hotel, and he was relieved when Nash agreed to wait. It would provide him with an excuse to spend as little time as possible with Webb. Nash went through into the adjoining room, ordering a drink from the desk clerk as he went.

'Bad business,' Webb said as Merrit sat opposite him. He watched Nash as he went, clearly unhappy at the man's presence. 'Bad business all round.'

'It's getting much cooler,' Merrit said. 'It's to be hoped that—'

'I meant with regard to all it suggests concerning our own work here. The child was always a liability. You must deny quickly and firmly any accusations regarding our – your – part in her disappearance.'

'Have any such accusations already been made?'

'So far, it's only whispers,' Webb said. 'Gossip. But you know as well as I do – as *they* all do' – he motioned to the people outside – 'that everything is fuel for this particular fire.'

'Is that why you came – to warn me?'

Webb looked quickly from side to side and then picked up a newspaper from the table beside him to reveal a large brown envelope beneath it. 'And to give you this,' he said.

He motioned for Merrit to take the envelope, which he did. It was heavier than he had anticipated.

'I hear Firth's own hopes and ever more desperate expectations have once again been dashed,' Webb said, unable to resist smiling. 'Meaning we'll be stuck with him for even longer, I suppose.'

The envelope was unmarked and Merrit slid the bound papers it held into his lap.

'It's my report,' Webb said as the sheets appeared.

'*Your* report? What report?'

'The report I have taken it upon myself, as Chair of the County Magistrates Association, to make to that body.' It was clear by his tone and the formality of the remark that he did not anticipate a favourable response to the revelation.

'A report on what?' Merrit was already guessing. It was why Webb was doing all this there, in the public eye of the hotel lobby. He looked through to the adjoining room, where Nash sat watching them.

'On your inquiry here. I felt it incumbent upon myself, as a leading figure in the Association, to keep its other principal members fully informed of the nature and the likely outcome of all our work here.'

'Meaning *my* work here,' Merrit said. He read the title page of the report, saw that Webb had included a full line of his initialled honours, memberships and qualifications, and then he quickly slid it back into the envelope and let it fall back to the table with a slap.

Webb looked at it there. 'You're a busy man, especially with this latest unfortunate turn of events, of course you are,' he said. 'I did you the courtesy of outlining my major points as part of my introductory remarks. A précis, if you will.'

'Of an inquiry that is not yet ended? Of an inquiry that has drawn no official conclusions of its own? An inquiry that has yet made no suggestions or recommendations regarding further investigations or possible actions to be taken as a result of those conclusions?'

But Webb only smiled at the barrage of words and the flimsy defence they erected.

'And a report, furthermore,' Merrit went on, 'which *you* – whatever your position here – had neither the remit nor the authority to make, let alone to submit elsewhere.' He felt more confident behind these particular ramparts.

Webb cleared his throat. '"Remit"?' he said. 'I see you appreciate the modern approach. And with regard to possessing the necessary authority, I feel certain that, as a representative of the County Magistrates Association, my decision to compile the report on their behalf will be met with their full support and approval.'

'The Assistant Chief Constable—' Merrit began to say.

'Was informed a week ago of my intentions. The same day I questioned the wretched Lisset girl and her equally wretched father and saw how little we were truly achieving here. I heard from his office by return of post that he considered this secondary assessment of events here to be a valuable thing. After all, if any further recommendations *were* eventually required to be made, then it would surely fall to both the police *and* the County Court to make and then enforce those recommendations.'

Even knowing the man as he did, Merrit was unprepared for this. He knew that the Assistant Chief Constable would have agreed to *anything* which raised another screen between himself and the events of the place; and he knew too that Webb, already well acquainted with the man, understood this better than he, Merrit, did.

Still covering your own back, he thought, remembering what Stannard had told him at the station. *It's all you've ever done, right from the very start.*

'Perhaps you ought to read what I have to say before you feel the need to censure or condemn me further,' Webb said, deliberately overstating the case and adding his insincere sense of hurt and outrage to that already uncertain equation.

'Later, perhaps,' Merrit said, unwilling to indulge the man further.

'When you and Doctor Nash have concluded your socializing, perhaps?' Webb said. He looked at Nash in the other room.

'We were out all day in the woods helping in the search for Agnes Foley.'

Webb smiled again at this. 'And I'm sure that you are both able to convince yourselves that it is a fitting and valuable and *proper* use of your time and expertise.'

Merrit refused to be drawn by the remark, but was then unable to resist saying, 'I imagine you – as a father yourself, something of which you have reminded the inquiry on more than one occasion – will know better than either of us what the girl's father is being forced to endure while his only child remains lost to him.'

Webb bowed his head slightly, but said nothing.

After a minute, he said, 'I might warn you in advance that I felt the need to be somewhat harsh – some might say critical – in my judgement of some of your own methods here – of their efficacy.'

'"Efficacy"?'

'You have indulged people, drawn no firm lines. You have been too eager to consider all sides, as they say, when the truth of the matter is only too evident to those who look at it clearly.'

'Meaning the girls were making everything up from the very start? Surely, you all understood that before I even arrived?'

Webb smiled again. 'Meaning simply that the Devil did not appear to them in the woods, nor attempt to seduce them in their beds.' He lowered his voice and barely mouthed the word 'seduce'.

'Then perhaps you have written no more or less than I have included in my own report on the proceedings,' Merrit said.

Webb shrugged at this. 'Perhaps.'

'But you still felt the need to say everything in advance of my own conclusions?'

'I have my reputation to consider. I have a certain standing in this place, a respected function. People look to me to—'

'To represent them honestly, openly and fairly,' Merrit said. 'So you said.' *And you still intend to become their next mayor.*

'Of course,' Webb said. 'Firth, Nash and I, we are fixtures in the place, a kind of compass.'

'Whereas I am not?'

The point — already made to him a hundred times over during the past weeks — was driven further home by a minute of determined silence.

Merrit looked again to Nash, who signalled to him with his raised glass. It seemed to Merrit that Nash was deriving some pleasure from what he was able to overhear of Webb's remarks, and that he might even concur with some of what the man was saying. Nash's trousers, like his own, were caked with mud to the knees, and Nash picked at this where he sat.

'The child should never have been returned home from

the asylum,' Webb said eventually. 'We might all have been spared a great deal.'

'And Mary Cowan?'

'Her? What about her? She won't stay here long. Her sort never does. She'll find her way to a city and never come back.' He guessed at a few places. 'That whole family have been troublemakers since birth. When a dog growls at you every day you learn to ignore it and live with it.'

'Are they all little more than animals, then?'

'Those are your words, not mine,' Webb said. He picked up his gloves and hat from the table.

'What do you expect me to do with this?' Merrit said, tapping the envelope.

Webb shrugged. 'Read it, discover that we are not so very far apart in our judgements and recommendations, and then perhaps consider what you have achieved here that I might not have achieved alone, at considerably less expense, and with a considerably more fortunate outcome.'

'If you imagine that the missing girl is about to be—'

'I'm not talking about her,' Webb said sharply. 'I'm talking about the watching, laughing world. The watching world. Your newspapers, your photographers, your so-called psychic investigators – all feeding off us here like jackals feeding off a corpse, or pigs fighting at a trough. *Us*, Mister Merrit. Us. And we are powerless to alter the course of things. They make all sorts of easy promises to us and then they break those promises without a second's thought or an instant of regret or shame.' He paused. 'Well, things must change, we must regain something of what we have lost, of what has been taken from us these past few weeks.'

'If you believe—'

'And to that end I have called an extraordinary meeting of the full Town Council to discuss that very matter tomorrow evening.'

Merrit felt as though a hand had been placed firmly on his chest and he struggled for something to say. 'While the search for Agnes Foley still continues?' he said eventually.

Webb shook his head at the words. 'You believe it makes any difference whatsoever to any of this whether the girl is found or not?'

The remark shocked Merrit. 'Not to *you*, perhaps, but I imagine that out of respect for—'

Webb laughed at the word. 'Respect? For what? For whom? The imbecile's father? The imbecile herself?' Webb grew ever louder as he said all this, gesticulating to emphasize his words. The few others in the room turned to look at him.

He finally rose from his seat, slapping the envelope with his gloves before walking away. People stepped aside to let him go and then watched him as he left the hotel.

Nash returned to Merrit a moment later and put a drink in front of him. 'I heard most of it,' he said, smiling. 'We all did. It's how he operates. Perhaps you heard the silent applause of his audience.'

'Did you know about his report?' Merrit asked him.

'Not specifically. I might have guessed. You should be in no doubt that he will have passed his judgement on you.'

'It counts for nothing.'

'It counts for nothing where you live. Everything here, perhaps, but nothing there. And Webb knows that. So, please, understand that, and then act accordingly. This was always too big a thing to be completely ignored by the Magistrates Association. And as much as they – spurred on by Webb, no doubt – resent your intrusion on to their territory here, so the Chief Constable – not his assistant, note – will similarly resent *their* endless prodding and griping. He is no more likely to take action upon Webb's report than your own masters are to act on yours. It's all a closely woven mesh of obligation, protocol, nicety and need, and we are all caught within it – you, me, everyone – like so many gasping silvery fishes.'

Both men laughed at the words.

'So will you attend his Council meeting?' Merrit said.

'Of course. And hail him as loudly as the rest of them when he's had his say and is left breathless and panting and with the applause of the room ringing in his ears.' He signalled for the nearby clerk to bring them more drinks.

As the boy delivered these, one of the constables arrived at the hotel, saw Merrit and Nash and came to them.

Merrit's first thought was that Agnes Foley had been found and that the man had been sent to tell them this.

But the constable shook his head. 'Not yet,' he said. 'I was sent to tell you that there's nothing to report except that the searching has finished for the day.'

It had ended at least three hours ago, with the last of the autumn light. Merrit thanked the man and told him to go home.

'Will you go back to Foley?' Merrit asked Nash, guessing that Nash would not now remain at the hotel.

Nash considered this and then shook his head. 'To what end? He knows as well as Webb does what the future holds for him – for the pair of them – so why add to his misery?'

'Is that what you truly believe?' Merrit said. 'That Agnes will be forcibly removed from him and that he's already resigned himself to this happening?'

'Whatever happens – whether the girl is found or not, suffering, dead or alive, whether she confesses all or continues to follow, copy and endorse the others, whether she is allowed to stay with him for the next fifty years or is taken away from him tomorrow and made a complete stranger to him – whatever happens, do you see anything to embrace and take comfort from in *any* of those prospects?' Nash drained his glass and put it down on Webb's envelope. 'Perhaps you could add that little speech as an appendix to your own report,' he said. 'And as for this one – you already know what it says.'

And then he too rose and left Merrit alone where he sat.

It was only later, as Merrit sat in his room, Webb's report still unread beside him, that he realized that Nash had been right in what he'd suggested about the immutable ties which bound the place together, and that the ties which bound Nash and Webb to each other remained considerably stronger than those which he, Merrit, might now wish to believe connected *him* to Nash.

All night long, people came and went in the square below, creating an air of unsettled expectation in the place. People had been told to search their homes and gardens, their businesses and yards and allotments for the missing girl. Every empty factory, warehouse and store was opened and searched. Every raised voice, every noise, it now seemed, might herald news of her discovery.

Merrit fell asleep where he sat, and when he woke, hours later, he struggled briefly to remember everything that had just happened.

And remembering all of this, he realized too that he was no longer at the centre of things, no longer a controlling or directing force in the town. He no longer served any true or accepted purpose there. He was adrift and rudderless, and every hour he now drifted on this tide of uncertainty and powerlessness took him further from that centre towards the outer reaches, and with neither a sign of the shore behind him nor a reliable beacon to guide him back there.

He went to his bowl and doused himself with cold water to clear his mind of these convoluted and wayward thoughts. The room around him, like the world beyond, lay in complete darkness.

23

THE FOLLOWING MORNING, MERRIT LEFT THE HOTEL EARLY to join the crowd of searchers gathering in the square. There seemed to him to be more constables among the townspeople, imposing a greater degree of order on the proceedings than during the previous day's impromptu searching. One of these newcomers stood on a cart and addressed the crowd through a megaphone.

Crossing the square, Merrit saw Firth and another man coming towards him. Firth signalled to him, indicating a space behind the gathering crowd. Merrit altered his course and met the two men beneath the awning of an ironmonger.

The man with Firth was short, slightly built and elderly, at least seventy. At first he was reluctant to speak in Merrit's presence, but finally acceded to Firth's urging.

'Mr Jessup is a member of our church,' Firth said by way of introduction.

Jessup took off his hat and held it in both his hands over his stomach.

Merrit began to regret having been diverted from his course. He searched the square for signs of either Webb or Nash, but saw neither. He saw Stannard writing in his notebook, and close by him stood Pye, the two men clearly already acquainted, each man now serving the needs of the other. And watching them, even from that distance, Merrit saw how alike both men were, how well suited and perfectly shaped to their mutual dependency.

'One of the few,' Jessup said, drawing Merrit back to them.

'Sorry?'

'One of the few. Members of Minister Firth's congregation,' Jessup said.

Firth smiled awkwardly at this unthinking remark. 'Mr Jessup is a neighbour of Foley's,' he said.

Merrit paid greater attention to the man.

'He has something to tell you that might have some bearing on all this.' He waved his hand at the tightening crowd.

'You saw something?' Merrit said.

'The night them two others were round causing trouble.'

'Before Agnes Foley disappeared, the same night?'

'I live next door,' Jessup said. 'I heard everything they shouted in at her. Hellions, they were. Their stones struck my own door and walls. They were there for an hour. They would have stoned the girl and her father if either had been foolish enough to go out to them.'

'Did *you* go out to them?'

'I had my wife with me. She's not well. She was terrified. Told me to keep the curtains drawn and the door locked and bolted.'

Merrit guessed he was going to be told all that Foley had already told him.

'Language something shocking. You wouldn't believe they were only children.'

'Did you hear any of their threats?'

'Telling the girl what they were going to do to her when

275

they got their hands on her for all *she*'d already been doing and saying.'

'Such as?'

'All sorts. Warning her to keep her mouth shut.'

'Was there anything that might help us now?' Merrit half-turned in an effort to hear what the constable was saying to the crowd.

Jessup looked at Firth, as though he had disappointed him more than Merrit.

'Tell him about afterwards,' Firth said.

Merrit waited.

'After standing in the street, they went round to the back of the houses,' Jessup said. 'There's an alleyway there. They finished all their language and throwing at the front then went round the back.'

'And did they continue threatening the girl from there?'

Jessup shook his head. 'No, that was the funny thing. Wild as animals and loud as fishwives round at the front, but the minute they got into the alley, they just stood and waited without making a sound. Pitch black, it was, near enough, and coming on to rain, but I could still see them.'

'What were they waiting for?'

'The girl. She climbs out of her window. I've seen her do it many a time before. She leaves the house without her father knowing. It's an easy enough thing to do, not much of a drop.'

'Do you think the girls were somehow signalling to Agnes Foley to go out to them?' It seemed unlikely after all their previous behaviour.

'I don't know about that. I doubt it. Not after everything that had just happened. It seemed to me more like they were flushing a rabbit from its hole. All that commotion from one direction and then waiting for it to bolt the opposite way. But she's done that before.'

'Been made to run from them?'

'No. What you said – gone out *to* them.'

Merrit shared a glance with Firth, who put his hand on Jessup's shoulder.

'Last time I saw her do it,' Jessup said, 'all four of the little – all four of the others were out there waiting for her.'

'And on this occasion two nights ago, Mary Cowan and Margaret Seaton were definitely waiting for her, whether Agnes knew it or not?'

'That's what it looked like to me. She climbed down out of her bedroom and over the scullery roof, and then the Cowan girl lifted her to the ground. Agnes jumped and fell and the Cowan girl helped her to her feet. Then she held her hand.'

'And Margaret Seaton?'

'She took the child's other hand.'

'And Agnes didn't struggle, didn't try to get away from them?'

'It didn't look like it. Besides, they had a good hold on her. You know what she's like. She can scarcely carry a thought in her head from one minute to the next. If anything, I'd say she seemed pleased to see them there. Perhaps she didn't even put two and two together and realize that they were the same two who'd been at the front of the house only a few hours earlier.'

Merrit considered all this and knew it was a likely explanation if Agnes Foley had gone off willingly with them.

'You ought to go and tell the police what you saw,' he said to Jessup.

The constable with the megaphone was still addressing the crowd with his instructions about the day's search.

'He came to me instead,' Firth said absently.

'I've got my wife to consider,' Jessup said. 'She wouldn't want the police all over the house upsetting everything. Besides . . .' He looked at Firth and waited.

'He's anxious in case the girls heard of what he'd reported and then turned up again to hurl their insults at him and his wife,' Firth told Merrit.

'Insults and stones. It would likely kill her,' Jessup said.

'Then let *me* talk to them,' Merrit said. 'The police.'

Jessup bowed his head and silently acceded to this.

'Was that the last you saw of the three girls?' Merrit asked him.

Jessup thought about this. 'They went off together towards the railway.'

'Not up the hill into the woods?'

'The railway, or at least in that direction. They were both still holding her, one on either side. I watched them until they turned the corner.'

'You should have let her father know then what you'd seen,' Merrit said.

'I know what I *should* have done. But, like I say, I'd seen it all before. How was I to know she wouldn't come back later? She always did before. I've seen her climb back up to the window in the middle of the night and in the hours before dawn after being out with the others. She might not be right in the head, but she's as stealthy and as capable as a cat. There were times when I was watching her when it seemed to me that she hardly knew herself what she was doing.'

'I don't understand,' Merrit said, prompting the man to explain.

'Like she was sleepwalking, or exhausted beyond all understanding of what she was doing,' Jessup said.

'Is that possible?'

'You've seen her,' Jessup said. 'She's biddable. I doubt she thinks even once, let alone twice about most of what she does.'

'Or what she's told to do?'

'Especially that.'

'Mary Cowan and Margaret Seaton were in their beds all night, according to their parents,' Merrit said.

'Then either *they*'re lying, or the girls lied to them,' Jessup said. 'It was turned eight when the three of them left the alley and I lost sight of them.'

'Almost twelve hours before Agnes Foley was reported missing by her father.'

At the far side of the square, the constable had finished speaking and the crowd was on the point of dispersing. Seeing the man preparing to climb down from his platform, Merrit ran to him, calling for all the others to wait until he had spoken to him. Some stopped moving at hearing Merrit, but just as many ignored him and continued walking away.

Undeterred by this, Merrit told the constable everything Jessup had just told him.

'He never said anything to us,' the man said suspiciously when Merrit had finished. 'The other girls were never out in the woods, not according to them or their parents.'

'They were lying,' Merrit said. 'They were with her. They took her with them.'

'You're saying they helped her to run away?'

'I'm saying they led her away from her home. I'm saying

279

she was with them, that they somehow *persuaded* her to go with them.'

'Go with them where?' The man's continued scepticism was evident in everything he said. 'How do you mean, *persuaded* her? Are you saying they took her, *abducted* her?' He pronounced each of the word's syllables with an equal, cold and unbelieving emphasis, and it was clear to Merrit that what he resented the most was this muddying of the clear waters of the plan he had just outlined to the impatient searchers. Two other young constables came to stand beside him, and he repeated to them everything Merrit had just said.

Waiting until he'd finished, Merrit said, 'You have to go back to the two other girls and make them tell you where they took her, how far they went with her, in what direction, where they left her, what her intentions might have been.'

'Intentions? Her?'

'He's just given everybody instructions on where to search,' one of the newcomers said, indicating the man with the megaphone. 'We've told everybody that time is of the essence. If we hold things up while we go back to question the other girls, we might be hours getting started again. I don't know if you noticed, but there wasn't *that* much enthusiasm for all this. Besides, there's more rain forecast for this afternoon, and the day's short enough as it is.'

'If they tell you where they left her,' Merrit said, suppressing his exasperation at the man's reasoning, 'then you'll save everyone a lot of wasted time and effort.'

The three constables shared a glance.

'Telling us how to do our job now,' one of them said, his voice low.

'Our sergeant says he sat up most of the night quartering

off the woods for each party of searchers. Says there's a proper *method* to what's happening today. Not like—'

'Use your *initiative*,' Merrit said. 'At least talk to Jessup.'

'Who's Jessup?'

'The man who saw it all.' He pointed to where he had left Firth and Jessup, only to discover that they were no longer there. He searched the thinning crowd, but still couldn't see them.

'He can't be *that* convinced of what he saw if he can't even be bothered to tell *us*,' one of the constables said.

'Besides . . .' another added.

Merrit waited. 'What?'

'What you're telling us, what you're *implying* . . .'

Merrit guessed what was coming next.

'What you're implying is that these other two girls – two girls, incidentally, who have spent the past few weeks running rings around you and your inquiry – that they were more than just walking with the missing girl into the woods.'

Merrit understood that the wisest thing to do in the face of this veiled accusation would be to retreat and to allow the men to follow their prepared and apparently unchangeable plan. But knowing what was now at stake, he decided against this.

'It's a distinct possibility,' he said. 'Especially, as you suggest, after all that's just happened here. Surely—'

'After all you *say* has just happened here.' The man looked at the others for their support. 'In fact, *you*'re the one saying that there's not much happened here at all, that the girls are just making up stories to get themselves in the newspapers, and that everything got out of hand. That's what *you*'re saying.'

281

Merrit struggled to frame his response to this vague and contradictory-seeming accusation.

'Meaning you think they've done her some harm?' one of the others said before Merrit could speak. '*My* understanding was that the three of them were close friends, that all five of them were. It's what *you*'ve been telling us for the past few weeks. Thick as thieves, if you're to be believed. All in it together. And now you want us to believe that they've done her a mischief? Why? To shut her up? Nobody believes a word she says, anyway, so what would be the point? Not that she ever says much that makes any sense in the first place. Nobody even listens to the child. Even *you* wouldn't have her in your court. She's a simpleton. It's clear to everybody who's been keeping an eye on what's happening that she only ever repeats whatever tales the others tell her, that she hasn't got a notion or thought of her own in her head.'

The three men nodded together, clearly convinced of the new-found strength of their argument.

'Perhaps we should put it to the vote,' one of them said eventually, indicating the remnants of the watching crowd of searchers, some of whom were now calling to ask why they were being delayed.

The three men waited for Merrit to say something.

But Merrit remained silent, knowing that whatever appeal *he* might make would be dismissed in favour of the resumed search, that his argument would count for little against this other, practical plan of action.

'The two girls still lied to you,' he said to the constables.

'Just like they lied to *you* in your court,' one said. 'And I don't see you getting too over-agitated on *that* particular score.'

'Then *you* go and see them,' another said.

The demands of those near by became more insistent, and the constables turned their attention to the loudest among these, relieved to finally draw themselves away from Merrit.

Merrit looked around him, hopeful of at least spotting Firth, but again he saw nothing.

He waited where he stood for a few minutes longer, watching as the last of the crowd dispersed. He knew it would serve no purpose to approach either Mary Cowan or Margaret Seaton directly with what he knew. They had become adept liars and they would deny easily and convincingly everything he put to them. And then he in turn would be accused of harassment, of persecuting the girls out of his own sense of failure. What little remained of his authority in the matter no longer protected him, and he understood this as clearly and as forcibly as the smirking constables and the vanished crowd now understood it.

Finally returning to the hotel, he again saw Stannard, now in conversation with Webb, who was dressed as though about to engage in a day's shooting. Stannard was asking questions of the magistrate and making notes of Webb's answers in his notebook. Merrit diverted to avoid the pair of them, but Stannard saw him and called him over to them.

It was clear to Merrit that Webb resented his presence.

'I was just talking to the judge here,' Stannard said.

'Magistrate,' Webb said.

Stannard shrugged at the correction. 'Magistrate. I was just recording his thoughts on this unexpected turn of events. Do *you* believe that all your questioning of the girls – some might say "hounding" – has led the Foley girl' – he looked quickly at his pad – 'Agnes – has led poor little Agnes to do what she's done?'

'No one hounded her,' Merrit said. 'Is that what's being said?' He looked at Webb as he spoke.

'Not "said", exactly,' Stannard said. 'But I'm led to believe by certain remarks and inferences that something like this – the child running off – wasn't entirely unexpected in some quarters.'

'What does that mean?' Merrit said. Everything the man said was a clutch or a grope in the dark.

Stannard flicked back several pages with his finger, making it clear to Merrit that he was repeating something Webb had just said to him.

'Magistrate Webb is participating in the search for the missing girl,' he said. 'He believes that there may be tragic consequences, a tragic outcome to these events.'

'I said no such thing,' Webb said, but with little conviction.

'That there may be tragic consequences,' Stannard went on. 'And that those tragic consequences might afterwards not unreasonably be seen to be connected to all that has just taken place here under your auspices. In fact, it is his opinion that you may have overstepped the mark in your questioning of the girl.'

'I said no such thing,' Webb repeated.

'You concurred.'

'I concurred?'

'With my suggestion. You seemed quite emphatic – adamant, even – on the point.' Stannard flicked his notepad again.

'Agnes Foley was never brought to the courtroom,' Merrit said.

'My understanding is that you insisted on questioning her privately, off the record, so to speak.'

'I spoke to her father, that's all. I never once—'

'I merely expressed an opinion,' Webb said. 'What I made very clear – what I made *absolutely* clear – is that what matters now is that every effort be made to retrieve the unfortunate child and return her to her family. She must be found, comforted, and then returned to safety. Whatever the reasons for her taking this course of action, our priority now is to find her.'

But Stannard had stopped listening to him. 'Is that why you're here?' he said to Merrit. 'To join in the search?'

Merrit knew better than to reveal anything of what he'd just learned to the man. 'Of course,' he said. 'I searched all day yesterday.'

'Some might consider that you were perhaps in some way assuaging your own conscience,' Stannard said.

'I daresay some might.'

'And so you would deny categorically that your insistence on questioning this girl – knowing what you do about her – has had any part to play in this most recent turn of events?'

'Neither of the two youngest – Agnes Foley or Maud Venn – was questioned either publicly or privately,' Merrit said. He looked again at Webb. 'Despite demands from some on the panel to attempt to do so.'

Stannard also looked at Webb. 'Can you confirm this, Magistrate Webb?'

'I . . . it . . .'

'Or perhaps you'll insist on refuting the suggestion that the child should have been pushed even harder into revealing the facts behind the lies and malicious behaviour of all the girls?' Stannard put the tip of his pencil to his lips and waited for Webb to draw an answer from his confusion.

But, outmanoeuvred like this, and unhappy at the mockery of his own authority, Webb could think of nothing to say.

'You try my patience,' he said eventually, and then he turned and walked quickly away from them, almost marching as he went.

Stannard put away his notebook, said to Merrit, 'I try his patience,' and laughed.

24

WAITING UNTIL THE SQUARE HAD CLEARED COMPLETELY, Merrit then went in search of Nash to tell him what he'd just learned.

Nash met him at the door of his surgery, drawing him into the building and then looking along the street on either side.

'Are even *you* now reluctant to be seen with me?' Merrit said, expecting Nash to laugh and deny this.

But Nash said nothing, merely walking ahead of Merrit to the small room at the rear of the building, where a fire burned. The two men sat in front of this and Merrit told Nash of his encounter with Firth and Jessup.

But even after hearing all this, Nash showed little true interest or concern, and remained preoccupied with his own thoughts.

Finally, realizing that what he was relating was neither an entirely unexpected revelation nor a genuine surprise to either of them, Merrit stopped talking.

It took several moments for Nash to notice this, but finally he looked up at Merrit and took a folded sheet of paper from his pocket.

'It seems to be the morning for surprises,' he said.

Merrit took the paper, opened it and read it. It was a note, poorly written and misspelled:

The Seaton Girl is with Her CHILD and has Once already Tried to DESTROY it. She has NOT acommplish and I have turned her away. NOTHING of this is My Doing.

'Meaning what – that she's pregnant and has attempted to—'

'To destroy the unborn child, presumably,' Nash said. 'The note was pushed through my door only ten minutes before you arrived.'

Merrit read the message again, but it gave him no further clues.

'I know there are two women – two at least – who are known in the town to perform that kind of thing,' Nash said.

'Would they admit it to you?'

'If they did, I should be bound to inform the authorities.'

It wasn't clear to Merrit exactly what Nash meant by this. 'If you confronted them with the note, it would quickly be clear which of them she had been to see,' he said.

Nash grew angry at the suggestion. 'Meaning if I turned up at the door with *you* standing behind me? Of course I could find out. But our concern now ought to be with Margaret Seaton. If she's already attempted something by herself . . .'

'Might she be injured?'

'There are half a dozen common methods, all of which have their consequences.'

Merrit considered this. 'She didn't appear pregnant,' he said. 'And neither, if Jessup's story is to be believed, was she suffering sufficiently from any failed attempt to abort the

288

child to be unable to play her part in the abduction of Agnes Foley two nights ago.'

'Thirty-six hours,' Nash said. 'She's fourteen. She'd hardly show until much later in her term. Besides, no one would be looking.'

'Is all this connected to her story?' Merrit asked. 'The man who was supposedly in her room?'

It was clear to him that Nash had already given the sequence and timing of these events some thought.

'It would be a convenient fiction,' Nash said. 'Especially if people believed her.'

'And all I've done is imply – insist – that she was lying, depriving her of the excuse she was trying to concoct,' Merrit said.

'It would still have been a lie,' Nash told him.

'Even so . . .' Merrit said. He began to understand the consequences of what he might unwittingly have done to the girl, the corner into which he might now have pushed her.

Nash understood this too. 'However this happened – whoever is responsible – the outcome would have been the same. What would she have tried to insist on next – an immaculate conception?'

Neither man spoke for several minutes.

'What will you do?' Merrit said eventually.

'Go and see her. If she *has* injured herself, she may not be in the care of her parents, who may themselves still be wholly ignorant of all of this. *Something* must have happened, judging by the alarm sounded in the note, however self-serving.'

'Perhaps the abortionist was visited only *after* Seaton had accompanied Mary Cowan into the woods with Agnes Foley.

Perhaps Mary Cowan going with *her* afterwards was part of the arrangement.'

'All still speculation and guesswork,' Nash said. 'We should concern ourselves now with the practicalities of the matter.'

Just as the constables and the searchers were more concerned with the practicalities of their search, Merrit thought.

After a moment, he said, 'Might she be bleeding?'

'Very likely. Blood poisoning is high on the list of those consequences I mentioned.'

Only then did it occur to Merrit that there was one further consequence of all this to be considered. 'The police,' he said, uncertain what to add.

'They would certainly need to be informed,' Nash said.

'And the girl – and whoever she approached for help – prosecuted?'

'Along with Mary Cowan, who assisted her,' Nash said. 'If that's what you truly believe – that there was some reciprocal arrangement.'

And again Merrit felt the implications and the consequences of all this – and of his own part within it – like a double blow.

'Is it always a bloody procedure?' he asked.

Nash nodded. 'It's always a child, of sorts, always flesh and blood. Most have no idea of what's happening to them until it's properly a child and they feel it start to live inside them.'

'A child within a child,' Merrit said. 'And by which time—'

'By which time, the abortionists can raise their prices, and the embarrassed and disgraced families can make their arrangements. There are plenty of girls here who are mothers at sixteen and seventeen.'

'But fourteen?'

'The child would be born far away and then either be put

290

into an orphanage or conveniently become the girl's brother or sister.'

Nash rose from where he sat and started gathering together pieces of equipment, bottles and packages of medicine. He pulled open a drawer and then stopped abruptly.

'What is it?'

From the drawer, Nash took out the piece of dirty cloth the dog had found the previous day. He gave it to Merrit. Part of it had been cleaned, revealing a pale-blue material beneath the ingrained dirt.

'I checked again,' Nash said. 'The Wilson baby. In the description circulated by the police, it was wrapped in a pale-blue shawl. Wool.'

Merrit rubbed the material between his fingers, feeling the rotted fibres separate. 'Did you guess this yesterday?'

'I'm not sure.'

'The dog didn't uncover any bones,' Merrit said.

'No. Small mercies.'

'Perhaps you and I should return to the spot and search further.'

'Like I said,' Nash said, 'it's a morning for surprises.' He took the material back from Merrit and returned it to the drawer.

'It could be anything,' Merrit said. 'Dropped by anyone. It was close to the kilns. Perhaps one of the burners or their wives or children dropped it.'

'Perhaps,' Nash said. He fastened the heavy clasp on his case.

Something else then occurred to Merrit. 'If all this – the note, its writer, the girl – if all this ever comes to light and you are accused of *not* immediately informing the authorities, then—'

'I know all that,' Nash said angrily. 'So are you suggesting that I should do nothing except pass it on and step back? Or perhaps I should wait until the unconscious, feverish and bleeding girl is finally found somewhere and brought to me, or wait until I'm called for to determine the cause of death by her ignorant parents, and that *then* I might confess or play my part in all of this?' He paused, breathing deeply. 'The note was delivered to me, not to you, and certainly not to your court. Whatever else you might have stirred up here, Margaret Seaton would still have been pregnant, the story still concocted, and the baby still growing inside her. The woman would still have been an abortionist and I would still have been a doctor.'

'I was only suggesting—'

'I know what you were only suggesting.' Nash signalled his apology to Merrit. 'Unfortunately, I live in a world where the privilege of true choice is in very limited supply, and available only to those who can afford it.'

'To people like me, you mean,' Merrit said.

'To people like you, yes,' Nash said.

'I shall have to rewrite my report on the girl and the incident in her bedroom,' Merrit said.

'Naturally,' Nash said. 'Wasted hours and days. An elaborate and filigree fancy reduced to a solitary drop of dirty, leaden fact.'

'The same might yet be said of *all* their tales and concoctions.'

'I know,' Nash said.

Again, neither man spoke for a moment, and then Merrit said, 'Why the Devil, do you think?'

Nash considered his answer before speaking. 'Because

in the end, any kind of fantasy is no more or less than that – a fantasy – and until it is exposed or confessed, the more outlandish and more carefully cultivated fantasy will always exert a greater pull and confer a greater power on the fantasist than a lesser, quotidian and more easily exposed one.'

'I suppose so,' Merrit said, knowing that their short time together was almost over, and that whatever their individual expectations of their endeavours, the outcome had disappointed them both equally.

'And when Agnes Foley is eventually found . . .' Nash said, interrupting Merrit from these thoughts.

'She'll point to Cowan and Seaton as her abductors?' Merrit said. 'By which time, Margaret Seaton's condition will have come to light. And then after that, perhaps even Edith Lisset and Maud Venn will see they have nothing left to either fear or lose and point their own accusing fingers.'

'Perhaps,' Nash said, turning away from him as he spoke.

'She will *be* found,' Merrit said. 'Agnes Foley.'

'Of course she will. Safe and well and soon, God willing.'

It had now been over twenty-four hours since the girl had been discovered missing, and perhaps half as long again since she had gone with Mary Cowan and Margaret Seaton away from her home.

'Webb seemed convinced that now that *he* was participating in the search for her, the child would be found by him personally,' Merrit said. 'Safe from harm, curled up asleep on a bed of sticks and leaves, and that she would then be carried rejoicing on his own broad shoulders back to her grateful father.'

'I can picture it now,' Nash said, and the two men shared a smile.

'I do understand what you're suggesting,' Merrit said. 'And I share your concerns.'

'I know. And Webb, without the grateful, happy child to parade home, would insist just as forcibly on picking up her limp and weightless corpse and carrying that, too, back along the same unhappy course with all the other searchers following in a silent procession behind him. Either way, he would be at the centre of things and making sure that everyone saw him there.'

'Whereas *I* shall be damned whatever the outcome,' Merrit said.

'Hardly that. Other accusing fingers will be pointed at you soon enough as the *cause* of all this distress and upset, but after that you'll be quickly forgotten.' Unwilling to continue this speculation, Nash patted his case. 'I ought to go.'

Merrit went with him to the door and then the two of them walked together back to the empty square.

'Perhaps you should take the piece of cloth to the police and tell them what you believe,' Merrit suggested.

'Not while all this is happening. It would only be considered an unwelcome diversion. Besides, even if the remains of the baby *were* to be found, what then? What would that prove? Nothing.'

The two men finally parted at the court door. The entrance was open, but the usually busy building was now deserted and silent.

'Will you let me know what you find?' Merrit asked Nash. 'Concerning Margaret Seaton.'

Nash agreed to this. 'Nothing I find will connect Mary

Cowan in any way to what's happening to the girl,' he said.

'I know that,' Merrit said. 'But perhaps the seriousness of what's now happening to Margaret might persuade *her* to reveal or confess something to me.'

'I think the time for confession is over,' Nash said, indicating the empty building behind them. 'Besides, whatever condition—'

They were interrupted by someone calling to Merrit, and both men turned to see Firth coming across the square to them, waving as he walked.

Nash left immediately. He raised a hand to Firth, but neither paused nor turned as the man arrived at the court.

Firth watched him go, waiting for an explanation from Merrit, which did not come.

'I'm finally holding a service,' Firth said eventually, unable to suppress the rising note of excitement in his voice.

'A service?'

'For the missing girl. In the hope that the Almighty, in His all-seeing wisdom, might direct our searching and return her to us. I have already tried to persuade her father – with some success, I believe – that the Lord has been watching over his lost daughter during her short absence, and that He has been doing everything in His power to ensure her well-being and safe return. If I—'

'It wouldn't be too much to ask, would it?' Merrit said, interrupting the man. He wondered if Firth had forgotten completely everything Jessup had revealed to them only two hours earlier.

'Sorry, I don't—'

'God – your God – and a small, imbecilic child,' Merrit said. 'It wouldn't take too much of an effort on *His* behalf, would it, to do all of those things? Perhaps if *He* forgot about the rest of us for a minute or two and concentrated all *His* energies on the girl.'

Finally understanding what Merrit was saying, Firth fell silent.

Merrit turned away from the man to look back at the empty court. 'I should go in,' he said. 'Loose ends.'

Firth smiled at the words. 'And you consider those loose ends – all this order and neatness and understanding that you insist on imposing on the world – you consider what little you have left to achieve in *there* to be of greater importance than the safe return of a lost child?'

It was the first time Merrit had heard the man talk like this. 'I didn't mean to be disrespectful,' he said.

'Of course you didn't,' Firth said.

'When is your service?'

But Firth was unwilling to say any more. He was even reluctant to be close to Merrit, and he took several paces away from him.

'I'll come,' Merrit said.

'Or perhaps you may be otherwise engaged,' Firth said. 'We must all seem such an unnecessary and profitless burden to you now that so little has been achieved here.'

There was nothing more Merrit could say to the man, and so he left him and went into the court, passing through the various corridors and ante-rooms to the chamber itself, where he sat in his chair and slammed his palms hard on the table in front of him, listening to the echo as the sound rang all around him like the slamming of distant doors into other empty rooms.

25

MERRIT WAS STILL IN THERE AN HOUR LATER WHEN HE WAS distracted from his work by a noise towards the rear of the room.

He looked up and saw Mary Cowan standing by the door and looking directly at him. She stood with her hands on the back of a chair, rocking it slightly and making the tapping sound which had alerted him to her presence.

Merrit's first thought was to wonder how long she'd been there, watching him as he'd worked; watching as he'd tried to pull back together all these rapidly unravelling and disintegrating threads. His second instinct was to check that she was alone in the room, that neither Margaret Seaton nor her father was with her or near by. But he knew by the way she stood and looked at him, by the sly and confident grin on her face, that this was unlikely.

He gathered up the papers in front of him and slid them into a folder and then his case. Always this tidying up, this closing away of raw and restless history.

When this was done, he looked back at her. She had come silently forward and now stood closer to the front of the room.

'What do you want?' he said sharply. He knew that even to suggest to her that he knew anything of her recent involvement with either Agnes Foley or Margaret Seaton would be to deny himself whatever small advantage he might still possess over her.

Moving a few paces closer, the girl mumbled something he did not hear. He knew that this was done deliberately – to force him to ask her to repeat what she'd said, whereupon her words would acquire a greater potency for having first been demanded and then being shouted at him.

Instead, he said, 'No one's listening. And certainly not to you. Not any more. They're all tired of your lies and your scheming. *I*'m tired of your lies and your scheming.'

She broadened her smile at hearing this. 'Oh?' she said.

'I imagine even *you* must be a little disappointed at how everything has turned out here,' he said to her. 'Particularly now that you're no longer at the centre of everyone's attention. Now that no one is prepared to listen to you any longer.'

'*You* still came,' she said. 'You still . . . all this . . .'

'I had no choice: I was sent. Your allegations saw to that. And I won't be the only one who wishes that everything you and the others concocted among yourselves had been either ignored or seen from the very beginning for what it truly was.'

'And what's that, then?'

But again Merrit refused to be drawn.

The girl folded her arms across her chest and looked around her at the empty room. 'They all still came to see and to have their say,' she said. 'Two hundred empty places, two hundred muted voices. 'At least I was—'

'No one cares what you *were*,' Merrit shouted at her. 'It's what happens now that is of concern to me.'

She looked up at the remark and all it might suggest, and for the instant that their eyes met, Merrit was convinced that she understood his concerns exactly. He considered telling her that Nash was at that very moment with Margaret Seaton and her parents. He considered repeating to her everything Jessup had told him about Agnes Foley's abduction. But he said nothing.

'I was—' she began again.

'And *this* is what you are now.' Merrit slapped his palm on the bulging files. 'A pile of stories and lies going round and round and round and finally disappearing into nothing. Your moment's passed.'

Mary Cowan considered all this and then shrugged.

'So what do *you* think happens now?' she said. She dropped her smile and pursed her lips, affecting disappointment. It was all still an act, still a provocation. She raised her folded arms slightly, causing her small breasts to appear more prominently at the open neck of her blouse.

'I didn't see you behaving like this when your father was looking over your shoulder,' Merrit said to her.

'Him?' She was caught momentarily off guard by the remark.

'Where is he?' Merrit said. 'Outside? Waiting for you? Waiting to hear what this pathetic little encounter throws up? Waiting for another ridiculous story to sell to the newspapers? Waiting to provide you with yet another alibi?'

She came even closer to him and sat down.

'Alibi?' she said. 'For what?'

When he refused to answer her, she said, 'We were all out looking for poor little Agnes earlier. Everybody was. Everybody who cares. *Her* father must be going mad with worry. Not knowing what might have happened to her – her being what she is, and everything.'

'Perhaps the Devil finally came back and this time took her off with him,' Merrit said.

She laughed at this, raising her feet on to the bench in front of her and causing the material of her skirt to rise over her knees. 'It's possible,' she said. 'All sorts of things happen in those woods. You'd only have to ask Margaret Seaton about that.'

'Meaning what?' Merrit said.

She waited before answering him. 'Meaning all *sorts* of things happen there.'

'Have you spoken to her recently?'

'Poor little wandering Agnes?'

'Margaret Seaton.'

'I might have. Why? Changing her story, is she? I don't think she's likely to do that, not now.'

And in that instant, Merrit was convinced that even as a younger child, Mary Cowan would have been more than capable of having killed the Wilson baby and then of protesting her innocence, whatever the suffering and cost to the mother.

'I imagine Margaret Seaton might have other, more pressing concerns than worrying about getting her own lies straight,' Merrit said, watching her closely while feigning indifference. And it occurred to him only then that this might be the purpose of her presence there now – to determine how much he already knew about the girl's pregnancy and her failed attempt at an abortion.

'I don't know what you're talking about,' she said. She licked her thumb and then rubbed at a mark high on her thigh.

'Don't do that,' Merrit said, regretting the words immediately.

The girl went on rubbing. 'The court isn't on – sitting,' she said. 'You can't tell me what to do and what not to do.'

Footsteps sounded in the corridor outside and they both waited in silence as these passed by.

'Why are you here?' Merrit asked her eventually.

The girl shrugged. 'To say goodbye? To let you know what a waste of time it was you coming here?'

'If I hadn't come here, then—'

'If you hadn't come here,' she shouted at him, 'then none of this would have happened. Everything would have ended, been sorted out and then soon forgotten.' It was a greater admission than she had intended, and she fell abruptly silent.

Merrit resisted responding to this outburst.

'You think you know everything,' she said, her voice lower.

'And is that what this little visit is about – to prove to me that *I* don't, but that *you* do?' It occurred to him that she might have been watching him earlier in the square, with Firth and then Webb, that she might even have followed him to Nash's, afterwards waiting until the crowd had dispersed, and knowing that he was alone in the court.

'I do know more than you do,' she said. It seemed another childish and telling boast, something else she could not resist saying.

'I don't doubt that,' Merrit said. 'But you're still only brave enough to say it when no one else is looking on or listening. Go and fetch your father or Margaret Seaton and let *them* listen to you without telling you to shut up.'

'What's *she* going to—' She stopped herself from saying more.

'Or perhaps you don't know where she is,' Merrit said. 'Perhaps she's out in the woods again helping in the search for Agnes Foley. Where's she looking, I wonder?' It was as much as he dared say.

'Who cares where anybody's looking?' she said. 'She's an imbecile. She should never have been here in the first place. Who's going to miss that idiot walking round and making everybody feel uncomfortable?'

'And would that include you?' Merrit said.

She smiled again. 'She wouldn't have told you anything,' she said. 'And besides, whatever she *did* say, nobody would have believed her. Questioning a lunatic? No wonder everybody was careful to keep their distance from you.'

'It was never my intention—'

'She's wandered off, that's all. She does it all the time. Except her father won't actually say that because it would mean he wasn't looking after her properly. Do you honestly think she gives a second's thought to any of the things she does?' She paused. 'Besides, you're only concerned now because her going off like that has interrupted all this.' She waved a hand around the empty room.

'Not really,' Merrit said. 'Everyone who wanted to tell me anything has long since had the opportunity to say it.'

'To tell you things about me?' She was unable to conceal her pleasure at this.

'About all of you.'

'I already know what people think about me,' she said. 'And I don't care.'

Had she been emboldened all those years ago by having been exonerated of killing the Wilson baby? Did she believe herself to be invincible? Were the buried baby and the tale of the appearance of the Devil in those same woods the beginning and the end of the same terrible story in which she constantly lived? Was the contrivance of the Devil – of all these associated tales – her way of bringing that endless fiction to a close? Was that all? Had a door been about to be gently and silently closed, and had *he* then appeared and then pushed at that same door until the whole country had heard its closing? Was that it? Was that all?

'You went to Nash's,' she said unexpectedly, drawing him back from these thoughts and confirming what Merrit had guessed about her spying on him earlier.

'*Doctor* Nash's,' he said, still struggling to clear his mind.

'So is someone ill?' She watched him closely.

'It's what doctors do – cure the sick and the suffering,' he said. 'Among other things.'

'Sick in the head, you mean, like poor little Agnes Foley? What doctor's ever going to cure her?'

'You didn't seem too concerned about her when you made her do your bidding,' Merrit said.

'Do my bidding?'

'You understand me well enough,' he said.

'And what about Edith Lisset and her vicious, plate-smashing ghost? Is Doctor Nash going to cure her, too?'

'She cuts herself,' Merrit said. 'It's a simple enough thing to treat. It gains her attention and sympathy, that's all. Attention, sympathy and pity.'

'And you think that's *all* it is?' she said. 'You don't think it's . . .' She pressed a hand into the material between her legs and laughed.

Then she rose from where she sat and came even closer to the table, standing immediately beneath Merrit and resting her hands on the table's edge.

'They *will* find her,' he said.

'So?'

'Everything that gets lost or hidden out there, one day gets found.'

'So?' She looked at the scattered items on the table. 'You even went to see that baby, Maud Venn,' she said. 'You and Nash. She sick too, is she?'

You're all sick, he wanted to shout at her.

'The talk here is that they're going to move away, the Venns. They never fitted in. Best thing all round if they just went and forgot about everything that's happened.'

This was news to Merrit, but no surprise.

She continued to look over the table. Where pieces of writing lay exposed, Merrit covered these.

'What if I screamed?' she said.

'What?' He wondered if he'd heard her correctly.

'If I screamed. Here. Now. What if I screamed as loud as I could? What if I screamed, pulled my blouse off and then threw myself down on to the floor, scattering these papers and files all around me? What if I screamed, begging you to get off me, not to hit me again, struggling on the bare boards to escape from you? I'd bruise myself and cut myself to pieces on that floor.'

Merrit struggled to retain his composure at the suggestion.

'And supposing I'd just done it instead of talking about it, telling you?' she said.

'No one would believe you,' he said, but the words dried in his mouth.

'Shall we see?' She took a step back from the desk and then watched him as he pulled more papers close to him. She laughed at this and held up her palms to him. 'Which way should I throw myself, do you think?' She looked at the floor around her. 'Perhaps I could slap my own face a few times, something to bring on the bruising and tears you'd caused me. Perhaps I'm no different from Edith Lisset and all her cutting.' She formed her hands into fists and pretended to thump her chest. Then she slapped herself gently on her cheek.

Merrit could not bring himself to speak while all this was happening, knowing that whatever he said might provoke her into doing what she'd threatened.

'Are you not going to say something?' she said. 'Are you not going to tell me how ridiculous I'm being? I see Minister Firth's having a service to pray for the safe return of the idiot. Perhaps you want to tell me to go to that, to stand up in front of everybody who's secretly thanking God that it isn't their own child who's missing, and then for me to beg for their forgiveness for all I'm supposed to have done.'

She continued gently slapping herself as she said all this, and the action seemed to Merrit like the ticking of a bomb.

There were further footsteps in the corridor outside, and for a moment he considered shouting to whoever might be there to come in to them. But that might also trigger the girl's threats, and all she would need would be a few seconds to throw herself to the floor and start screaming. It was all anyone coming into the room would see and hear; his own explanation would count for nothing.

She, too, heard the footsteps and turned to the door.

'Are you going to shout for help?' she said, smiling at him. 'You could tell them that *I* attacked *you*. That I confessed everything I'd done and then threw myself at you when you told me I needed to be punished. Perhaps you could tell them that you were about to administer that punishment yourself,

305

here, now, while the two of us were alone together. You could even tell them I'd agreed to it – anything so long as the police weren't involved.'

'They'd know I was being ridiculous,' Merrit said.

'Not if I said the same thing. I could tell them that I was happy for you to punish me. I could tell them that you'd made me see the error of my ways and that I knew I deserved to be punished, that I *wanted* to be punished. Anything to bring an end to all this.'

And again he saw how skilfully she had outmanoeuvred him. She laid her small traps for him and he walked into them. And when he did this, she either laughed at him or applauded him. And then she led him to the next.

The footsteps in the corridor had receded by now.

'Too late,' she said. Then she surprised him by walking away from the table and sitting down again.

Merrit sensed that a crisis had passed, that whatever she was there to prove to herself, she had accomplished.

She raised and lowered her legs, and then she yawned and stretched her arms before resting her hands on either side of her.

'Perhaps you should just go,' Merrit said to her.

'Meaning I should never have come here in the first place? The rest of them will be back soon, all the searchers.'

'With Agnes Foley, I hope.' He watched for her response, and just as it seemed she was about to speak to him, there was the sound of running footsteps in the corridor outside, followed by the voices of several people calling his name.

Mary Cowan seemed not to notice this; or if she did, then she behaved as though it were of no consequence whatsoever to her.

There were other running feet, other raised voices, and the hitherto silent and empty building seemed suddenly to be filled with an air of alarm and urgency.

Merrit rose from where he sat, and as he did so the door was pushed open by one of the constables he'd spoken to earlier. The man was panting, unable to speak, and he leaned forward with his hands on his knees to catch his breath.

Merrit waited. Directly in front of him, Mary Cowan never once took her eyes from him, never once turned to look behind her at the cause of all this sudden commotion.

Eventually straightening, the constable saw Merrit and the girl together, and he watched them for a moment, sucking in air and puffing out his cheeks before finally regaining his composure and motioning for Merrit to go to him.

26

'THEY'VE FOUND THE MISSING GIRL,' THE MAN SAID. 'NASH told me to come for you.'

'He was searching?'

'On his way back from the Seatons' house.'

At this mention of the Seatons, Mary Cowan finally turned to the constable.

'And the girl herself?' Merrit said.

The man shook his head and then tilted it to one side before holding up an invisible rope.

'What, man?' They were at cross-purposes. Merrit had asked him about Margaret Seaton's condition.

'Hanged herself,' the constable said.

'Margaret Seaton?'

'What? No – the Foley girl. Hanged herself in the Skene tunnel.'

'I don't – what tunnel?' Merrit struggled to grasp what he was being told.

'The Skene cutting. Railway tunnel a mile south. We only just got round to walking through it on account of the trains. Half a mile long. Unlit. They've stopped the trains at either end. Sending them through at a crawl while we're looking.' He became exasperated at Merrit's lack of understanding.

'And is Nash still with her?' Merrit said. He remembered the tunnel from his night with Stannard at the station.

'For what good it'll do her,' the constable said. 'He said for you to go to him. He said to tell you, and then to make sure her father stays where he is. Said to send Minister Firth to him.' He stood watching Merrit intently, as though waiting for all these instructions to be either confirmed or acted upon.

But instead, Merrit looked back at Mary Cowan. Her concern at the mention of Margaret Seaton had given way to a lack of interest in all that had then been revealed about Agnes Foley.

She knows, he thought. *She already knows.*

The girl now avoided looking at either man.

'What shall I do?' the constable said. 'About her father, the minister?'

'Do exactly what Nash told you to do,' Merrit told him.

'By rights, I should report back to my sergeant,' the man said. 'I told him yesterday we should have searched the tunnel sooner. If we'd been allowed in there yesterday, then the chances are *I* would have been the one who found her.' He was clearly disappointed at having been denied this opportunity.

Mary Cowan locked her fingers together and then clasped her hands over her knees.

'Where will she be taken?' Merrit said.

'Taken? Who?'

'Agnes Foley. Where is she being taken?' It seemed as though everything he now said to the man was being deliberately misunderstood by him.

'Taken?' The constable wiped his face with his sleeve. 'She's dead. Nobody's taking her anywhere. At least not yet. Nash said for you to be sent for. You're the one in charge here.'

'Not of this, I'm not,' Merrit said.

The constable shook his head at the denial. 'Took me ten minutes to get here,' he said. 'Ran.' He studied the stain on his sleeve. 'There's a police medal in this for somebody. Hanged herself. Poor bloody mite. Who would have thought it? Still, with her being' – he spun a finger at his temple – 'and everything, it was always on the cards, I suppose. This, something . . .'

It's why she came here, Merrit thought, watching Mary Cowan. *That same ridiculous game in which she always insists on remaining ahead. She knew the searchers were going into the tunnel, she must have done.*

But whatever he believed, or wanted to believe, he knew he could suggest nothing of these suspicions to the constable. And so to remove himself from all temptation of this, he told the man to lead the way back to Nash and the tunnel.

As the two of them went, he looked again at Mary Cowan where she still sat.

The girl looked back at him and held his gaze. 'What shall *I* do?' she said. 'Are you leaving me here all alone?'

He refused to answer her.

'She can't stay unattended in the court,' the constable said. He indicated the table and its scattered papers.

'Get out,' Merrit said to her. 'Now. Go.'

The constable was surprised by the harshness of this command. 'She'd be best off at home until all this is over and done with,' he said.

Now he, too, would be part of her alibi.

'I don't care where she goes,' Merrit said. He grabbed Mary Cowan by her arm and pulled her to her feet.

The girl made no protest at this rough treatment, merely

smiling at Merrit as their faces came close, and then whispering, 'Whatever you say,' to him.

He released his hold on her and she smoothed her sleeves and the front of her blouse and then walked slowly ahead of them out of the room.

Outside, in the corridor, the constable called for a clerk to lock the door and for him then to call on Minister Firth to go to Agnes Foley's father.

Merrit waited for the two men to finish talking, watching Mary Cowan as she continued at the same slow, measured pace along the corridor towards the street. The place was bathed in late-afternoon sunlight, shining yellow on the tiled floor and wall, and she seemed to fade and then reappear as she passed through the blocks of dusty light. Before leaving, she turned and looked directly back at Merrit. She raised her hand to him, waiting, smiling again, and again confident – or so it seemed to Merrit – of the role she would play and the tales she would tell in the days ahead as the events of the past few days overtook all that had recently happened there.

But Merrit made no gesture in return, and so after a moment of waiting like this, the girl turned her back on him and continued at the same slow pace through the thickening light.

'Just go,' Merrit said beneath his breath. 'Just go.'

The constable returned to him and the two of them left the building together.

Outside, Mary Cowan was nowhere to be seen, but there were others, including some dismissed searchers, already gathering in the square, and these men and women paused in their excited conversations as Merrit and the constable passed through them. Merrit acknowledged those he recognized, but few did anything other than nod silently or bow their heads and then turn away from him at his approach.

Leaving the centre of the town, the constable led the way to the railway crossing on the lane running from the rear of Agnes Foley's home. Descending to the track, he pointed to the right, and then led Merrit along the sleepers towards the distant walled embankment.

The tunnel entrance stood a few hundred yards further on, hidden from the crossing by the gentle curve of the rails. Men stood at the side of the track and rested on the steep enclosing slopes. A brazier had been lit and some congregated around this. Merrit could already hear barking dogs, their excited noise amplified by the tunnel.

Approaching the stone arch, and seeing the great height of the wall above him, Merrit felt suddenly reluctant to enter. Lamps had been lit along the line of the track, and others burned from hooks in the curved brick roof. There were more men here, and they came and went from the darkness swinging their own lights.

He searched for Nash, but couldn't see him. The police sergeant was shouting orders to his gathered constables. He paused at Merrit's appearance and came to him.

'Doctor Nash is still inside,' he said to him. 'It's definitely her. He wanted you to see her before we started dismantling.'

'Dismantling?'

'The scene. It's the phrase. Before we take her down. The railway company is anxious to get the trains moving properly again. Some of the newspaper photographers have already tried to get in there.' And as he said this, both Stannard and his photographer were manhandled from the blackness of the tunnel. Stannard saw Merrit, and upon his release he came to him.

The sergeant warned the two men not to try and enter the tunnel again and then returned to his constables.

'Bad affair,' Stannard said to Merrit.

'What do you want me to say to you?'

'A few words would be useful. How far, for instance, do you account for what's happened in there with regard to your own work here?' Another of the man's airless, self-fulfilling questions.

'I don't,' Merrit said.

The photographer wandered away from them, adjusting his equipment as he went, and it occurred to Merrit that he might already have secretly taken a photograph of the dead girl and now be protecting this.

'A bit disingenuous,' Stannard said. 'Or is that my headline – "OUTRIGHT DENIAL BY CHIEF PROSECUTOR"?' He lit a cigarette and drew hard on it.

Merrit smiled at the empty threat. 'I was never that,' he said.

'It hardly matters to my eager readers. All *they*'ll want to know about is why that poor, suffering, innocent child was driven to do something like this.'

'Have you seen her?' Merrit said.

Stannard hesitated before nodding. 'We were on the tracks when the call came. She might have been – you know – but she was smart enough to take herself as close to the middle of the tunnel as she could get before . . .' He blew smoke over Merrit's shoulder. 'So, do you accept no responsibility whatsoever for her death?'

Merrit said nothing.

313

'There aren't many here who don't see at least *some* connection between recent events and what's just happened,' Stannard said.

'The same people, presumably, who were only too happy to pour out their own angry complaints against the girls, including Agnes Foley, to you?' Merrit said. 'The same people who were happy to indulge themselves in all their talk of the Devil and poltergeists and demons in the night for their own excited amusement? The same people calling for at least some kind of punishment or redress now?'

Before Stannard could respond to any of this, Merrit pushed past him and followed the rails into the tunnel. Men passed him in the opposite direction, but few recognized him in the gloom and then the growing darkness.

After walking for a few minutes, he saw a group of men ahead of him, visible in the cluster of their lights. He called to them. Lanterns were raised, and some of the lights moved along the track towards him. Then Nash called out to him, and Merrit, relieved that Nash was still there, continued walking.

Nash finally emerged from amid the others and gave Merrit a lantern.

'Where is she?'

Nash nodded over his shoulder. 'In one of the recesses.' These were set into the brick wall at regular intervals, intended for the protection of men working in the tunnel when a train passed through.

'She's high up,' Nash said, his voice a whisper. Every sound was amplified and made sharper in the confined space.

'I don't—'

'High up. She's hanging from a lantern hook seven feet off

the ground and with nothing beneath her to suggest how she might have climbed up there.'

It was clear to Merrit that Nash shared his own suspicions.

'Has anything been said?' Merrit asked him.

'By the police? Not yet. It's why I wanted you to see her where she was. I persuaded them to wait.'

'In the hope that I might take on some responsibility for whatever happens next?'

This response disappointed Nash, and he shook his head. 'I just wanted you to see her,' he said. 'That's all. It seemed fitting.'

'After all I've set in motion here, you mean?'

This time, Merrit's answer angered Nash and he turned sharply away from him and walked back to the others.

Merrit picked up the lantern and followed him.

The nearby men dispersed at their approach, and most of them crossed the rails to avoid Merrit.

'She's here,' Nash said, raising his lamp to reveal the girl hanging in the recessed brick alcove.

Agnes Foley's face was level with Nash's own, her bare feet at his waist. He stepped aside to afford Merrit a closer look at her.

The girl's arms and legs hung limp and straight. Mercifully, her head was bowed, revealing only her long hair, which covered her face and hung to her waist. Her nightdress was wet and blackened. Water dripped all around her, seeping through from the earth above. And there had been trains through the tunnel, filling it with their soaking steam and soot-filled smoke. To Merrit, the brick wall looked like the wall of a tomb in which the girl had been stood upright like the small statue of a saint in its enclosing niche.

She even looked carved in stone because of the smoke's discoloration, and because of the dripping water which had added its own glistening sheen to the hanging corpse. Every line and curve and angle of her small body was clearly outlined beneath the thin, near-transparent material of her nightdress.

'I'm sorry,' Merrit said. 'My remarks.' He looked closer at the rope around Agnes Foley's neck.

'It's heavy-duty,' Nash said. 'God knows where it came from or where she might have found it.'

'You don't believe that,' Merrit said quietly, but received no answer.

Nash came to stand close behind him.

'Mary Cowan turned up in the courtroom,' Merrit said.

'To what end?'

'To gloat. To exercise the last of her power and to impress upon me yet again the true and exact nature of my own particular brand of powerlessness here.'

Nash shook his head at hearing this. 'Does Agnes's father know yet?'

Merrit was uncertain. 'I imagine everyone in the place knows by now,' he said. He moved closer to the hanged girl and took her hand in his own. 'How long has she been here?' he said. It was beyond him to lift her chin, or to push the wet hair from her face with his fingers.

'Difficult to say,' Nash said. 'The tunnel's warm, the steam . . .' adding suddenly, 'Margaret Seaton's parents refused to let me see her.'

'What did you say to them?'

'What *could* I say?'

'But you think they knew?'

'Her mother was wringing her hands and crying all the time I was there. Her father blocked the entrance to the stairs.'

'I see,' Merrit said.

'We all *see*,' Nash shouted. 'We all *see*.'

Merrit waited in silence for a moment, until Nash's words had completed their fractured, reverberating passage out of the tunnel, sounding to Merrit like nothing more than the frantic flapping panic of a trapped bird.

Eventually, he released the girl's hand and stepped back from her.

'I considered sending another constable,' Nash said. 'For Firth and Webb to come here.'

'Did you want Firth to say a prayer?'

'Something,' Nash said. 'I suppose, above all else, I just wanted *them* to see, too. You know how people feel about suicides.'

'Perhaps Firth feels the same,' Merrit said. It was a terrible suggestion to make – as terrible as the realization of what both Agnes Foley and her father would be denied by the manner of her death. In addition to which, the last thing the place would want or tolerate now would be a second inquiry so soon after the last.

'Perhaps,' Nash said.

Waiting a moment longer, and imagining they were both now saying their own silent prayers for the dead girl, Merrit went back to Agnes Foley and lifted her by her legs so that she fell limply against his chest and shoulder, and so that the rope above her slackened on its hook. Nash came to help him, swinging the rope free and then untying its simple knot so that the girl could be lowered to the ground and laid amid the scattered lanterns there.

Merrit set her down gently, drawing together her thin legs and then crossing her arms on her chest. He finally took the rope from around her neck and threw it away from them.

'It may be evidence,' Nash said.

'I know.'

There was a broad, dark bruise across Agnes Foley's throat, and Merrit rearranged her hair to hide this.

'What are you doing?' Nash asked him.

'I just thought . . .' Merrit continued, wiping the girl's face with his fingers, revealing the pale flesh beneath the wetness.

Across the tracks, the watching men bowed their heads and began murmuring their own low prayers for the dead girl.

Finally, Merrit rose from the ground, and Nash knelt and took his place there, lifting Agnes Foley into his arms, standing slowly and then motioning for Merrit to pull the girl's nightdress straight and to lay her arms against her sides.

Nash balanced the girl against his chest, settling her head into the soft fold of his arm. Water dripped from her fingers and her feet, and ran from her hair across her face and neck like tears.

Then Nash left the side of the tunnel and walked along the centre of the tracks. The praying men fell silent at his approach, and then walked ahead of him towards the tunnel entrance, the yellow light from their lanterns swaying and shifting over the curve of the brickwork like the vaporous flames of a rising fire.

Approaching the entrance, Nash paused briefly and then straightened his arms, raising Agnes Foley higher across his chest. One of the girl's arms fell loose and Nash waited as Merrit laid this back in place.

Ahead of them, alerted by the lantern carriers, all those still gathered at the embankment fell silent and then arranged themselves into parallel rows as Merrit and Nash and their small, weightless load emerged from the darkness of the tunnel and came slowly out into the full glare of the setting sun and the final, vivid moments of the day's dying light.

The London Satyr
Robert Edric

1891. LONDON IS SIMMERING under an oppressive summer heatwave, the air thick with sexual repression. But a wave of morality is about to rock the capital as the puritans of the London Vigilance Committee seek out perversion and aberrant behaviour in all its forms.

Charles Webster, an impoverished photographer working for famed actor-manager Henry Irving at the Lyceum Theatre, has been sucked into a shadowy demi-monde which exists beneath the surface of civilized society. It is a world of pornographers and prostitutes, orchestrated by master manipulator Marlow, to whom Webster illicitly provides theatrical costumes for pornographic shoots.

But knowledge of this enterprise has somehow reached the Lyceum's upright theatre manager, Bram Stoker, who suspects Webster's involvement. As the net tightens around Marlow and his cohorts and public outrage sweeps the city, a member of the aristocracy is accused of killing a child prostitute . . .